GOOD CLEAN MURDER

A Plain Jane Mystery

Also by Traci Tyne Hilton

The Plain Jane Mysteries

Good Clean Murder
Dirty Little Murder
Bright New Murder
Health, Wealth and Murder
Spoiled Rotten Murder

The Tillgiven Romantic Mysteries

Hard to Find
Dark and Stormy

The Mitzy Neuhaus Mysteries

Foreclosed
Eminent Domain
Buyer's Remorse
Frozen Assets

To Daniel, of course.

This is a work of fiction. All characters, places, and incidents are used fictitiously. Any resemblance to actual persons either living or dead is completely coincidental

Proverbs 31
House

Good, Clean, Murder: A Plain Jane Mystery

CHAPTER 1

THERE HAD BEEN A STORM IN THE NIGHT and twigs and blossoms littered the long sweep of concrete front steps at the hundred-year-old stone mansion the Crawford family called home. Jane Adler had two hours to get the six-thousand square foot house whipped into shape. Then she was off to her next client to do the same thing. Jane was alone on the cool spring morning. The neighborhood was a quiet, haven of sunshine and fresh green gardens. She wished she could trade jobs with the gardener today, just so she could stay outside and enjoy the long-awaited sunshine.

On her way back to the front door she watered the early hyacinth and late crocus in the mossy urns that lined the steps. She fished the errant petals out of the bubbling fountain, and gave the brass fish that leapt out of the splashing water a quick polish.

Spring had finally come, and with it, her last term at Harvest School of the Bible. Jane was one semester away from graduation. Then she would fly away to the mission field. There were a few hurdles in front of her still: joining the right organization, fundraising, convincing her parents she was ready to leave the country for good.

Jane dusted the lid of the copper newspaper box and flipped it open. The morning paper was still lying inside.

Had the paperboy been late? Jane leaned around the pillar of the front portico to look down the street. She didn't see any newspapers lying on the vast front lawns, but odds were most of the homeowners had boxes like the Crawfords'.

Jane turned the other way, but didn't see the paperboy on his scooter. She expected as much. He had to be sitting in school by nine in the morning.

Jane carried the newspaper around to the back of the house with her broom and her watering can.

The special directions for today's work would be waiting by the door in the mudroom. She prayed it wouldn't be a Cinderella day. Cleaning the rugs, drapes, and fireplaces would destroy her tight schedule.

Jane swept the back steps, wiped the mildew from the windowsills, and used her rag to polish the brass porch light before she let herself back into the house.

As Jane racked the outdoor broom, her cell phone rang.

Caller id showed it was her roommate, Samantha. She sighed.

"Hey, Sam." Jane slipped her Bluetooth around her ear so she could talk and clean at the same time.

"Get soy milk, okay?"

"And when should I do that? At nine tonight when my class gets out?" Jane stared at the bulletin board. The usual slip of paper was missing.

"Oh, are you doing that again?"

"Going to school? Yes." Jane dropped to her knees and fished under the decorative storage bench for the list of instructions. She couldn't feel anything so she pulled the bench away from the wall. The scraping sound on the slate floor made her skin crawl. "Was that it? Milk?"

"Soy milk, Jane. I'm lactose intolerant." It sounded like Sam was chomping gum while she spoke. Jane grimaced.

"Did you see the paper this morning?"

"Funny you should mention the paper. It was still in the box when I got here." Her directions weren't under the bench, but she'd been cleaning the Crawfords' home for two years now and knew the Monday schedule like the back of her hand. She knew everything except the special little things that were usually left on the bulletin board.

"Mr. Crawford didn't have it lying out for all to see this morning?"

"What do you mean? Is he in it? Or one of his kids?" Jane shoved the bench back against the wall. She stood up and looked around the room. Nothing. If she could get Sam off the phone, she could text Pamela just to be sure there wasn't something extra she needed to get done.

"Do you have it handy? Turn to the business section."

Jane carried the newspaper into the kitchen. She hit the lights on the way in and sniffed. Something was missing. She sniffed again. Coffee. Had no one made coffee this morning? She twisted the lid off the coffee carafe. Empty. No coffee. No cups in the sink. No signs of life.

Jane gave the carafe lid a tight twist and put it back on the coffee maker. Then she slid onto a stool and opened the newspaper on the kitchen island. "Sorry. Were you still talking? I got distracted."

"Yes, I was," Sam said. "I said, get the soy milk on your way *to* school, and you said sure."

"Not likely."

"Did you open the paper yet?"

"Umm, hmm."

"Front page of the business section, below the fold."

Jane turned to the page. Near the bottom, she found the headline that said, "Big Bob Crawford Bows out of Burger Business."

"What is this?" Jane ran her eyes across the short article. Bob Crawford was closing the chain of burger restaurants his father had opened in 1950. He apologized for how his family business had contributed to the obesity epidemic in America.

"Wow. I knew his heart attack had affected him, but I never expected this." Jane's heart sank a little. This meant the end of free dinners on the days she cleaned the Crawford house.

"When you see him, ask him what he's planning on doing now. Maybe he'll get into the smoothie business."

"I can't ask him that, Sam. It's none of my business and he's my boss."

"You and your boundaries. If I were in your position, I'd ask."

"Like you'd ever clean houses for a living." Jane scratched at a blemish on the granite top. A dinner spill, maybe.

"I bet this is why things are so strange around here this morning."

"What do you mean?"

"They didn't leave any directions, or make coffee. All the lights are out. It's just a little weird. Maybe closing the family business has put them off of their schedule."

"No coffee? Poor you."

"No kidding. Hey, I'm going to let you go. I've got to get this house put together before they get back."

"Fine, but see if you can get Jake to tell you more about this."

"If I see him, I'll ask, okay?" Jane couldn't remember the last time she had seen Jake Crawford and didn't expect to see him anytime soon. Under those circumstances, it was an easy promise to make.

"Good enough. Get the soy milk, yeah?"

"Nada. I've got work to do."

"What evs. You're a rotten roommate." Sam hung up.

Jane frowned at her phone. Sam's attitude problem was nothing new, but losing Roly Burgers was quite a blow. Jane's stomach grumbled. Free burgers had been a great perk.

Jane tied a pink bandana around her head to keep her wispy brown hair from shedding while she worked. Fast and thorough. She would try to make life for the Crawford family as easy as possible in the face of massive changes, but get in, get clean, and get out was her main goal.

Jane folded the newspaper back up. She set it on the kitchen desk, next to the charger station. She wondered what her dad would say when he found out about the end of the Burger with the Roly-Poly Bun. Running a Roly Burger franchise had made her parents' early retirement possible

The Crawford family home in the exclusive Laurelhurst neighborhood of Portland and all of the lavish lifestyle that went with it was entirely thanks to the second-generation burger chain.

Jane stared out the front window. How many people would lose their jobs when the restaurants went dark? She closed her eyes and said a silent prayer for them all. Portland did not need more layoffs.

After his heart attack, Bob Crawford had been morose. Depressed even. He had spent weeks on end huddled in his office, unshaven and wearing a bathrobe. Eventually he had cheered up, and it occurred to Jane that his new lease on life was probably due to the decision to quit making burgers.

Jane tried to shake off her own morose thoughts. If Bob didn't want to make burgers any more God must have something else in store for the people who relied on him. She felt a catch in her throat. It might be true, but it was hard to believe. God let a lot of people suffer more than even the poorest of Portlanders. While she believed that God had his hand on the Roly Burger family of employees, she still felt a little sick about their impending loss of work.

Jane needed to get her mind out of the shadows. She recited the beatitudes as she made her way upstairs, in an effort to get her own attitude in order. "Blessed are the poor in spirit, for theirs is the kingdom of heaven." She pulled out a rag and dusted the deeply-carved wooden frames that lined the staircase. "Blessed are those who mourn, for they will be comforted." She turned back and ran the rag down the banister. "Blessed are the meek, for they will inherit the Earth."

She tried not to hurry as she rubbed the dust off the stair-rail spindles. Pamela Crawford always noticed dust on the mahogany. "Blessed are those who clean others' dirt for they will be able to pay for their schoolbooks."

Jane tucked her lemon-Pledge-soaked dust rag back in her apron pocket and moved on to the laundry room, the chemical citrus wafting away with her. She needed to strip the beds and get the laundry going if she was going to get out to her next house on time. On her way past the laundry room, she grabbed a hamper.

Then she stopped. Monday was laundry day. Laundry day and *payday*. The envelope full of cash was always pinned to the bulletin board with her directions. That envelope was supposed to buy her books today. Standing still with the hamper on her hip she debated. Stop now, call Pam, and ask for directions and money, or just keep working? The laundry would take two hours, whether she was paid or not, so she moved to the master bedroom. She could call Pamela after she had the first load in the machine.

Jane pushed open the bedroom door with her hip.

In a smooth set of motions perfected over her two years as a housekeeper, she set the hamper down, grabbed the end of the comforter and pulled all of the bedding off the bed. Then she looked up to grab the pillows.

Bob was still in bed.

"I am so sorry!" she whispered. She backed away from the bed.

Bob hadn't seemed to notice her.

Heat rose to Jane's face. What a complete moron! She should have knocked. She could have given him the chance to wake up a little. She looked away from the bed, waiting for him to speak.

He didn't say anything.

In fact, Bob hadn't moved a muscle when his covers had come flying off him. Surely, if a big guy like him had moved, she would have noticed.

She stepped back to the bed.

Bob was very still, and his face was pasty.

Jane's heart thumped against her ribs, like a small, hard fist.

Bob was not well.

Her feet felt like bricks as she pulled herself across the Persian rug to the side of Bob's bed.

He was wearing an A-line tank top—a wife-beater. His huge shoulders were covered in brown wiry hair. She had never seen Bob's naked shoulders.

Jane placed two shaking fingertips under his jaw, and turned away.

She couldn't feel a pulse. She moved her fingers across his thick neck, trying to find even the faint hint of life, but it wasn't there.

Jane shoved her hand into the pocket of her jeans and yanked out her phone. *911. Must call 911.*

"Ambulance, Police, or Fire Department?" The voice of the 911 operator was steady, solid.

"Ambulance, please!"

"Where are you located?"

Jane gave the operator the address of the Crawford home.

"An ambulance will be right there. Can you stay on the line with me?"

"No, I can't. I've got to call his wife."

"I understand. We'll be right there."

Jane ended the call and began scrolling through her phone for Pamela's number.

Pamela could be at the gym right now, or at the salon, or with the board of directors dealing with the business. She could be anywhere.

Jane found their daughter Phoebe Crawford's number first and hit send.

"This is Phoebe." Her voice was rough like she had just woken up.

"Phoebe, it's Jane Adler. I'm at your parents' house and your dad—" Jane's voice broke, but she took a deep breath and continued, "I called the ambulance. I think it was another heart attack. Can you get here?"

"Slow down, what?"

"I'm at the house, and I think your dad has had another heart attack. The ambulance is on its way. Can you make it over here? Do you know where your mom is?" How did Phoebe not understand? Jane walked to the window to watch for the ambulance. Her knees felt like water.

Phoebe yawned on the other end. "That's awful," she said. "I had a rough one last night. Call me when he's at the hospital and I'll be right there, okay?"

"But I'm just the cleaner…you need to be here. Or your mom."

"Oh, you're *that* Jane. I wondered who this was. Call me when you know what hospital he is at and I will meet him there, okay? It's just another heart thing. He'll be fine."

"I don't think he's going to be fine." Jane saw the ambulance turn the corner, its lights spinning and siren blaring. A fire truck was right behind it.

"Okay, so call me later." Phoebe yawned again and hung up.

Jane pressed her lips together.

Bob was definitely not fine.

She needed to call Pamela. She scrolled through her numbers again but didn't see it. Bob's cell. Phoebe's cell. Jake's cell. Even Pamela's sister-in-law's number.

The ambulance pulled into the driveway.

Jane ran down the stairs to let them in. She threw open the door and directed two paramedics up the stairs. "The door at the end of the hall!" she hollered as they passed.

Jane followed them, with another paramedic right behind her. She reached the room just in time to see one of the men grab Bob by his feet.

Another man grabbed Bob's shoulders. Together the paramedics pulled him to the ground.

Bob landed with a thud. Jane's stomach twisted at the sound.

The man at Bob's shoulders grabbed the neck of the tank top and ripped it down the middle. He began chest compressions, counting in a low voice.

The woman who had followed Jane pulled out the defibrillator.

Maybe Phoebe was right. Maybe they could start his heart again. The paramedics stuck wires at his chest and hip, and then applied the charge.

The man who had ripped Bob's shirt attached an oxygen mask.

"How did you find him?" The third paramedic asked. She had been busy pulling things out of her medical bag and handing them to the two who were performing CPR.

Jane jumped. She hadn't been expecting a question. "I just, I opened the door and went to strip the bed and there he was. He didn't look right so I checked for a pulse."

The paramedic nodded, encouraging her to continue.

Jane shook her head. "There wasn't one so I called 911. Is he going to be okay?"

The paramedic tilted her head, her mouth in a small frown.

Jane looked back at her phone and scrolled through the numbers. She needed to find Pamela Crawford. Now. She went through them all three times, the numbers and names swimming. She closed her eyes and pressed the heel of her hand over one eye. She counted to three. She opened her eyes and scrolled through one more time, slowly.

"Pamela's mobile." Under P, instead of C with the rest of the Crawfords.

Jane hit send.

The paramedic on his knees looked up at his partner and shook his head. The partner pulled out a cell phone.

A phone rang in the master bathroom.

The woman who had spoken with Jane put her hand on Jane's back. "Would you like to answer that call?"

Jane held out the phone in her hand and pointed at her Bluetooth headset. "I'm trying to get a hold of Bob's wife."

The paramedic nodded and went back to work.

When Jane's call went to voice mail, she hung up. What message could she leave Pamela? Thirty years of wedded bliss were likely over?

The phone in the master bath had stopped ringing, but Jane thought she'd check it. Maybe Pamela had been trying to call Bob, trying to find out where he was.

Everything went in slow motion as she moved to the bathroom. The doorknob clicked as it turned, as though it needed to be oiled. The door caught on the threshold as she pushed it in. She scrubbed that floor every Friday and could feel, in her fingers, exactly how much higher the bathroom tile was from the bedroom floor.

The voices behind her sounded like they had gone into slow motion as well. One voice said, "Get the declaration of death," but the words went on forever.

Jane pushed against the doorknob, but it stopped against something. She pushed harder. It seemed to be hitting something that had a little give, but couldn't be pushed out of the way just by opening the door.

She put her shoulder to the door but couldn't bring herself to shove it open.

Bob was dead.

The paramedic who had spoken with Jane put her arm around Jane again and led her from the door. "It's been quite a morning for you. Sit down." She led Jane to a large wingback chair by the window. "You might be in a bit of shock. Just relax, and keep breathing, okay?"

Jane looked at the paramedic. They were about the same age. They had the same brown hair in the same ponytail, at the middle of the back of their heads. Jane nodded, and then closed her eyes.

The conversation of the paramedics was like a low throb around her. She couldn't follow it. She could hear the words *declaration of death* repeating in her head like they were still being said. Would she have to tell Pamela, Phoebe and Jake that Bob Crawford was at a funeral home?

"Hey guys, look at this." An urgent voice rose above the murmuring.

Jane opened her eyes. They had gotten the door to the bathroom opened a little farther and the paramedics were squeezing themselves through the gap.

The noise of their conversation rose louder and louder.

She heard someone say, "Get the coroner here."

Another voice said, "Look at the bruising on her wrists. Go check the other body for bruising."

Jane sat as still as she could, but all of a sudden she couldn't catch her breath.

She leaned forward in her chair, letting her head drop. With her head between her knees, she held her breath and counted to three. Then she exhaled. She repeated it until her heart seemed to calm down. She hadn't noticed that her arms had been shaking until after they had stopped. When her whole body felt still, she stood up.

She took one more slow, deep, breath, and walked to the bathroom. The door was open several inches, but she didn't try to push her way in. She peered through the opening instead.

Pamela Crawford, a woman almost as large as her husband, lay crumpled on the bathroom floor, her face red and bloated.

One of the paramedics held her wrist in his hand. He looked at the other and shook his head *no.*

The female paramedic looked at the other two. "I'll get her out of here." Jane watched her mouth say the words, but her voice was almost silent.

"Jane, right?" she asked.

Jane nodded.

"Why don't you come downstairs with me?"

They walked downstairs and into the kitchen.

"Why don't you sit down while we wait for the police? They shouldn't take long to get here."

Jane sat down.

"You've had a shock. Will you be able to take the rest of the day off?" The paramedic had a sympathetic look on her face.

"Yes, I think I can." Jane looked at her hands. She had her phone in a white-knuckled grip.

"Then why don't you arrange that, okay? I need to get back upstairs." The paramedic didn't move or break eye contact.

Jane nodded and stared at the phone in her hand. She could call her next two clients and tell them what had happened. It was just two calls, but they were both friends of Bob and Pamela. What could she say to them?

"I should be here, for the family. I should change the linens and put the laundry in and make lunch."

The paramedic shook her head. "We're just gonna leave things the way they are for a little while, okay? Until we know what's been going on."

Jane pressed her fist into her knee and took a deep breath. "But it was just a heart attack, right?"

The paramedic nodded, "It looks like Bob may have had a heart attack, and Pamela as well. We wouldn't expect to find both of them on the same morning. The officers should be here any minute. Sit tight, okay?"

Jane listened for the sound of distant sirens. She let go of her phone and smoothed out her apron.

The paramedic tapped the table with her knuckles and lifted an eyebrow. "You okay down here?"

Jane nodded and the paramedic ran back upstairs, taking them two at a time.

"Blessed are those who hunger and thirst for righteousness…" Jane began the beatitudes where she had left off, in the faint hope of keeping her panic at bay.

A sharp knock on the door interrupted her.

Jane snaked her way up the curvy hill to her school. Her little car quivered with its last ounce of energy, but Jane prayed it to the top.

The school was nestled into a flat spot midway up a hill, overlooking rolling hills of vineyards. Supposedly the hillsides were facing the sun in such a way that they produced award-winning harvests.

Jane pulled up the ebrake. She looked at the little church building with the three-story dormitory behind it. Perhaps this place, which faced the *Son*, would also produce a good harvest.

Dusk was falling and the dorm windows began to spark to life as lights were switched on for the evening. To pay for school, Jane had to work. To work, she had to be in town early in the morning. She needed to work to pay for school, but she could not live in the dorms and still maintain a solid work schedule. She was this year's lone commuter student, but it would be worth it. Community College would have been cheaper, but she wanted—needed—Bible training, not poly-sci and biology.

Classes met in the basement of the church. All of the administration happened in the ground floor of the dorms. Jane crunched her way across the gravel parking lot to the dorms. She filled her lungs with the fresh, clean air of the spring evening, always a welcome contrast to days filled with the chemical scents of ammonia, bleach, and polish.

The building the students used as a dorm had once been a tubercular hospital. It was over one-hundred-years old now, a petite three-story concrete and cast-iron building. In years gone by it had been the last place of refuge for hopeless cases. The church building across the parking lot had been drastically remodeled from what it had been when it was the chapel for the hospital, but Jane liked to think that hopeless cases could still come here for healing.

She pushed open the heavy glass doors and trudged to the office. She knew she wasn't the first student to take only night classes and finish a certificate in two years instead of taking the full-time nine-month program, and surely she wasn't the only student to run out of money right at the end. All she needed were books and tuition for her last class. The Crawford paycheck would be enough…when it came.

Glenda, the administrative secretary, was at her desk. Her hair was pulled back in a high bun, stabbed through with a pencil. She had dark circles under her eyes and her glasses were low on her nose.

"Yes?" Glenda's voice was raspy like she was coming down with something.

Jane cleared her throat. She looked down at her hands. "You're wanting your books, aren't you? I don't think they are in yet. Something about the class change. I got the old order stopped in time but I haven't gotten the new ones yet. You are here for class tonight, right?"

Jane nodded. Class change? No books? She wasn't sure if she should praise God for this or not. "What do you mean, 'the class change'?" Her schedule had been arranged so carefully. This last class was required for her certificate.

"Donald had to go back East. Something about a crisis at the Debriefing House. We had to cancel Reverse Culture Shock, but the new class should be really good."

"Don't I need Reverse Culture Shock? I mean, it was required, right?" Jane ran the course requirements through her mind. She was sure RCS was a requirement for the Overseas Ministry Certificate.

Glenda prodded her glasses with her knuckle and looked up. "We can't offer it again until summer, but this class is good, you'll like it."

"But what about graduation and the certificate?"

Glenda took a deep breath. "Can I be honest, Jane? You live out in the real world and have a job, so I think you can appreciate this."

Jane swallowed.

"The certificate is just a piece of paper. We give one to everyone at the end of the program. You'll get a certificate. If you want to take Donald's class you can take it in the summer."

"I know it's just a piece of paper, but I want to go overseas, so I want to be trained…" *The piece of paper didn't matter?* Jane's knees felt weak. Two years of hard work scrubbing floors and studying late and the piece of paper didn't matter?

"Their franchise had three locations. Two outside of town and the one on the Eastside."

"Hmmmph." Marjory turned back to the lady at the desk. "Let's finish this up later today, all right?"

The admin frowned at her computer screen. "I need to get the statement off to the franchisers as soon as possible, don't I?"

Marjory glanced at Jane and shook her head.

"What do you need?"

"I'm waiting for Jake."

"Ahhhh." Marjory let out an annoyed sigh. "You went to Presbyterian Prep with him, didn't you?"

"Yes, ma'am."

Marjory raised an eyebrow. "This is an early date." Marjory turned her eyes to the front window. "Getting breakfast?"

Jane didn't like what Marjory's tone implied. "Jake needed to pick up his car. I was at the house anyway so I gave him a ride."

"Oh?"

It was getting worse. Jane stammered and closed her mouth.

"Did you stay over, then? And his parents dead just a few days."

"Ma'am. I'm the cleaner. I come Mondays, Wednesdays and Fridays."

Marjory raised an eyebrow. "Oh, yes. I remember Pam saying that the Adler girl cleans houses. You're not still coming are you?"

Jane opened her mouth to speak but Marjory didn't give her a chance.

"Oh I suppose she set up auto pay. Well you'd better keep coming then until the estate is settled. I don't want to be paying you for nothing."

Jane stood up. "Ma'am, the thing is…"

Marjory held her hand up, "Not now, please. We are a family in crisis. I really don't have time for whatever problems the housecleaner has." She turned from Jane, and let herself into the office marked "Bob Crawford."

Jane sat down again.

Jake burst through the office door. "Aunt." He kissed Marjory on the cheek.

Marjory frowned.

Jake dropped a to-go bag on Jane's lap. "Thanks, Janey. You're a real sport."

Jane gripped the top of the paper bag in her fist. "Whatcha doing tonight?"

"I've got class." The warm, familiar aroma of the Roly Burger breakfast sandwich sent Jane's hunger into hyperdrive. All she wanted to do was slip away and eat.

Jake snorted. "Have fun with that then." He opened the door and let himself back out again.

Jane followed him. "Wait a second, Jake."

"Yeah?" He smiled, one dimple popping in his cheek.

"Marjory said something about me cleaning until the estate is sorted out. Because of auto pay—but I'm not on auto pay and I really need my last paycheck. Err, cash. Your mom always paid cash."

Jake frowned. He narrowed his eyes. "Is that so? She always paid cash?"

Jane nodded. "I'm sorry. I don't mean to be a bother, it's just that my budget is tight and every little bit makes a big difference."

Jake looked at his watch. "Sorry. Auntie Marge is right. You're just going to have to wait until the estate is sorted out." He looked up and smiled, but not with his eyes. "I wouldn't quit cleaning if I were you. It would make your case for another 'cash' payment pretty hard."

Jane crossed her arms. "And if I quit you'd have to clean up after yourself."

Jake's eyes relaxed a little. "You got it. Listen, you keep coming and I'll see what I can do about getting you paid. Deal?"

"What other choice do I have?" Getting a new client sounded like a good choice to her. The idea of serving the family in crisis nagged at the back of her mind. "I'll do what I can, okay?"

"You and me both." Jake opened the door to his Camaro. "See you around."

Jane decided to drive back home to eat her free breakfast.

Sam wasn't at the apartment, which was a welcome relief. Jane sat on her bed without putting the screen up. Her Roly Breakfast Burger and hash brown sticks were cold, but it still tasted like heaven.

According to Isaac, God had put her in his class so she could minister to the Crawfords. According to Marjory she was obliged to clean until the estate was sorted out. According to Jake she ought to do the cleaning so he wouldn't have to.

According to her budget she needed over $500 if she wanted to keep her place in Sam's apartment, get her books for class, and continue to eat. She expected $300 from her clients on Monday, but the Crawfords were her big-ticket family. They paid for a month of service all at once and paid much more per hour than the others. The $300 on Monday just wouldn't cut it.

Jane created a new flyer for Plain Jane's Good Clean Houses and printed them out. She'd start soliciting referrals at her next house. She checked her watch—she had just enough time to whip up a batch of cookie dough before she left.

When Jane had cleaned her way down to the main floor of the Larsen house she spooned the chocolate-chip dough onto the cookie sheets she had brought with her. She would bake them so that when she left the house it would smell like heaven. Several of her fliers would be waiting with a tray of fresh-baked cookies. She would write a little note explaining that she had room in her schedule to add a new client. She closed the oven door and said a little prayer.

Jane had left a lot of unfinished work at the Crawfords' because of the little breakfast run. If she went to the Crawfords' house before she hit the laundry mat she would feel much better about her day. As a bonus, she'd be less likely to run into Sam getting ready for another night of clubbing.

And she'd leave Jake a batch of cookies too. Not that anyone he knew was looking for a housekeeper, but it was a little thing she could do for Jake. And Phoebe, of course.

Nothing much had changed at the Crawford house since she had been there on Monday, but she decided to complete the usual cleaning tasks. When she got to the bedrooms her heart flipped in her chest. She knew that Bob and Pamela were long gone, but she knocked on their bedroom door first anyway.

Everything in the room was the way it had been left on Monday. Her mind raced. Was she allowed in her yet? Should she call the cops to find out if she could clean? Call Jake to find out? Just clean anyway and claim ignorance? Maybe Marjory had directions for her. Her phone was in her pocket as always, so she pulled it out again. Her fingers trembled as she held it. She should call the cops first. She began to dial 911, but she didn't hit send. 911 was the emergency number. What was the regular police number? She tapped her pointer finger on the screen. She should just call Marjory. Marjory would know what to do.

Jane scrolled through the numbers and pulled up Marjory Crawford. "Hello, Marjory?"

"Yes?" There was a hint of irritation in Marjory's voice.

"This is Jane Adler, the housecleaner. I spoke with you this morning. I was just wondering about the master bedroom. Am I allowed to clean it?"

"Excuse me?" Her voice was thick with irritation now.

"I just, I mean it hasn't been touched since the police were here. Do they want to keep it a crime scene or something?"

"The room hasn't been touched, *Jane*, because you are the housecleaner and you haven't touched it. In other words, yes. Do your job."

Heat rose to Jane's face. Marjory had hung up on her. Of course. Cleaning this room was her job. And just because it was unusual for both Bob and Pamela to die on the same morning doesn't mean it was a crime. Jane stuffed the phone in her pocket and stripped the bed. It looked like her quick stop at the Crawfords' was laundry day as well.

She knocked on the next bedroom door. There was no reply so she let herself in. She did not use her tricky one-swish bed-stripping maneuver, but pulled the blankets off slowly and carefully. There were six bedrooms in the Crawford house. If she expected a corpse in every bed the laundry would never get started, much less finished, but she knocked on the third bedroom door anyway.

There were no corpses waiting for her. No cobwebs either. She stripped both single beds as fast as she could, leaving the duvets in a pile on the floor.

She pushed open the fourth bedroom door.

"Well, hello there."

Jane jumped back and knocked into the door behind her. "I am so sorry."

"Doesn't bother me." Jake was standing in front of a mirror jelling his hair in nothing but a short towel. "Need something?"

Jane looked out at the hall. "I'm just stripping the beds. I'll come back."

"Don't rush out. You can strip with me here." Jake chuckled.

"No, I'll come back." Jane pulled the door shut behind her. She held on to the doorknob for a moment and tried to compose herself, but she was shaking with embarrassment. The door twisted in her grip.

"Hey now, don't lock me in here."

Jane dropped the handle and hurried down the hall.

Jake stepped out. "It's no biggy. Just grab my sheets when you get a chance. I'll be downstairs."

Jane didn't turn around. She heard him run down the steps. She was a maid. Seen and not heard. Seen and not heard. She sorely wished she hadn't been seen or heard.

At bedroom number five she knocked again. When no one said anything, she let herself in.

She stared at the bed for a moment, not exactly understanding what she was seeing. She closed her eyes and opened them. Luggage. It was just luggage. Three matching Louis Vuitton suitcases on top of the bed. She hefted them off of the bed and stripped the blankets. Her first guess was that Phoebe had come home, but this wasn't Phoebe's usual room.

Could be Marjory, but Marjory had a house twice as big as this back in Maywood. Why would she move to the second-best guest bedroom at her brother-in-law's house? When Bob's brother William had died while Jane was still a kid, Marjory had demanded that everyone leave her alone. Surely she wouldn't push herself on her niece and nephew right now, but then, who else could it be?

The question of who this luggage belonged to didn't matter. What mattered was getting the sheets in the laundry. She added them to the basket and went to the last bedroom.

Phoebe had moved out at the beginning of the year, but you couldn't tell it from her room. Jane followed regular procedures and left everything alone except the sheets. These, she pulled off as fast as she could and dumped them in her laundry basket. She turned a blind eye to the dust and clutter. It wasn't her house so it wasn't her business.

She hesitated at the door. Half-naked Jake could be anywhere right now, but she thought she could avoid him if she stuck to the back stairs, the cleaning closets, the laundry room, and the cellar. Basically anywhere work might get done. Too bad she still needed to clean the rest of the house as well.

She braced herself and shouldered the door open. Eyes firmly ahead she made it to the laundry room without distraction. She popped the door open with her hip and set the basket down.

"Hey, one more idea." Jake was sitting on the laundry machine with his bare legs hanging over the round, glass-faced door. He was still in his towel.

Jane sighed. "Yes?"

Jake hopped down, to the detriment of the arrangement of his towel. He snatched it up and clutched it in front of him with a chuckle. "I have too much to do around here. I need live-in help."

Jane trained her eyes to the ceiling and said nothing.

"What do you think?"

"I think you need to get dressed." Jane held the laundry basket in front of her like a shield.

"Heh-heh. Yeah, but I also need someone to cook and do the laundry and stuff. Are you interested?"

"I'm not a live-in maid."

"It's a big house, Jane. Have some sympathy for an orphan."

Jane looked up at him. "I think you are in shock, Jake. How are you dealing with losing both of your parents?"

"Terribly, Jane, just terribly. Won't you move in and take care of me? I can't stay here all by myself."

"All by yourself? Someone is in the guest bedroom." She motioned toward the hall with her basket.

"Never."

"No, really. Someone is in the second best—the yellow room."

"You're crazy. What makes you think someone is staying here?" Jake walked over to the door and stood in front of it, one hand holding his towel up, the other resting on the doorjamb.

"The matching set of Louis Vuitton luggage sitting on the bed makes me think it."

"But who is it?"

"Jake, really? Where is your head?"

"It's in mourning, Jane. Have some sympathy. Let's go see whose luggage is in the yellow room."

"Feel free. I have to do the laundry." She motioned to the machine with her hefty basket of sheets.

Jake gripped his towel with one hand and grabbed Jane's elbow with the other. "Come on. Let's see who horned in on the family riches."

Jane set her basket on top of the machine. She let Jake pull her out of the laundry room. She was running out of time to get everything done before school started, but she was curious who was staying at the house.

In the bedroom Jake popped open the first suitcase. "Cotton nightgown, size huge? Real rabbit fur slippers? Any guesses yet?" He tossed the slipper on the floor. "I have one. Aunt Marjory. Let's see." He pulled a smaller case to himself and flipped over the luggage tag. "Mrs. M. Crawford. That would be the lady herself. The Aunt-in-question. But when did she get here?"

"Sometime after we got breakfast?"

"Or was it before? We could check the status of her bed if *someone* hadn't stripped it of its clues."

"Sorry." Jane turned to the door. It wouldn't be pleasant for her if Marjory were to pop in right now. "Can I get back to the laundry again?"

Jake tucked the ends of his towel in a little tighter and took Jane by both of her hands, "Not until you promise to move into the third-best guest room. You wouldn't leave a nice innocent boy like me in a house like this with a woman like that, would you?"

It was tempting. To not leave him, that is. "I can't move in here. Marjory wouldn't like it at all."

"Another good reason!"

"I'm going to do the laundry."

"Can I bring you a load? You might have noticed, you might not have, but I have nothing to wear."

Jane sighed again. Another hour to wash his clothes too? Why not? "Yes, yes, bring them in. But I do have to get to school today."

"Whatever." Jake dropped her hands and sauntered out of the room, his towel slipping just a little as he went.

Jane turned away again. She absolutely did *not* want to be Jake's live-in maid.

CHAPTER 4

CLASS TIME CAME AS A RELIEF after the long day. The musty basement with the flickering fluorescent lights felt like a retreat. Jane sat at her desk next to Sarah. Getting to the end of Jake's laundry and the rest of the cleaning had taken her to the last minute. She hadn't had time to run home and change much less get to the laundry mat to do her own clothes. She smelled like a combination of fresh baked cookies, lemon pledge, and hard work, but hoped her friend wouldn't notice. She thanked the Lord that books for her class hadn't come in yet, since she still didn't have money to buy them, much less time to read them.

Jane typed furiously as Mr. Daniels lectured. Her hand cramped as she hit the keys, but attempting to get down everything she heard helped her stay awake.

Night class. Jane yawned. She looked at her computer screen. The words "let's take five" were in front of her blinking cursor. She smiled at them. It was a good thing she was taking notes, since she was clearly not paying attention.

"Earth to Jane." Sarah waved her hands in front of Jane's screen. "Want to run out to the cart and get a coffee?"

"Not if I want to be at work on time tomorrow."

"You don't look like you could even remember where you are going tomorrow."

"I'll remember in the morning." Jane rested her head on her fist. "It's been a trying week."

"Want to go out after class then? You seem like you need some kind of break."

"Don't you all have curfew?"

Sarah smiled and opened her fist. She held a big silver key. "What's curfew when you have a key?"

Jane rolled her eyes. "I know it's no fun to be stuck in your dorm at ten every night but...how do I say this..." Jane looked around the room full of almost-adults. "You all live in Honeywell. What on earth would you do here after ten anyway?"

"Drive to town, of course. Are you in?"

Jane sucked on her bottom lip, a laugh bubbling up inside her. "Let me guess, I get to drive."

Sarah grinned. "Well, you know. Eddie is the only one with a car and he's not likely to sneak out after curfew, is he?"

Jane spied out Eddie. His head was in his Bible. "No, he's not likely."

Jane toyed with the idea. Cram her Rabbit full of repressed eighteen-year-olds for a night on the "town" or go home and sleep?

Before she could voice her opinion, Isaac Daniels caught her eye. He smiled and crossed the room to join them.

"How did it go this week?" His voice was low and he sat with his back to Sarah.

Jane could feel a blush coming on. She was not even remotely interested in sneaking Sarah and her friends off campus. "I don't know, really. There isn't much family around to minister to."

"It's early days. Have patience. Sometimes the small stuff, done faithfully, makes a bigger impression anyway."

"That's what it comes to. My only trouble now is they don't want to pay me until the estate is settled, but I need the income."

Isaac frowned, his brows pulling together. "Can they do that?"

"Anyone can do anything, I guess. I need to figure out who is in charge of the estate and discuss it properly. Someone assumed I had some kind of auto-pay, but it has always been cash. I have to sort out that misunderstanding first thing. Well, I need to get another client or two first thing." Jane rubbed her pencil's eraser on her desk, making a small square with the pink rubber. "Or sort out the issue with Marjory first. Or do them both at the same time. Right? The best way to handle a problem is to be unfocused and distracted."

Isaac choked on a laugh. "Sorry. I shouldn't laugh, but I get it. Talk after class?"

She looked up from the eraser doodle. He watched her with big, sympathetic hazel eyes, but the corner of his mouth was turned up in a smile.

"Maybe we can brainstorm a solution."

"Sounds good." Jane smiled a little too.

Isaac resumed his spot at the podium with a bounce in his step. His smile was slightly out of line with the data on families in crisis he quoted. And considering the thin line Jane was walking, her smile felt a little out of line as well.

The last half of class flew by. Jane found her notes harder to concentrate on and Isaac easier to watch.

Jane lingered at the back of the class until the rest of the students had filtered out. When the room was empty Isaac joined her. "I have to head back to town." He ran his hand through his hair.

Jane's heart sank. "Oh, okay."

"You head back to town too, right?

"Yes." Jane sat up straighter.

"We could meet at Starbucks."

"Yes, let's."

"To talk about how you can be a light right now." Isaac kept her eyes locked in his as he spoke.

"Of course." Jane blushed again, she just knew it, but, at the same time, she didn't mind.

Jane and Isaac left the classroom.

She followed him into town, admiring his aging Range Rover. She had a light, fluttering feeling in her chest for the first time in days. As sure as she was that it was against Bible school rules, she was fairly certain this was a date.

Her suspicions were confirmed when he paid for the grande non-fat latte, decaf, that she ordered.

The aroma of fresh-brewed Starbucks, warm pastry, and Isaac, standing close to her, made Jane forget, for a moment, that she was still a mess from work.

Once they sat down, Isaac appeared more confident, and younger too. The diffident, unsure manner he had used to invite her to coffee had been replaced by a cheerful smile and a more relaxed voice. Plus he had left his jacket in the car.

He leaned forward in his chair with his elbows on the table. "So you have more problems right now than you expected on Monday, I'd say."

"I do. I don't know how it spun out of control so fast, but I'm kind of up a creek."

"Because you are expected to work for no pay, right?" Isaac picked up his paper cup and held it in front of his mouth, blowing lightly into the lid.

"Exactly." Jane copied his motion, but not on purpose. The warm cup was a comfort. She took a sip that was still too hot.

"Do you have a lawyer?"

Jane choked on her coffee. "A lawyer? Far from it. Why would I need a lawyer?"

"If you need to quit working for them to pick up more clients to meet your bills, the family might make things difficult. Well, only if they truly believe you are being paid still or have been paid in advance." Isaac's jaw tensed.

"I can't imagine who would sue me." Jane furrowed her brow. She had expected him to recommend some Bible verses, to pray with her, to make small talk.

"Sorry. My dad is a small claims court judge so problems tend to appear litigious to me. They might not sue, but even if they don't you still have trouble."

"Yes. Well...I am seeking new clients now so that should help. And you haven't given any homework yet, so, you know, I've got time."

Isaac grinned. "Yeah...I haven't. Do you think that crowd would do homework?"

"What do you mean?" Jane blew into the lid of her coffee. She wanted to hear what his thoughts on the little Bible school were. Her own concept had been so recently called into question.

"Well..." Isaac flushed. "I mean it's not exactly Harvard, is it?"

"I suppose it can't draw quite the same caliber of professor."

Isaac shifted in his seat. "Touché."

"Sorry. I didn't mean that. What do you think about this school? What's the deal with it?"

"You tell me. You're a student there."

"I'll say this much: The catalogue made it look like a great training school for someone who wanted to serve overseas."

"It is that."

Relief swept over Jane. She tilted her head from side to side, stretching her neck out. That was all she wanted to hear. She was well-trained for the mission field.

"But it's not as good as seminary."

Jane lifted her eyebrow. "Oh?"

"Look at it this way. At the Bible school you studied some pretty basic theological concepts, some pretty basic intercultural stuff, some pretty basic linguistic skills, and you learned how to get along with PKs."

Jane rolled her eyes.

"Or not how to get along with PKs. Either way it was a pretty basic education. Kind of the Junior College version of seminary."

"So then why are you teaching there?"

"PhDs are expensive." Isaac shrugged. "Sorry. I don't mean to be a drag about your school. I guess I just figured since you are an adult, and live in town rather than in the dorms, that you would get it. Considering all of that though, why are you at Harvest?"

"Because I want to be a missionary and I didn't see the point of studying biology and essay writing. I wanted to focus on my goal."

"What is your goal?"

"The ten-forty window."

"How do I say this…" Isaac set his cup down. He was suppressing a smile.

"I know." Jane scrunched up her mouth.

"You can't get into the ten-forty window with a Bible school degree."

"I said, I know." Jane did her best not to sigh. She had learned a lot in her almost-two-years at Harvest, including that she needed something besides a Bible school certificate to get into her ideal mission field.

"But if you knew that, why did you pick this school?"

"Well, I didn't know that when I started, did I? But I need to finish what I started. I'll get where God wants me to be. I'm not worried about that part."

"You look worried." Isaac took a drink from his paper cup.

Jane looked down at her coffee cup. Why had she said she wasn't worried? Of course she was worried. "Okay. I hadn't been worried until Monday. When my clients both died and then Glenda told me that the Bible school certificate was meaningless, I began to have some serious doubts about what I was doing."

Isaac reached across the table and grabbed her hand. "I can believe it, but listen, we can straighten out the ministry thing at least—we can figure out how you can serve these guys in their need, because in reality, this one family in this major crisis could be the whole reason God has you at Harvest School of the Bible."

"God has arranged the last two years of my life so that I could be in your class?"

Isaac's face lit up as he smiled. He tried to pull his features into a more somber look, but it didn't work. "Would that have been so bad?"

Jane liked the way his hand felt on hers—rough and strong. A shiver ran down her spine. "I plead the fifth."

Isaac let go of her hand and took a big drink of his coffee. "So can you anticipate any needs your clients may have in the coming week?"

They brainstormed household chores that Phoebe and Jake might have until the coffee shop closed up for the night, and then they parted ways. Jane watched Isaac drive off in the opposite direction from her. She assumed he wouldn't have lied about where he lived, but from the direction he was driving away it did not look like he had needed to come all the way into town.

CHAPTER 5

THE WINDOW IN JANE'S APARTMENT that faced the parking lot was dark. Jane checked the clock on her dash as she parked. It was just after eleven. Sam rarely had the lights out by eleven, even though Jane slept in the living room.

Her two years in the cramped quarters of a junior apartment with a girl she met on Craigslist were beginning to tell on Jane. She sat in her car and stared at the dark window. Disappointment washed over her like a cold wind. She ought to have been asleep in that dark room. She needed to be up by five tomorrow.

Her parents had cautioned her against sharing a junior suite—a space distinguished from a regular studio by a partition between the "rooms," but with no real bedroom door. Her parents had told her not to look for a roommate online either. Her parents had told her to move to Phoenix with them, enroll in Arizona State, but, Jane reminded herself, she knew what she wanted.

And that, apparently, was a small apartment with a stranger and a half-hearted education.

Jane turned her ignition off. At least the light was out so she could go straight to sleep.

Jane ambled up the steps to her front door counting the weeks left until the end of school and attempting to ignore the smell coming from the dumpster at the foot of her staircase.

May was coming, and with it, freedom from her classes and her commute. She could move to Phoenix with her parents and start her fundraising. Good things were coming in May. A little pang of disappointment hit her. In May she'd be done with Isaac Daniels' class.

The front door light was burnt out. The sheltered entry to the apartment was pitch black. Jane stumbled over something as she crossed the landing to her door. She looked down and discovered a small cardboard box with her blanket on top. She frowned and kneeled down. She removed her blanket to discover her pillow, her books from last term, And her half a bag of Chex Mix.

Was Sam kicking her out? And if so, where were her clothes? She quickly recalled they were in her car, waiting to go to the laundry mat, but what about the rest of her stuff, like the futon she called her bed?

Jane pulled out her keychain and clicked on her L.E.D light. By its small glow she read a note scribbled on the side of the box. *Rent overdue. Evicted.* She bowed her head. "Oh dear God, what on Earth?" She didn't pray it, so much as turn the question over and over in her head. She was too confused to pray. She was absolutely certain that her rent was *not* overdue. She pressed the palm of her hand to her chest. Her heart thumped against her hand like a drum.

"Okay, Lord. Just give me my next step." The words of the Psalm came to her mind. *"Your word is a lamp to my feet and a light to my path."*

What did the Bible say she should do? No stories of twenty-year-old girls on their own kicked to the curb in the middle of the night came to mind so she pulled out her phone and called Sam. She hoped the phone would wake her up from a deep sleep. Anger was beginning to replace her confusion.

The phone seemed to ring forever, but right about when voicemail should have clicked on, Sam answered.

"Let me in," Jane said.

"I can't. We're evicted."

"What do you mean, 'We're evicted'? Just let me in to get the rest of my stuff at least."

"I can't, idiot. We were evicted."

"But rent wasn't late. What do you mean 'rent was late'?" Jane rocked back on her heels.

"About that…"

"Samantha, did you not pay the rent?"

"I was going to, but something came up." Sam's voice was slurred.

"How often did something come up, Sam?"

"Listen, I have a lot of expenses and I had to use the money for some stuff and now we are evicted. Deal."

"Where are you?" Jane's mind was spinning. Some unbefore-met part of herself wanted to find Sam and punch her in the nose. The rest of her just wanted to find a place to spend the night.

"I'm out of town. Sorry about this. Hey. I didn't box your stuff up, the landlord did. Talk to him about it."

"But my furniture? My bed? My dresser? My privacy screen? What about that stuff?"

"Yeah, so, he needs that to sell for the past rent or something. I don't know. My dad came and cleared my stuff out for me. Maybe your dad can come. The landlord is kind of a bully, but whatever. I'm busy right now. Just get a hold of him yourself and deal with it." Sam disconnected the call.

Jane stared at her phone. Unless her lock-box was in the cardboard box on the front-step, her emergency credit card would still be inside the apartment.

Jane stood up. She brushed the dirt from her knees. With a shaking hand she pushed her key into the lock and attempted to let herself in to the apartment. The lock resisted her key. It had already been changed.

She stepped backwards from the door and tripped on the box of her stuff. Her little safe had to be in that box. She pulled out the blanket and the pillow and the bag of Chex Mix again. She dug through the short stack of textbooks. She pulled out the pile of fashion magazines that were actually Sam's. No lock-box. No emergency credit card. No place to sleep.

Jane looked down at her rag-top Rabbit. Even with her winter coat on she was shivering in the early March night air. She'd freeze to death if she tried to sleep in her car. She grimaced. She wouldn't actually freeze to death, but it would be *really* cold. She tapped the face of her cell phone. She wanted to call her daddy to make it all better. He could pay for a hotel room over the phone, couldn't he?

She paused. Her parents were on a cruise. Did she really want to panic them in the middle of a vacation they couldn't leave?

Something Isaac said over coffee came to mind. *Sometimes serving others meets our own needs in ways we didn't anticipate.*

Isaac wouldn't have wanted her to move in with Jake, would he? Could that have been the message God was sending her?

Jane sat down and folded her cold hands. She closed her eyes. "Okay, God." This time she prayed out loud. "I don't want to move into the Crawford house. I don't want to live in the same house alone with Jake. I don't want to be a live-in housekeeper, but is this your plan? Is this what you meant for me to do?" Somewhere outside of the apartment complex an owl hooted. Jane waited in silence until her legs went numb.

She would go to the Crawfords' house because she had nowhere else to go.

In ten minutes she had reached the Crawford house. She pulled into the side drive and parked around back by the mudroom door. One hundred years ago, when the house had been built, it was considered the servants' door. Very appropriate. She left her car in the little round drive where Pamela had directed her to park on the days she worked.

The whole house, like her small apartment, was dark. She didn't want to go in. The night couldn't have been warmer than thirty and the cold nipped at her cheeks as she sat in her car.

There was an empty, warm bed inside that house. There was probably an old school friend inside that house, and according to the luggage she saw today, there was a dragon in that house.

Jane shivered from cold. Marjory might be a dragon, but she was asleep. The cold night was awake.

She let herself into the mudroom and took her shoes off. She tucked them under the bench and shuffled in her sock feet to the door. She pulled the door open slowly, hoping it wouldn't groan. It didn't. She was desperate to get in unnoticed. This morning's invitation might well have been forgotten. Or the inviter might already be gone.

She debated which bedroom to take herself to as she made her way to the bottom of the back steps. The third floor of the Crawford house was mostly the original ballroom, but behind the ballroom were two small bedrooms for staff that the family who originally built the house used to keep. Like the other bedrooms, they were dust-free and had fresh linens. Barring the bodies in the master bedroom, the Crawford house was always ready for company.

The third step of the back stairs squeaked, but otherwise the trip up the first flight of stairs was uneventful.

The second flight of stairs squeaked twice at the top so there was no getting away from it. She reached the first of the servants' bedrooms and slipped in. She shut the door behind her with a click and sat on the bed. It was just after midnight now. In the morning she had to go clean the neighbor's house. Possibly, if she was going to be staying on here as some kind of live-in maid, she'd have to make breakfast as well.

Jane shifted her winter coat off. She plucked her phone out of her pocket and pulled up Jake's contact info. Better now than never. "GNite. CU AM" She texted. "Will U want BFast?" She flopped down on her pillow and hit 'send.' Did a text count as a contractual agreement? She wondered what Isaac's dad would have to say about that.

Isaac.

Was tonight's coffee really a date? Did she want it to be? Was it against the rules for her to date an instructor? These questions were far more welcome than the question of how Marjory would take it when she saw Jane in the morning.

CHAPTER 6

SLEEP WAS HARD TO COME BY, but waking up was a breeze. Jane whipped herself out of bed, still wearing the same clothes she had spent the day before in. Her laundry was moldering in the Rabbit. Maybe when she negotiated her new position with Jake he would throw in laundry room privileges.

The bathrooms on the top floor were clean and had soap and towels—Jane was particularly glad she never scrimped on the upstairs work—but no bathtub. She gave herself a quick scrub up and did her best to smooth her crumpled clothes. She wasn't a pretty sight. Marjory couldn't possibly know her schedule so Jane's current plan was to sneak down the back steps, retrieve her shoes from the mudroom and then enter the kitchen as though it were all perfectly normal.

Jane flicked the light off and shut the door.

"Hey!"

Jane jumped.

"So what's for breakfast then?" Jake seemed to fill the narrow hallway. He leaned on one wall with his outstretched arm, his legs crossed at the ankle all the way to the other wall. He smelled like he had been drinking, and like Jane still had on yesterday's clothes.

"Whatever you like." Jane tried to duck past.

Jake stood up. "I'm glad you decided to have sympathy on me."

"It seemed...like the right thing to do."

"Eggs. And pancakes." Jake let Jane pass.

She hustled down the stairs, but he stayed at her heels.

"Scratch that. Eggs, bacon, and waffles. Do we have any bacon?"

"I'll look."

"Jane, tell me again why you clean houses?"

"To make money, Jake."

"Yeah, but don't you have money? I mean, I thought you Adlers had money."

"My parents have money. And I have work, so, that's like having money, in its own special way. You wouldn't know." Jane rounded the corner into the kitchen. The sun had yet to rise. The kitchen windows were black as night above the checkered café curtains.

"It's too early for sarcasm." Jake caught up with her, but bumped into the doorjamb. He leaned on it, making puppy eyes at Jane.

"My apologies."

"I understand *jobs*, but if your parents have money why aren't you a sorority sister like Phoebe?"

"Where is Phoebe, by the way?" Jane turned on the kitchen lights. She went straight for the coffee pot. She could not manage Jake at five in the morning without coffee.

"She's at school still. No point in coming here until the funeral, right?" Jake shuffled into the kitchen, and heaved himself onto a stool.

Jane rested her hands on the kitchen island. "Jake, I'm a little worried about you. Your parents…"

"Are dead. I know."

"But how are you doing? Do you know what the stages of grief are? It's early, I know, but I think you may be in shock." The coffeemaker burbled in the background. It was beginning to smell like something worthwhile. Jane took a deep breath, letting her nose fill up with the smell of hope.

"I'm self-medicating. It works. Where do we keep the bacon?" Jake opened the refrigerator.

"What time did you get in last night?"

"What are you, my mom?" Jake tucked his head into the fridge like a dog digging for a bone.

"I'm just concerned." Jane found her favorite coffee mug. She drummed her fingers on it, waiting for the coffee machine light that indicated she could commence with waking up.

"If a young man in crisis is going to properly self-medicate he can't be expected to come home, okay? It takes a full night to wipe away the grief." Jake pulled himself out of the refrigerator. "There isn't any food in there."

"I can't believe you are joking about this." Jane couldn't wait any longer. She pulled the stainless steel carafe out of the machine. There was almost enough in it to fill her cup. She took a drink. It was probably psychosomatic, but it helped. She stood up a little straighter.

"I can't believe you are a housekeeper. Look at yourself." Jake stood in front of the fridge with the door still open.

Jane replaced the coffee carafe. She didn't answer. She knew what she looked like right now. And, if her hopes for her future came to pass, she would look a lot worse than this more often than not. The two-thirds world was not a glamorous place.

"But really, what happened? I mean, what, we graduated high school like yesterday and you've come to this already? You need to come out with us tonight, like old times." Jake leaned against the open door of the refrigerator.

"Close the door, Jake."

Jake turned around. He stared at the door for a moment. He shut it, but he crossed himself first. "There, but for the grace, go I."

"I didn't party in the 'old times,' Jake."

"Don't I know it. What was with that? We had a good scene at the old alma mater. Were you playing hard to get? Because if so, it worked. You had all the boys salivating for you." Jake slumped onto his stool again.

"I just don't party." Jake looked rotten. He looked physically ill. She turned away from him. He needed coffee at least. She pulled another mug down from the cupboard. It said, "Prez Prep Key Club." Must have been Phoebe's.

"We don't have any bacon, Jane. Both of my parents are dead and we don't have any bacon."

"You just got in, didn't you?" Jane poured his coffee and set the mug next to his elbow. She wondered a bit if he would pass out and knock it over or pick it up and drink it. Jake's eyes were red and his nose as well. He had deep bags under his eyes. "You're still drunk."

"Don't say it like that, Jane, like it's a bad, bad thing. I'm medicating my depression and grief, remember?"

Jane pulled the mug of coffee back to herself. "Go upstairs, Jake. Go get some sleep. And then…and then we'll talk about your grief."

Jane had cried every night for three days when her parents pulled the U-haul away. Three nights of weeping in the junior suite she shared with Sam, just because her parents had moved away to Phoenix. What would she have done if they had died?

"Janey, will you put me to bed, please?" Jake wilted over on the counter top, resting his temple against his hand. His eyes fluttered shut.

Marjory entered with resounding footsteps. There were three early risers in the house, apparently. "Oh!" She stopped in the doorway to the kitchen. "I didn't realize. I see. Well, good then. I'll take my breakfast in the dining room." Marjory bounced her keen gaze back and forth from Jane to Jake.

"She can't, Aunty. We're out of bacon." Jake let his head roll off his fist. He began to sob.

Jane closed her eyes and took a deep breath. This was the family in crisis that needed her help. She could take it.

"Get that boy upstairs. He's a shame to look at." Marjory stared at him with a furrowed brow.

"Yes, ma'am." Jane took Jake by the arm and led him to the front staircase. His sobbing calmed down as they walked.

"Janey, will you snuggle me? I'm pretty sad." He flopped his head over onto her shoulder.

"Just go to bed and forget about this night, okay?" Jane whispered.

"Please for snuggle?"

Jake didn't look any older than he had looked when they graduated not so long ago. His cheeks sported a barely visible blond scruff. And far from bulking up he had grown an inch or two taller, but looked ganglier. He looked so young and vulnerable, leaning on her as they marched up the stairs, that she was sorely tempted to snuggle him until he fell asleep.

But he stank like he had washed up in a bathtub full of hooch so the tempting sympathy passed.

"Get to bed. I'll get some bacon so you can have breakfast later today."

"Janey does love me."

Jane pushed him into his bedroom and shut the door. He'd have to put himself to bed.

"Ja-ane?" Marjory must have been at the foot of the stairs, her voice carried straight up to Jane.

"Coming!" Jane scurried down the stairs.

Marjory stood in the entryway looking out the front window. "Jane, I'm going to need a lot of help today. Do you think you can manage?"

"It depends. I have other clients today as well."

"I see. And so you don't have time in your schedule for us?"

"I have some time, ma'am. So it depends on what you need help with." Jane wrapped the edge of her t-shirt around her fingers. It really depended on how much per hour Marjory was willing to pay. She didn't want to agree to anything without establishing her boundaries first.

"Obviously this is related to our recent loss. You can see I am in no condition to go looking for more help." Marjory looked Jane up and down, her lip curling in disgust, "You really will have to do."

"What is it you need?" Jane thought Marjory looked perfectly competent still, but she cautioned herself against judging too quickly. Only God knew what was going on in Marjory's heart.

"We are about ready to schedule the funeral. This whole house needs to be cleaned in preparation for it. I can't imagine what you have been doing for my poor sister, but I can't have all of the guests here with the house in this condition. Can you fit a deep clean into your schedule?"

Jane took a deep breath. The house looked gorgeous, like always, and it raised Jane's hackles to hear otherwise. Pamela had done nothing but praise her work. Besides, she honestly couldn't fit a deep clean in, if for no other reason than she couldn't get the house any cleaner than it already was, but she decided to try. She needed extra work, and this job was conveniently located. "Yes, if you don't mind my working late evenings and early mornings to get it done, and if you will give me a list of the specific jobs you want done." She paused and tried to smile. "My rates are fifty dollars an hour."

Marjory lifted an eyebrow. "Ah."

Jane kept quiet. Only the Crawfords paid her that much, and they had suggested it in the first place.

"Can we set that up as an auto payment?" Marjory glanced at the computer with a frown.

"Usually Pamela left my payment in an envelope with the day's instructions on the first Monday of the month." Jane squared her shoulders. This was her one shot to get her affairs in order. She didn't want to chicken out.

"Mondays?"

"Yes, ma'am."

"Then you were already paid for this week?"

"No, ma'am. I wasn't."

"Hmm...I suppose you can't *prove* you weren't paid." Marjory pulled out the desk chair. She rested her hands on the black leather headrest.

Jane looked Marjory in the eye. She supposed she couldn't prove it either, but if she could get enough hours of deep cleaning in it would help make up for the loss. "Because of the lost wages I would need to be paid half up front."

"Indeed?" Marjory said. "Well, I'll think about it."

"I plan to book my schedule this morning, ma'am. So if you would like to book me you'll have to decide now." Jane felt like she was holding Marjory up, rather than serving her.

"Fine, fine. You *are* a live-in maid, correct?"

Where to start with that question? "I am, but only at the recent request of Jake."

"You've moved in with Jake?" Marjory's knuckles turned white as she gripped the chair.

"No, ma'am. Not in the manner you are implying. The morning we met you in the office to get his car he asked me to move in as a housekeeper because the place was too big for him to manage alone."

"And you just jumped right on that offer?" Marjory's lip curled up in disgust. "Now that he is going to inherit, the *maid* moves in."

"Like I said..." Jane's voice cracked. The conversation had been going so well until the question of her housing came up. She didn't want Marjory to think she was a gold digger. She wasn't anything of the kind.

"All right. That's fine. Don't make a scene. We'll discuss this later."

Jane stood her ground for a moment. She prayed silently. *The meek shall inherit the Earth.* But that was the point, wasn't it? She wasn't trying to inherit anything. Just trying to have a safe place to sleep at night. *The meek shall inherit the Earth.* She may not want to marry the Roly Burger heir but that didn't change what God was whispering to her. *Be meek.*

"Yes, ma'am." She left the room as quietly as she could. She wasn't sure that Marjory still wanted breakfast, but better safe than sorry. She went back to the kitchen and started to cook.

Marjory was somewhat less than impressed by the toast and fried egg, but Jane couldn't fault herself. Buying groceries and cooking had never been on her to-do list. If Marjory wanted to add it now, she'd have to pay for it.

As she scrubbed the yolk off the china plate, Jane wondered about the etiquette of contract negotiation during a time of mourning. Not for the first time her mind wandered back to Jake and what he might think about it. *No, Isaac.* She shook her head. She wanted to know what *Isaac* thought of this situation. Not Jake.

She wiped the plate dry. She had better get out of the house. She had no interest in confusing her feelings for Isaac and Jake. Jane reached up to put the plate in the cupboard and got an unfortunate whiff of her unwashed self. Laundry. And a shower. She couldn't go to her next client's house, or anywhere for that matter, like this.

From her spot tucked in the corner of the recently remolded kitchen Jane listened to Marjory on the phone. She wasn't trying to eavesdrop. She just wanted to sneak out to her car to grab her laundry while Marjory was distracted. From what she could hear the conversation Marjory was having was complicated and heated. When Jane thought she heard the door to the late lamented-Bob's office close, she made her break for the car.

She felt eyes on the back of her neck as she popped open the Rabbit. She even turned around, but every curtain was closed. Jane pulled her laundry basket out of the car. If she wanted to be clean, it was now or never.

She lugged her canvas bag of dirty clothes upstairs to the laundry room. The real problem was going to be waiting for the clothes to get clean before she took a shower. She shoved a small load in the machine, just enough for the day, and set the machine to quick wash. Had her life really come to this? Skulking about in someone else's home trying to hide while she washed her clothes?

She had used her own detergent in an effort to take as little as she could from the Crawfords while she stayed at the house. She sat down on the parquet floor of the laundry room and leaned against the wall. She stared at the rose-covered wallpaper across from her while her laundry spun in the machine.

Jake was right. He was sleeping off a hangover in the other room, but he was right. The Adlers did have money. Money they would have been happy to spend on her if she had only picked a real university and a real degree. They were even willing to help her reach her goal of being a missionary, but like the washing machine, whose digital timer ticked down with painful slowness, a four-year university education had sounded like it would take forever. Why should she spend four years studying econ and literature if all she wanted to do was spread the gospel to the lost?

Jane closed her eyes and rested her face in her hands. "Oh, dear Lord, I am homeless and broke, and I am afraid it was all for pride. Who am I to say that I know better than my parents? Do you want me to call them? To quit all of this and go home?"

"Well, I don't. If you go home, who will wash these for me?" Jake dropped a pile of laundry next to her with a thump. "Who knew I had so many filthy clothes? Who usually does the laundry around here? I swear no one has touched my clothes since Christmas."

Jane lifted her head. "Shouldn't you be asleep still?"

"Can't sleep. Terribly depressed. Grief."

She tried to read sincerity into his words, but it was difficult. "Have you given yourself the chance to grieve yet, Jake?"

Jake turned away. He covered his face with his hand.

There was a sharp knock at the door and Marjory stepped into the laundry room. "Jacob, leave her alone. She has work to do."

Jake straightened up like he had had an electric shock. "Yes, ma'am."

"And go find your sister. She's not answering any of my calls."

Jake turned and snapped his heels together. He saluted his aunt. "Yes, ma'am."

"And don't be a brat. Get out of here." She gave Jake an awkward pat on the shoulder as he marched past.

She turned her attention back to Jane. "You must forgive him. He's not just young, but also obnoxious. I really don't know what your role here was while Pamela was alive, but seeing as how Jake has hired you to be live-in staff, I have a job for you."

Jane stood up and tried to straighten her clothes. "Yes?" Her schedule didn't feel like it could take another assignment, but it was better to listen first and discuss after.

"This afternoon I have several men from the business coming over. I will need you to serve coffee and…refreshments. I don't care what, but I need you to be on hand to prepare, serve, and clear."

Jane nodded, but kept her tongue.

"They will be here at two this afternoon."

Jane cleared her throat. "I can be here for that, however the kitchen is empty, as far as I can tell. Will you be getting what we need or leaving me cash for that?"

Marjory let out a heavy sigh. "That's right. I noticed breakfast was slim today. I'll leave an envelope of cash. I won't be having dinner here, but you will probably need to get something to feed Jake as well. I doubt he knows how to feed himself."

Jane nodded. The words, 'an envelope of cash' were the best ones she had heard in a week.

Marjory looked at her watch. "All right then, I'll see you at two." She turned to leave, but paused with one hand on the door, "I know this is all very awkward, Jane, but loss is like that. Things will get back to normal eventually." Marjory pulled the door shut behind her.

Jane slumped against the wall. As soon as her clothes were out of the machine she was taking a shower and leaving. The idea of skipping town with the envelope of cash brought a brief smile to her face, but she wouldn't. She'd slip away to the library, spend some time in the Word, clean the home of her paying client, and then do the shopping.

Things were looking up.

CHAPTER 7

BACK IN THE CRAWFORD KITCHEN, Jane finally felt refreshed. Clean clothes and a shower were nothing to the hour she had spent in the library in prayer and meditation. God's words had soaked deeply into her heart and she felt strong. The Lord was her tower and refuge, so she would never be truly homeless. His word was her daily bread so she could never truly go hungry. Plus the other client she had cleaned for this morning had left her a beginning of the month bonus. They had never done that before.

She pulled a pan of heat-and-rise dinner rolls out of the oven and replaced it with a pan of miniature cinnamon rolls. She set the hot pan on the granite counter to cool. In addition to the rolls, she was serving a veggie tray, cold cut platter, broccoli and raisin salad, cinnamon rolls which were baking in the other oven, fruit platter, cheese plate, baguette and brie, fresh hot coffee, and unsweetened ice tea. The piles of food in the refrigerator did her heart good. She had also stocked up on the basics for the Crawfords' breakfasts, lunches, and dinners. No one was going to go hungry while she was in charge of the kitchen.

She half-expected Jake to pop in while she arranged the food, but he didn't. She carted the first tray out to the library where Marjory was meeting with the business associates, a twinge of disappointment nipping her heart.

She let herself into the room as quietly as she could, her slippered feet whispering across the polished hard wood floor. At a nod from Marjory, Jane walked to each of the three businessmen with the tray held out in front of her.

The men were all in suits with polished shoes. All but one looked old enough to be her father. Considering they had some kind of important role in the Roly Burger corporation they probably knew her father. She kept her eyes down. When she had made her way around with the fruit and veggie tray, she exited.

She'd refill coffees in about five minutes, offer the meat, bread, and cheese, and then close with the sweet rolls. She was making it up as she went along, but no one seemed to mind.

They barely noticed her at all, in fact. Their discussion seemed heated, and their angry voices carried down the hall. Not quite all the way to the kitchen, but as she toted her emptier, lighter trays back she could still hear them speaking.

"This is what Bob wanted." The speaker's deep voice was like a growl. He was the man who was wearing wire-rim glasses, she was sure. A Mr. Vargas, who she had met at past Roly Burger company picnics.

"But until the investigation is over we shouldn't make any changes." Marjory didn't sound angry, but she was loud and forceful.

"If we shouldn't make any changes, then I say the plan that is already in effect needs to keep going." Jane didn't recognize this voice so she assumed it was the man in a green tie, someone she had never seen before.

"How can it keep going if we haven't begun? I blame the newspaper. I don't know how they got wind of Bob's plans." This was Vargas again.

"We can't let some reporter make business decisions for us." Marjory's sentence faded away as Jane entered the kitchen.

She could see their dilemma. Did they continue to shut down all of the local Roly Burgers the way that Bob had planned and had been reported or did they wait, keep the status quo, and let the new leader make his or her own decision?

And who would the new leader be? Did Bob's sister-in-law Marjory come into leadership now or did his eldest son, Jake? For as long as Jane could remember Marjory had been a social member of the company—at all of the picnics and openings, not running a location of her own, or a member of the

board. At one time Marjory's deceased husband had been a
board member, but that was years ago.

Jane carried the coffee carafe to the library door and
waited. She didn't want to walk into the middle of an
argument—but from the sounds of it, she would have to wait a
long time before they cooled down.

As before, she tried not to eavesdrop but certain words
grabbed her attention. Words like "murder" and "motive" and
"we'll call our lawyers." She lost track of who was making the
worst of the accusations, but Marjory had said "motive" in a
shocked kind of voice. And Vargas had said he'd be calling his
lawyers. The fourth man in the room, a man she remembered
was called Walker or Waller…something like that…was trying
to calm the group down. At least that was what it sounded like to
Jane. When she heard him say "Peace, peace" for the third time
she turned the knob and slipped into the room.

Marjory was standing, red-faced, staring at the man with
the green tie. He was also standing. He looked flustered, ashen-
faced even. He was blubbering something. It sounded like "but
Bob, but Bob, but Bob," over and over, the most literal
blubbering Jane had ever heard.

"Ahem." Jane cleared her throat into her fist.

Vargas stood up with a violent thrust. "I *will* be calling my
lawyers." He shoved his way past Jane and left.

The blubbering man turned and watched Vargas leave.
"What does it mean?" He almost wailed as he spoke.

"It *means* that we all need to contact our lawyers."
Walker—or Waller—stood up as well. He nodded at Marjory
and moved to the door, not seeming to notice Jane and her carafe
of coffee. "And you, *my dear*, had better contact your own
lawyer, because the corporate lawyer will do you no good." He
exited less dramatically than Vargas had done.

Jane turned to Marjory.

Marjory shook her head. "Drama queens," she huffed.

The blubbering man nodded at her, his mouth agape.

"You're the worst of them, Fitch, I swear. How hard is it
to nod your head and agree? We need to press pause on all
corporate decision-making until after the investigation of the
deaths is over and the estate has been settled." Marjory looked

over Jane's head at the open library door. "It's like those men don't even care that my husband's brother and sister-in-law are dead."

Fitch swallowed and nodded. He looked to the door but stopped, his eyes glued to Jane. "You're that Adler girl," he said.

Jane nodded. He knew her?

"I managed your dad's locations until last year." The color was slowly returning to Fitch's cheeks.

"Ah," Jane said. He still didn't look familiar.

"Don't worry about calling a lawyer." Marjory's voice had gone soft. "Those men are bluffing."

Fitch nodded. "Yes. All right. I won't."

If he had been managing burger restaurants for her father, Jane was certain he didn't have a lawyer, or the money to call a lawyer. No wonder he had been reduced to a blubbering pile by the other men in the room.

"Go back to work. Business as usual for you."

Fitch nodded. "Business as usual for building and maintenance." He exited the library, leaving Jane and Marjory alone.

"Well...that didn't go as I had hoped." Marjory stood with her hands clasped behind her back, facing the window. "Thank you for being available."

There was a softness to Marjory's words that caught Jane off guard.

"That's why I'm here, ma'am." It was the truth, as far as it went. Jane was here, right now, to serve a family in crisis. Or so she kept reminding herself.

"Please clean up this mess." Marjory turned and waved her hand to the food that had hardly been touched.

"Yes, ma'am." Jane picked up the plates from the small tables scattered around the room and balanced them with her empty hand. As she headed back to the kitchen she wondered what conversation she had stumbled onto. Were the suspicious deaths murder after all, and was someone in that room responsible? She shivered at the thought. From what she had heard, Fitch had been invited as a yes-man, to agree with whatever Marjory proposed. The Waller/Walker man and Vargas were muckety-mucks in the Burger with the Roly-Poly Bun business. Would either of them have wanted Bob and Pamela dead?

Would Marjory have wanted them dead?

Jane stretched plastic wrap over the untouched tray of meats. She had enough food to feed herself, Jake, and Marjory for several lunches, unless the cops came and arrested Marjory, in which case the meat would last even longer.

Jane bit her bottom lip. Marjory was acting like she was in charge of the family business. Seizing control of the family business seemed like a good motive, but was it true?

Jane needed to find out what role Vargas and Waller/Walker played in the business to understand what their motives would have been. After stowing all of the food away in the much fuller side-by-side stainless-steel fridge, Jane trod slowly back to the library. This wasn't any of her business, but so long as she was hearing half conversations through closed doors, it seemed wise to attempt to understand what was going on. And, in its own way, digging into the suspicious deaths was sort of like serving a family in crisis. Jane wondered, with a little smile, if she could get extra credit for finding out who had killed the Crawfords.

CHAPTER 8

JANE HAD MANAGED TO GET all of her clients cleaned despite the additional work that came with cooking for Marjory and Jake. By the time Friday night class rolled around, Jane felt tired, but satisfied. The fluorescent flickers and the aroma of dust greeted her like an old friend. She had made it back to class again after the most trying week of her life. However, try as she might, she still struggled to pay attention to the whole lecture.

Three hours of lecture was long at the best of times, but when trying to sort out the major players in a suspicious death, plot a plan to retrieve her confiscated belongings, and keep her face from blushing magenta every time she looked at the tall, dark, and disarming lecturer, it was a Herculean event. And she wasn't Hercules.

Hercule Poirot, perhaps, but not Hercules.

She had a list of people she needed to talk to about Pam and Bob, and next to each name she had noted what she knew of their psychology.

Since she had grown up with Phoebe and Jake at their exclusive Christian prep school, they were easy.

Jake: lazy, self absorbed, emotionally stunted. She scribbled possible motives onto her paper next to his name, but they seemed foolish. Seize power of the company. Scratch. If it had been a motive he certainly hadn't exerted himself to do it. Escape being sucked into the family company? That one seemed more likely, but with Bob's plans to shut the burger business down being public it seemed unnecessary. What company was Jake at risk of being sucked in to? Unless she came up with something better than the last one on the list, "Erratic behavior indicates mental imbalance," Jake was not her first suspect.

She considered Phoebe. Despite being on campus at a university a mere two miles from her parents' home she hadn't been seen since the deaths were reported. Well, Jane had to admit, she herself hadn't seen Phoebe, but Jake, Marjory, or any number of their other family members may have. Under psychological notes Jane listed: Determined, driven, hardworking. In general those were good qualities and only applied, as far as Jane knew, to Phoebe's soccer career. The notebook paper line allocated for motive was blank. Why would Phoebe want her parents dead? They were paying a pretty penny so she could play soccer for a team that had recently won the national championship. One doesn't hamstring one's gravy train, usually.

Marjory was a different story. Marjory, Bob's sister-in-law via her marriage to his deceased brother, had grabbed the reins of the business that had funded her lifestyle all these years. When William had passed away, his shares had gone to her. Or were they shares? Is that what it was called? Jane had to admit that she didn't know what kind of financial stake Marjory had in Roly Burgers.

Financial stake. Marjory wanted status quo…that's what Jane had gleaned from the bits of conversation that had fallen by the wayside. If she were financially dependent on the burger business would she have been willing to kill to keep it running?

Or, by status quo, did Marjory really mean they needed to continue Bob's plan to shut it down? Jane picked through her memories of overheard conversations.

Jane scribbled big X's across all of her notes. It didn't matter. It wasn't her business, and it was distracting her from the real and present danger of not getting her lock-box with her emergency credit card back from the apartment. Plus her futon, privacy screen, side table, locally-sourced honey mustard, alarm clock, iPod, swimsuit, Excedrin migraine, shower foof, the OED on CD Rom and Nave's Topical Bible. She stopped. Was that all she owned in the world besides the junk in her car and the laundry that she had finally managed to wash? No, she also had the complete works of L M Montgomery, a hummingbird feeder, a pair of Gucci sunglasses, her Birkenstocks, and one pair of high heels. She ran her pencil down the list. That looked exhaustive. And pathetic. But she had needed to keep her possessions to a minimum. She did not need a bunch of first world baggage in the 10/40 window.

She was still staring at her list, bouncing her thoughts between facing down the bully landlord and what could be keeping Phoebe from coming to the house when Sarah sat on the desk.

"Earth to Jane. You have a serious case of senior-itis."

"How can I? This place doesn't have 'seniors.'"

"It's a great mystery, but either way, our lecturer stares at you for hours at a time and you ignore everything he says."

Heat rose to Jane's cheeks. She looked up to see if he was anywhere near them.

"It's okay, he took a call in the hallway. What's up with you two? The last two classes, you two couldn't keep your eyes off of each other and then tonight you hardly know he's alive."

"Nothing's 'up.' I've just got a lot on my mind right now."

"What is so important that you can't make time for a hot guy like Mr. Daniels?"

Jane tried to suppress a smile. *Mr. Daniels.* She called him Isaac, herself. "Did I not tell you that I was evicted because my roommate stole my rent money instead of paying it and now the landlord has all of my worldly possessions under lock and key?"

"You are kidding!"

"I'm not. It is pretty bad. I have a place to stay right now—as a housekeeper, but I'd kind of like to get all of my stuff back, you know?"

"I can imagine, at least."

Jane laid her hand over her suspect notes. "I admit though, the attractive lecturer has distracted me from making any progress."

Sarah's eyes popped open wide and her mouth made a little "o." She shook her head in a tiny motion. Jane's heart dropped. It was that shocked-but-laughing look people get when someone you are talking about is right behind you.

Jane raised an eyebrow.

Sarah looked over her shoulder, but turned her head as though following someone with her eyes. Then she let out a long breath. "He passed. I don't think he heard you."

"I'm probably a really big idiot." Jane picked up her pen and tapped it on her page of notes.

"No, I can assure you, as an expert at seeing who digs who, however attractive you find Mr. Daniels, he thinks the same, but double, about you."

The smile snuck back on Jane. Her heart did a little flip. She held the same opinion, after their coffee earlier in the week, but they hadn't been calling or texting or any of the other things people do when they like each other, so she had begun to think she was imagining it. Of course, they hadn't exchanged phone numbers, but that was a part of her disappointment.

Sarah stood up. "Stay at your desk after everyone leaves. He always walks out of class immediately after you do. This time, just don't leave."

Jane nodded.

The rowdy students, hopped up on coffee from the cart in the lounge, seemed like they'd never leave at the end of lecture. Isaac had been in the middle of a lively conversation with several of them. It didn't seem to Jane that he had noticed her waiting. While she debated on paper whether to call her parents over the weekend, when she knew they'd be back from the cruise, Isaac and the students she thought of as "kids" argued over the L in John Calvin's TULIP. As far as Jane was concerned John 3:16 said *God so loved the world* so there couldn't be any limit to his atonement. She was glad to hear that was the side Isaac took as well.

"You just believe what your seminary taught you," an eighteen-year-old Calvinist called Duncan said. He thumped his Bible with his knuckles. "If you took the Bible literally the way you claim you do, you couldn't deny that Christ's atonement isn't for everyone. Jeesh, all you have to do is look around and see that not everyone is saved."

"You are confusing your L and your U, Duncan. Not everyone is saved because not everyone is elect."

"You're both just rebelling against your parents. It's dangerous and stupid." Sarah flailed her hands while she spoke.

"We all grew up together at Fair Havens Baptist and you know you don't really believe this Tulip nonsense."

"Be careful," Isaac said. "Just because we don't subscribe to it, doesn't mean it is nonsense."

"But it is dangerous and foolish. What's the point of missions if everyone who is going to get saved will get saved and can't escape it anyway?"

"Thank you, William Carey. There is more to salvation than that."

"Of course there is. That's my point!" Sarah face-palmed.

Jane rested her head in her hands. Free time. That was the problem with the live-in students. They had too much free time. If they had some real work to do they wouldn't have time to waste arguing about election and all of that. She could wait three more minutes. If they weren't done arguing in three minutes she'd have to leave, no matter how much she wanted a few moments alone with Isaac.

They didn't stop. At one moment Jane thought she caught Isaac glancing her way, but he didn't extricate himself from the group.

Jane packed up her small computer and her notebooks. She left without looking behind her.

As Jane turned into the Crawfords' driveway her phone rang.

"I hope you don't mind. I got your number from the class list."

Jane's heart raced. "I don't." She felt like her heart was going to break out of her chest.

"It's been a while...I was just wondering how you are doing."

"Okay...hanging in there. Um...when I got home after coffee I found out I had been evicted." Jane unbuckled, but stayed in her car.

"What? Are you kidding? I'm so sorry I didn't follow you home. I should have followed you. It was so late. What did you do?"

"I'm okay. It is okay. It might have been weird if you had followed me home." Jane couldn't suppress the smile. Maybe, just maybe, he was interested.

"Yeah, that's what I thought at the time."

"You were right." Jane drummed the steering wheel with her fingers.

"Do you have a place to stay? You must since it's been days, but do you need any help with anything?"

"I hate drama. I'm sorry if this seems like a lot of drama. Drama is totally not my thing." In fact, Jane thought, she might die if he thought this was normal life for her.

"I can imagine."

"So, my roommate stole my half of the rent for what seems to have been several months, and that's why we were evicted, but the landlord has all my stuff locked up, something about selling it to make up for back rent. Is that right? Can he do that?"

"You should talk to a lawyer, Jane. Do you want to? I can connect you with my dad."

"I really can't afford a lawyer." Her envelope full of cash that had represented hope didn't have enough to pay a lawyer's consultation, much less any real help.

"No problem, just meet my dad for coffee or something. Let him talk you through it just once."

"But would he do that? For free?" Jane tapped her toes in rhythm with her drumming fingers. She couldn't have been more excited if he had actually shown up at the house. She dearly wanted to turn the conversation away from her predicament.

"He'd help a friend of mine, sure."

Jane bit her lip. She'd only known this guy for a few days, but so far absolutely everything about him was wonderful.

"Let me talk to him and then I'll give you his number, okay?"

"Thank you so much, Isaac."

"I know you are pretty busy but I was wondering if you were free for dinner next Saturday?"

Jane closed her eyes and pictured her schedule. The date of the funeral was still unannounced. Unless that changed, she was still free. "Sure, I'm free," she said.

"Great. Dinner then? Can I pick you up?"

Jane looked up at the Crawfords' brick mansion. "Let's just meet this time."

Isaac didn't answer for a moment. "Oh. Okay."

"Just because I'm staying with clients. I don't know if housekeepers get to go on dates, you know?"

"Ah! Okay then. Can you meet me at Hudson Station at seven?"

"I'd love to. See you then." She hadn't meant to end the call, but the "see you then" and the awkwardness of arranging a first date took the wind out of the conversation.

"See you then," Isaac repeated, and ended the call.

Hudson Station. That was a nice restaurant. She'd been there with her parents before. This was a real date. Not just a quick coffee or hanging out to talk about her drama. Too bad she didn't have anything to wear.

CHAPTER 9

JANE WAS SHIVERY WITH EXCITEMENT on her drive down to the Mini-Missions Fair. She felt like she had some kind of a handle on how God was using her in the life of the Crawfords, but cleaning up for local families wasn't her destiny. Cross-Cultural Evangelism was.

Last year she had felt a strong connection with the Village Friends. She wasn't a Quaker, but after research and prayer she felt like she could sign their statement of faith with an honest heart. The work they did with women in the 10/40 window made her heart flutter. She could picture herself settled into village life, learning from the women and sharing with them. The representative last year had been encouraging as well. She and Jane had hit it off. They had even exchanged emails on and off over the last year. Jane planned on hitting up the Village Friends booth first thing to reconnect and even, maybe, begin the application process.

Of course, Jane reminded herself, there were many great organizations to work with. She'd have to attend the fair with an open mind and heart, listening to God's call. She just hoped, and prayed, that His call would involve Village Friends.

The missionaries' cars filled the back parking lot at the Harvest campus. Jane tingled with excitement. Today looked to be a day of unalloyed pleasure.

She parked in front of the dorms and headed to the old sanitarium building. Like last year, the organization booths were arranged around the perimeter and down the middle of the dining hall. The keynote speaker would be using the chapel/classroom and the library and boys' and girls' community rooms in the dorms would host the break-out sessions.

The dining hall was packed tight with booths, tables, tri-folds, even video projectors. Missions recruiting seemed to have taken a high tech turn since the year before. The aroma of stale cafeteria food had been replaced by the smell of thousands of freshly printed pamphlets and excited kids. The room was bright, hot, and loud.

There looked to be about twenty-five tables and a missionary for every student. Weaving her way through the bustle wasn't easy, but it was fun. Jane kept her eye open for the Village Friends logo but it wasn't one of the first booths.

She tried to ease her way past the Youth Mission Adventures table, but her bag snagged on something. She turned to see the strap of her bag firmly in the hand of Amelia Long, her closest friend from last year's class at Harvest. "Amelia!" Jane dove to hug her. "When did you get home?"

"We made it in last Tuesday. Just in time for the Harvest Fair. I begged them to let me come rep here." Amelia squeezed Jane. "You're almost done, right? Are you ready to fill out your apps? I've been dying to have you on the field with me."

"Amelia—you know I'm not joining YMA. I've got my sights set on something long term." Jane tilted her head away from Amelia, in search of the familiar brown logo.

"This is such great experience, though, Jane, I don't think you should dismiss it. So many of our staff move on to long-term missions after they serve with us. I think you would really benefit from a term with YMA." Amelia grabbed a handful of pamphlets and shoved them at Jane. "Just reconsider it? If you join the Uruguay Station we could serve together!"

Jane took the pamphlets. "I'll pray about it. How does that sound? I promised myself I'd keep a completely open mind despite what my personal longing is."

"Thank you. Thank you, thank you!" Amelia threw her arms around Jane again and squeezed her. "We've got break-out sessions in the dorm lounges this year. Make sure you come to mine. I'm sure you won't say no after you hear us share."

Jane nodded. She had already dismissed the conversation in her mind. Her year of hanging out with Amelia and dreaming together about missions work seemed so long ago.

Jane moved on from the Youth Mission Adventures table. She had spotted Village Friends around the corner. A knot of students encircled one of the representatives, but there was also an older woman sitting at the table, doing some kind of handwork. Jane pushed through the crowd.

"Good morning," Jane said.

"Ah, good morning, my dear."

"What is that you are making?" Jane spoke with a quiet reverence. The woman in front of her looked to be in her early seventies. She wore some kind of tribal dress that looked hand-embroidered. As she worked on a piece of her own embroidery, her hands shook. "This is suzani, a traditional Kirghiz embroidery."

The unbleached fabric was covered with soft cotton thread in vibrant primary colors. The hook looked like a crochet hook, but was sharper, and seemed to work like a regular needle.

"This is the tambour," the missionary said, directing Jane's eyes to the hoop. "And this is the suzan, or needle. It's rather different than your needles at home, isn't it?"

"Yes." Jane watched as the missionary pierced the taut fabric with her needle.

"This is what I spent many, many years doing with the women of Chong-Tesh. Mothers and daughters work the suzani together, and share wisdom. We find that letting the women of the village teach us their work is the best way for us to share our savior with them."

"I'm Jane, a friend of Sandra Obwey." Jane stuck out her hand. She was too excited to keep talking about the suzani. She wanted to skip right to the paperwork.

The missionary set down her tambour. She took Jane's hand in her own thin, warm hand. "Lovely to meet you. I am Margaret Stowe, but you may call me Macha, my Kyrgy name for the last forty years."

"Wonderful to meet you, Macha. I'm really excited about graduating Harvest this year. Sandra and I connected last year and I've been interested in partnering with Village Friends." Jane scanned the table. Intricate handiwork covered the whole table. There wasn't a flier or leaflet in sight.

"Sandra and I really connected. I was hoping to get more information today. Maybe an application."

"Please, take a seat." Macha indicated a folding chair at the corner of the table. "Do you sew, Jane?"

"Not yet." Jane's cheeks were beginning to hurt from her smile. Patience. She needed to be patient with Macha.

"It would be a good idea to learn as much about sewing as you can. I don't know where God is planning to send you, but all of the work we do with women centers on sewing. You should also know quite a bit about cooking."

"Oh, I do. I've been living on my own for two years." Jane bit her lip. It sounded true before it came out, but as soon as she said it her life of ramen noodles and frozen pizza flashed before her. That, she was sure, was not what Macha meant by cooking. "At least, I should say, I've got a start. I'm learning."

"That's very good. Young ladies do so much better with us if they have spent some time keeping their own homes. We find that women with a family connect much more deeply with the women we serve than single women do. In the 10/40 window marriages tend to be arranged and being a single woman is unusual."

Jane nodded. She hoped Macha wasn't saying what it sounded like she was saying.

"When I began my years of service, single women went into the mission field. We went all over the world. I began as a nurse you see, so I had something to offer the women." Macha stitched as she talked. Her voice had the slow, sing-songy rhythm of reminiscence. "We could still use nurses. Nurses are welcome everywhere. But we have found, through the years, that standing out makes connecting at the heart level more difficult."

Jane nodded. More difficult to be single. Nurses welcome. She plastered the smile back on her face. She was going to keep an open mind. She wasn't going to crumble at the first roadblock. Village Friends had sounded like the right place for her, but it wasn't the only place.

"What do you do, Jane?"

"I'm a housecleaner." Jane licked her lips. She was hard worker, doing a humble job—wasn't that somewhere near the heart of missions?

"What do you want to do?"

"Well, I want to be a missionary, Macha. I want to go overseas and spread the gospel."

"That's good, since you are at a missions fair, but what do you want to do on the missions field? How do you want to serve?" Macha's eyes never left Jane's face.

"When I started school, I didn't know about tent-making missions, but I've only got this one term left and I'm ready to go. I thought if I wasn't a tentmaker, it would be okay. I want to do what you do." Jane bit her lip.

"Are you married?"

"No." Jane dropped her eyes to her hands.

"What I do works so much better if you are married, but Village Friends isn't the only organization, my dear. Why don't you look around the fair a little? You might find a good fit." Macha turned her eyes back to her needlework.

"Thank you for your time, Macha."

"You might also consider continuing your education. Perhaps you could go to nursing school."

"Thank you." Jane stood up quickly and turned away. Sandra Obwey hadn't mentioned that she needed to be married, or a nurse. Maybe Macha was wrong. Jane tried to make sense of the milling students and missionaries. Macha might be wrong, but her heart told her not to make a snap decision. God hadn't called her to be a nurse, but that didn't mean he wasn't going to.

The milling crowd overwhelmed Jane. She needed to get a breath of fresh air and a moment of quiet. She grabbed a schedule as she passed a student handing them out. Jane found a quiet seat on the front steps to read it, but before she did, she closed her eyes and prayed silently. *Dear Lord, give me the heart of a servant, and a heart to follow your lead. I'm scared that I'm going to make a mistake, Lord. I just want to serve you, however you have planned.* She sat with her eyes closed for several moments, listening to the calm quiet, and being still before God.

She opened her eyes again, but stared into the distance at the views of the farmland around her. *The harvest is ready. Pray for the workers.* This was what she had always been taught, what she believed, and what she had dreamed of. She did not dream of cleaning toilets, frying bacon, and solving murders. She was certain that the Crawfords were the trial of the moment, not her future life's work. But what *was* her future life's work?

Jane spotted Isaac leaving the Chapel. He had a spring in his step. When he spotted Jane he loped across the gravel parking lot. "Hey there!"

He took a seat on the step next to Jane. "I just got here. This looks like a pretty good fair."

Jane frowned. "Yeah."

"What's wrong?"

"Sorry. It's nothing." Jane set the schedule across her knee so they could both look at it.

"Trouble at home?"

"No, nothing like that." Jane pointed at the Youth Mission Adventures session on the schedule. "My friend Amelia is speaking. I might go listen to her."

"Pause. Don't move on yet. I really do want to know what's bothering you. I would have thought the Next Steps Fair would put a smile on your face, if nothing else would."

Jane chewed on her bottom lip. "It's nothing really. I am keeping an open mind and trying to listen to God's will."

"But you got disappointing news inside?" Isaac leaned away from Jane so he could make better eye contact.

"Yeah, kind of."

"What kind of news?"

"It's just that I really like one organization, but they kind of want married women, or like, nurses. I feel…unprepared."

"If you need to be married, I'm glad you're unprepared." Isaac's face broke into a big smile. "Let's go in and find a different organization. One that knows what you have to offer." He grabbed her hand and stood up.

She stayed seated, but her heart felt a little lighter. "I just need to figure out what it is I have to offer first."

Isaac tugged her arm. She stood up and smiled. He put his arm over her shoulder. "I'll do what I can to help. You have a good head on your shoulders. You're a hard worker. You make people smile just by walking into a room."

Jane felt her cheeks heat up. "All admirable qualities, but useful overseas?"

"You know your scripture. You care about people who are hurting."

"That's a little more tangible." Jane's heart was in her throat. She walked into the Mini-Missions fest with Isaac—*Mr. Daniels'*—arm around her shoulders. What would the other students think? What did she think?

"How about ELIC?" Isaac asked, stopping at the first booth.

"That's short term." Jane led him away.

"YMA?"

"Also short term."

"Have you considered the Evangelism Fleet?" Isaac grabbed a glossy pamphlet from the table with a cruise ship model.

"Short term. Am I picking up a theme here?"

"Can I help it if I don't want to send you away forever? I did just meet you, after all." Isaac stopped in front of the Summer Institute of Language/Wycliffe table. "Ever considered translation work?"

"No, I'm mostly interested in Evangelism."

The Church bell rang. According to the schedule this was the signal to go to Chapel for the morning keynote speaker. Isaac stood still, his arm around her shoulder, as the students flowed out of the room around them. "You didn't want to hear the keynote, did you? It's the director of YMA. You know, the short term people."

Jane rolled her eyes and laughed. "Maybe I could skip this one."

"I wouldn't want to waste your time on something that wasn't a lifelong commitment after all." He grinned. "Where can two people go for a quiet conversation around here?"

Jane stepped out from under his arm. "This way, to the library."

The Bible school library was a small room filled with donated biographies and commentaries. The dusty, almost vanilla, smell of old books greeted them as Jane opened the door.

She sat at the library table. Isaac straddled a chair across from her.

"Okay, I'm just going to lay this out there. Missions work, in the end, is like any other job. You either need experience or skills."

"And that's what my time at Harvest was for." Jane folded the corner of her schedule back and forth.

"That's what you intended it for, but it's not enough. I know, you want it to be enough, but I think if you are serious about missions you need to consider short-term work."

"I went on short-term trips in high school. I don't want to go backwards when I could spend my time learning the language and the culture. It will take a long time to be fluent enough to preach in a 10/40 language. Wouldn't more short-term stuff just waste time?" The corner of the paper ripped off in Jane's hand. She rolled it into a ball between her thumb and finger.

"Untried missionaries waste time too. High school missions trips are equal parts helping the teenagers grow up and helping the community they travel to. What if you got to your dream closed country and you just weren't up to it?"

Jane pressed the ball of paper until it was tiny and hard. "Do I look like I wouldn't be up to it?"

"Couldn't say until you try. You keep saying 'short-term,' but a full year immersed in a new culture won't feel short. I think missionaries need to try it before they throw themselves into a dangerous field."

"And I think they don't. So one of us is wrong." Jane pressed the small paper ball onto the table. When she picked her finger up again it stuck. She looked at the small white dot pressed into her fingertip. It wasn't what she had anticipated when she took out her nervous energy on the paper, but it was what happened. She turned her finger over before she made too much of it. She couldn't always predict results, but that didn't mean she couldn't sometimes predict them, when given enough information.

"Yup. One of us is wrong." Isaac was still grinning, basically from ear to ear. His happiness, in spite of her saying he was wrong, was infectious and she found herself smiling again.

"That's more like it. They call this a Missions *Fair*, after all. Not a Missions Gauntlet."

"Maybe they just named it wrong."

"From the crowd in the other room, it sure felt like it! Where are you going next?" Isaac pulled the abused schedule from Jane.

"What *long-term* organization is hosting a break-out session?"

Isaac laughed. "You could sit in with Pioneers. You'd like them."

"I do like them," Jane said. "Are you coming?"

"Wish I could. I've got to get back to my school. Seminary waits for no man." Isaac stood up.

"I'll walk you to your car?" Jane stood up as well.

"Please do." Isaac opened the library door for her. "Take good notes today and show me after class on Monday."

"Will I get extra credit?" Jane looked up at him from lowered eyelids.

"Ha! You know, for a second there I kind of forgot you were the student and not another instructor." They were at his car. He picked up her hand and squeezed it. "See you Monday?"

Jane nodded, smiling. He forgot she was a student. That was definitely a good sign. In fact, she felt pretty sure he was interested in her, a novel twist to the end of her Bible school era. With that happy thought she went back to the missions fair. If she kept her heart open to God's plans, she couldn't help but succeed.

CHAPTER 10

MONDAY MORNING CAME EVEN THOUGH Jane had hoped that it wouldn't. The Missions Fair had left her head swimming with contradictory ideas. Go, right after graduation, with a short-term organization and get tons of experience fast. Stay, and learn a trade that she could take with her as a tentmaker. Go, right away, and serve while she still had her verve and energy, before she got tied down by life at home. Stay until she had developed the wisdom and maturity she would need to have a life-long career overseas. And above all else, serve your current calling faithfully, because those who are faithful with the small things will be blessed with more opportunity and responsibility.

Jane had peeled herself out of bed an extra fifteen minutes early just to have some time alone in the kitchen. She tried to turn off her whirling thoughts so she could focus on serving the Crawfords faithfully. She had slipped in and out of church on Sunday, trying to go unnoticed. She didn't want to have to attempt to summarize her missions fair experience in casual conversation with friends. It was much too soon.

Jane shut the door to the kitchen in the hopes that the rich aroma of fresh coffee wouldn't travel upstairs to wake up the rest of the household. Over a breakfast of leftover cinnamon rolls and cold cuts, Jane watched the morning news on the little kitchen TV. The Human Liberation Party was picketing a Roly Burger, blaming the animal fats for the deaths of the Crawfords and for the obesity epidemic in America. It was a long shot since the Roly Burger Franchise hadn't spread East of Idaho yet.

The reporter held a microphone up to a skinny, leathery woman with feathers hanging from her ears. "We were promised these temples of human depravity would be closed and we demand they be closed!" Her blue eyes looked huge in her skeletal face. The text running under her picture read, "Rose of Sharon Willis, local head of the HLP."

"What does *Help* plan to do to force the Crawford family into keeping their promises?" The reporter asked. The reporter was about twenty-five. She had shellacked black hair and a face that looked like her skin and lips and eyelashes were made of plastic. Jane was fascinated by how the reporter could speak without appearing to move. She was also aggravated by the way the reporter assumed the HLP (or Help, as they were called locally) was correctly reporting the Roly Burger situation.

"Help will Help!" The crowd behind "Rose of Sharon" were chanting.

Rose of Sharon glowered over her microphone. "We shall overcome!" she shouted.

Non-answers like these drove Jane crazy. Were Rose of Sharon, or HLP making a real threat? Were they planning to keep protesting? To do a sit-in? To vandalize? Their current activity plus several local "unsolved" cases of vandalism at fast food restaurants indicated each of these were a possibility.

"Is there a message that Help wants to send to the people of Portland and the Crawford family right now?"

"The Crawfords may be dead, but their legacy of crimes against humanity live on in these corrupt places and Help won't stand for it. Today we picket—tomorrow we conquer!"

The plastic faced reporter turned to the camera. "Back to you, Francis."

The TV flipped back to the news desk. "We'll keep you updated with the latest as the Human Liberation Party enacts their policy of forcing businesses known to harm the health of the citizens to shutter their doors." The newsman shuffled his papers and smiled into the camera as the TV turned to a commercial for toaster strudels.

Jane turned it off. She should know better than to watch television news. The Roly Burger location that was being picketed was not too far out of the way on her drive to the Larson's house, which she had to clean today. If nothing came up before she had to leave she'd drive past it to see how long HLP's picketing energy had lasted.

Jane rinsed the crumbs from her plate and racked it in the dishwasher. She could hear Marjory coming down the hall.

"Good morning." Marjory didn't sound happy, per se, but she didn't sound angry either. Jane pulled a stool up to the kitchen island and sat down.

"I've been going through all of Bob and Pamela's papers and came across this." Marjory slid an enveloped marked "March Housekeeping" across the table. "According to their Quicken records they pulled this cash out for you the night before they died."

Jane stared at the envelope.

"I'm sorry you had to wait so long for your pay." Marjory cleared her throat.

Jane looked up. Tears brimmed Marjory Crawford's eyes.

Marjory slid another piece of paper across the granite. "We'll be having the reception at the house, right after the memorial service. I've made the list of jobs that need to be done." Marjory laid another envelope on top of this list. "I expect it won't take you more than fifteen hours to get through this list. I calculate that this would be half down, as per your request."

Jane stared at the pile accumulating before her. It looked like it would be enough money for everything she needed, plus some.

"Do you have time in your schedule to fit in fifteen hours of work if the memorial is Saturday afternoon with the reception following?"

Jane nodded. Saturday was six days away. She could make it happen.

Marjory stared over Jane's shoulders as she spoke. She appeared distracted and tired. "I should say, four of those fifteen hours are for setup, service and cleaning after the reception."

Jane nodded. That meant she had to fit fewer hours of cleaning into her regular schedule. That would be more than fine.

Marjory pulled her eyes back to Jane. "Saturday will be formal. Please wear black."

Saturday. Jane's heart sunk. She had a date for Saturday night. She'd have to call Isaac. She had his number on her phone now. Or maybe she could text him. Was that too impersonal? She couldn't remember. In the three years since she'd left high school behind her she hadn't dated at all. Did she text to reschedule to show that it was a casual thing and not any kind of drama, or did she call to show that she still really, really, wanted the date but the change couldn't be helped?

"I'm sorry." Marjory was shaking her head. "I'm at sixes and sevens today. I really am. This is all for Saturday in two weeks. Make a list and leave it on the desk in the office if you are going to need anything from me." Marjory left the kitchen without waiting for a reply.

Jane stared at the small stack of papers in front of her. Money. Lots of money. And she could still make her date. She was glad she was sitting down. If she hadn't been she might just have fainted.

On the way to the Larson house, Jane drove to the bank to deposit her windfall.

She was back to the Crawford kitchen by lunch. She had driven past the protest on her way home. News helicopters were hovering over the scene and two television news vans were parked out front, so it was hard to see anything. Perhaps that was HLP's plan: block all of the driveways so no customers could get in. The crowd of protesters looked less impressive in person. There were about a dozen skinny, dreadlocked hippies lounging on the sidewalk in front of the door. Jane was flipping through the television channels to find the newest report on HLP, but she figured they had assumed positions of fatigue to illustrate that they were making a hunger strike. It was the same move they had played at the end of last summer right before the last Pig-N-Pancake packed up and left town. At least a hunger strike wasn't destructive.

Before Jane could find the station with the news, Jake and Fitch from building-and-maintenance sauntered into the kitchen.

Jane straightened up.

"At ease," Jake said.

"Can I get you all anything?" Jane motioned to the refrigerator.

"Just coffee. We're having a business meeting, aren't we Fitch?"

Fitch shrugged. "You called. I came."

"That's right, I called. We need to get those yahoos off of my property."

Fitch raised an eyebrow. Jane leaned against the sink, trying to be inconspicuous. Jake had property? This was news to her.

"The courts always decide with Help, Jake." Fitch took a stool.

Jake pulled three coffee cups out of the cupboard. He filled them, adding plenty of cream in one and a dash of Irish Crème in another. He handed her the coffee with cream and kept the coffee with liquor for himself.

Fitch accepted the black coffee. "I mean it. We can't make them leave. The police won't touch them after that last lawsuit."

Jane took a sip of her coffee. Just the way she liked it.

"You are right, but you can do something."

Fitch gestured with the hand that held the coffee cup. Coffee sloshed onto the counter.

"Show a little respect for Janey here." Jake wiped the coffee spill with his shirtsleeve.

"Spell it out for me, Jake. Pretend I'm the dumbest man in the business. Tell me exactly what you think I can do."

Jake snorted. "Pretend?"

Jane blushed. Poor Fitch. She had never heard her father call him dumb.

"Condemn my building, building-and-maintenance man. Get the hippies off of my property."

"Is that one yours?" Jane asked.

"You can bet your sweet bippy it is. I could care less about HLP, but they are standing there talking nasty about my parents who aren't even cold in their graves yet. I want them gone."

"Condemning property doesn't really work like that, and, um, you know, I just handle the equipment and stuff."

"If the restaurant is full of rats they'd condemn it," Jake said.

"I wouldn't know." Fitch stared at his coffee cup.

"If you want your business to keep running you don't really want it overrun with rats." Jane took another drink of her coffee. *If Jake owned a Roly Burger of his own and he didn't want it to be shut down...was that a good motive?*

"I don't care if the business runs, Jane. Dad was buying back all of the franchises so he could shut them down. I'm good with or without the burgers, but HLP cannot spread their filth all over my business while talking smack about my dead parents."

"Your dad could afford to buy back all of the franchises?" Jane's hand shook. She set her coffee cup down.

"Yes. We're rich. Bet your parents wish they had stayed in the game a little longer."

Jane shook her head. "I don't know. Maybe. Maybe not."

"The Adlers did just fine in their deal," Fitch said. His thin lips were pursed. *Had Fitch done well too?* Jane wondered if building and maintenance paid as little as managing fast food restaurants did.

"If you can't condemn it, what can you do?"

"I can." Fitch looked up and to the left. Jane watched him think with fascination. His mouth moved in tiny subtle motions like he was sounding out his ideas before he spoke. "I could order new equipment. Lots of big trucks to haul in and haul away. They'd have to clear the property if I ordered enough."

"Make it so."

"It will be expensive, and unnecessary."

"We're very, very rich, Fitch. Money is no object, and I'm the one who decides what is necessary. I want new everything from every vendor. Understand? I'm not selling my franchise back to the family."

"But I thought you didn't care..." Jane watched Jake. His thoughts didn't play out on his face like Fitch's did, but his body spoke volumes. He stood with his chest out and his shoulders squared, almost bouncing on his toes like he was about to take off on a fast run. He wasn't thinking—just taking action.

"That was five minutes ago. Keep up." Jake looked from Fitch to Jane and back again. "That's it. Make it so. You can reach me on my cell." He turned back to Jane, "And you know where you can reach me." He winked. Then he bounded out of the dining room.

"Well!" Jane said.

"No kidding."

"Are you going to do it?"

"Might as well. It would clear out the protestors, and if Jake wants to keep running the business he might as well have new equipment. That location was his graduation gift and he hasn't done much with it yet."

Jane got a laptop for her graduation. Jake got a restaurant. The Crawfords were really, *really*, rich.

"So, I guess I'd better get back to the office." Fitch hesitated, sliding his cup back and forth by an inch on the counter top. "Will your parents come up for the funeral?"

"I suppose so," she said. "I guess I'd better give them a call."

Fitch nodded. "Say hi for me."

"Sure, I will."

Fitch nodded again and left.

Jane turned the TV back on. She found a channel playing the news. She'd watch it while she had her lunch just to see what else they had to say about HLP.

Jane wondered if HLP might have had an interest in killing Bob and Pamela. Of course, it was their deaths that were keeping the businesses open, so technically HLP wouldn't have liked that. Unless HLP wanted the publicity more than they wanted the hamburger industry to disappear.

CHAPTER 11

"JACOB TERWILLIGER CRAWFORD, you cannot put it off any longer."

"I'm terribly busy, ma'am."

When Jane had passed through the mudroom, Jake hadn't looked busy. He had been spread across the mudroom bench with his feet propped against the floor-to-ceiling shelves. He had been poking at his iPhone with one hand and holding a steaming cappuccino in the other. The aroma of coffee mingled with the odor of rain boots and wool sweaters that hung around the mudroom all winter had followed Jane to the rack of velvet curtains she was steaming at the far end of the hall.

Marjory stood in the mudroom doorway with her arms crossed over her chest. Their loud, if obscure, conversation was as clear as day, try as Jane might to not eavesdrop. So far Marjory had repeated the demand to "not put it off" and Jake had repeated how busy he was. It sounded as though they had already been arguing for some time before their voices rose to the point that Jane could hear them.

Jane put the steamer wand down and slid the wrinkle-free velvet curtain down to the "clean" end of her clothes rack. She pulled the next curtain into place and picked her wand up again. Marjory was so loud she could be heard over the hiss of steam and the whirr of the machine.

"We have the funeral home booked, the caterers scheduled, and the announcement ready to print in the newspapers. You need to get down there today and sign the papers."

Jane had hoped the argument was about something a little more interesting than that.

"I don't want to be responsible for paying for this circus." Jake's words were muffled, like he had his mouth on the lid to his coffee cup already.

"It doesn't matter what you want, young man. You are the next of kin. You have to sign the papers. For the love of all that is holy, I've already paid for everything, but they won't take one action until you have signed."

"But I just don't like cremation."

"It was in their preplanned funeral arrangements! And after all the time we've made the funeral home wait you would be much happier with a cremation."

"Watch it. That's my parents you are talking about."

"I wonder that you realize it. Get down to the funeral home today and sign the papers. Jane can go pick up the last effects. I won't make you exert yourself overmuch."

Jane worked over a stubborn wrinkle on the green drape. She felt defeated. Not that she didn't want to go pick up the last effects, wherever they might be, but the dragon that had been Marjory just days ago *sounded* defeated and it was having its effect. She sounded…small, even, and Jake, the star of Presbyterian Prep's basketball team and straight-A student, sounded like the worst kind of snotty slacker. When she was done with the drapes she had to call Phoebe. This house needed an infusion of new blood.

Steaming all of the drapes to be found in the five-story, 100-year-old-home took several hours, and by the time Jane was finished she was a sweaty mess. Her arms shook as she carried the last set into the living room to be re-hung, and the sun was setting. She was determined to call Phoebe as soon as the last drapery clip was clicked together.

She slumped into the wingback chair next to the window and took a deep breath. Phoebe hadn't been interested last time she had called. Jane hoped that was because she had been woken up from a deep sleep.

Jane scrolled through her phone and found the number. It only rang once.

"Hello?"

"Phoebe? This is Jane Adler, from your parents' house."

"Oh. Hi." Phoebe's voice had the same defeated sound in it that Marjory's had had while arguing with Jake.

"I, um, I was wondering how you are doing."

"As well as could be expected."

Jane fumbled for her next words. *Help? We need you? We're falling apart here? I know I'm just the maid, but....* She decided to go with that one. "I know I'm just the maid, but...things are really tense around here and I just thought that maybe it would help if you, um, you were to come and stay for a while."

There was silence on the other end.

Jane waited.

"Yeah, um. I was kind of rude last time we spoke. You know, you aren't 'just the maid.'"

Jane wasn't sure what Phoebe was referring to, but was too exhausted to pursue it. "See," Jane began, "it's just your aunt and Jake here and it seems like they could really use you."

Phoebe let a heavy sigh out that crackled over the cell phone. "Why? They've got you. If I've heard it once I've heard it a thousand times. 'That Jane is a real crackerjack. She's going places.'"

"Um..." Jane was really at a loss now. "I just think that your brother...and your aunt..."

"I'm sure you've got things under control, Jane. When have you not? If Aunt Marjory is lonely she can call her own kids, and as for Jake...I'm sure you can comfort him just fine."

"Phoebe, I know this has all been really hard for everyone..."

"Listen, don't call me again. I'll be where I need to be, when I need to be there."

Phoebe hung up.

Jane stared at her phone. Since when had Phoebe hated her? They had known each other a little bit, via company picnics, and at school, but Phoebe was a freshman at college this year and really their circles had barely crossed at school. Jane closed her eyes.

If she just had a few grates to clean her transformation into Cinderella would be complete, evil stepsisters and all.

Jane heard the soft padding sound of Marjory's leather-soled boots coming down the hall. She rubbed her eyes and tried to perk up.

"Ahh, there you are." Marjory looked her up and down, like a specimen. "I need you to get to the Medical Examiner's office to pick up the last effects." Marjory looked at her watch. "You should still have time today."

Jane's mind was working slowly, and Marjory was gone again before she could ask where the ME's office was.

Her trusty laptop was waiting in the bedroom on the third floor, so, ruing her not-so-smart phone for not the first time, Jane trudged her tired body upstairs to find out where the ME's office was and if she really had time to get there. It was, after all, already four in the afternoon.

Her laptop took an unearthly long time to warm up and connect to the spotty wi-fi. In fact, she was halfway back down the second flight of stairs before it picked up a signal, but eventually with the help of St. Google she found what she needed. "Oh, thank you, Lord." The prayer of thanksgiving slipped out like breathing.

The state ME's office was not downtown, as she had feared. It was still six miles away, but she could avoid the rush back home from work by taking surface streets. Jane was pretty confident she could make it there before it closed at five.

Jane pushed open the door to the ME's office ten minutes before closing. The drive had been fast enough for surface roads, but it was a bit farther away than Jane had anticipated. She paused just in front of the heavy glass door and looked at the reception desk. The room was cold and smelled like antiseptic and the biology lab at her old high school.

A middle-aged woman with heavy gray hair hanging in thick bangs over her forehead sat with her eyes glued to a computer screen. A wall of bullet proof glass, with a small pass through in it separated the receptionist from the waiting room.

Jane cleared her throat and went forward to the desk. "Excuse me, I'm here to collect the last effects of Robert and Pamela Crawford." Her voice inflected up like a question.

"Are you the next of kin?" The lady at the desk looked up through her wide plastic glasses.

"I'm the housekeeper."

"I can only release the last effects to the next of kin."

Jane took a deep breath. "Could we call him and have him tell you I can take their belongings home?"

"It doesn't work that way." The woman turned to her computer again.

"Could you let me know how it does work? I'll need to explain it when I get back to the house."

The lady looked up again. "I can't release anything to anyone who is not the next of kin. Not the personal effects, not the investigation report, nothing. Just let them know."

Investigation report? Jane perked up. She hadn't known she could get a copy of that. Well, that is to say, she couldn't yet, but if she came back with Jake she could. "And how do you prove the next of kin thing?"

"Picture ID. Is that all?"

Jane looked at the wall clock. Technically she still had three minutes. "About that report...would it tell the cause of death?"

The receptionist let out a heavy sigh, her shoulders sinking in apparent aggravation. "That is the point of an autopsy, isn't it?"

"So we would know the cause of death..." Jane spoke under her breath.

"Everything but the results of the blood work. It can take several weeks to get the report back on blood work."

"But if it was just a heart attack?"

"It's always just heart failure."

"What?" Jane straightened up.

"I'm sorry. I'm exhausted. I don't mean to be short with you. The heart always fails when we die, so between you and me, most deaths are labeled 'cardiac arrest.' That or pneumonia. People with aids die of pneumonia. People with cancer die of pneumonia. Everyone who doesn't die of heart failure dies of pneumonia."

Jane looked back at the clock. The receptionist sounded like she was ready for a new line of work, but as long as she was feeling chatty Jane thought she should take advantage of it. "So, a drug overdose could be written as cardiac arrest, or heart failure or something?"

"Yes, it could. They're supposed to write the cause of the heart failure, but it doesn't always get recorded." The receptionist straightened up and looked nervously toward the door behind her. "The medical examiner always does it right, of course. I'm just talking about the regular doctors, and I shouldn't have said that much."

"But what about murder? Or something like that?"

"Every suspicious death comes here and the ME does a very good job of determining what caused the…heart failure." She smirked at the last word, obviously still annoyed by the nature of death certificates.

"But if you don't get the blood work back for several weeks what does the ME write on the death certificate?" Jane leaned forward on the counter in front of the protective glass, trying to appear interested and friendly at the same time.

"Without blood work or obvious trauma? Well, that would be heart failure or pneumonia, wouldn't it?" She shrugged. "Send the next of kin in for the personal effects, and, um, do you mind keeping our little chat to yourself? I'm, um, I have a migraine."

"I completely understand. You should hear me talk about cleaning houses when I have a migraine. I'll let Jake know he has to come here himself. Thanks for everything."

The receptionist nodded and turned back to her computer screen.

Whether the receptionist thought the ME's report would be helpful or not, Jane was pleased that she had the chance to get her hands on it. She'd love to put to rest the idea that the Crawfords had been murdered—she might be the only one thinking it so far, but she'd love to make that thought go away.

CHAPTER 12

JANE WASN'T IN A HURRY to get back to Marjory empty-handed, so she made her trip home go past the protesters at the Roly Burger. The news helicopters were gone, but one news van remained. Jane parked behind it.

The protestors seemed to have increased since the news broadcast. There were at least thirty now. Jane scanned the parking lot—she counted three Priuses, a Smart Car, and a several road bikes. It looked like the protestors had all come straight from their day jobs.

Most of them lounged in front of the double glass door, but five protesters surrounded a family in the parking lot.

Jane got out of her car. She leaned on the rag top roof and watched, the smell of grilled burgers and fresh-baked bread tempting her to get closer.

A mom in sweats and a hoodie held the hands of two medium-sized boys. Jane guessed older grade-schoolers, wearing dirty soccer jerseys and shin guards. A man who was possibly their dad stood with them. He was a big guy, broad, and hefty, and wore a hoodie that said "Coach" on the back.

The scrawny protestors in their Toms and dread-locks were bearing down on the family.

Jane took a deep breath. Talk about a family in need. She crossed the parking lot, praying with each step. She didn't want to escalate the drama, but those poor boys looked like they had just finished a game. If so, they were starving.

Jane pushed her way past the family and stood in front of the protesters. "Let these people in."

"To poison their children? Never!" The speaker was a skinny yellow woman with thick blond hair in a braid that went to the waistband of her hemp pants.

"They aren't going to poison their children. Just let them pass." Jane crossed her arms over her chest.

"Mo-om, I need to use the bathroom." One of the kids behind Jane had a desperate twinge to his voice.

"Listen, everyone." The dad seemed to be using his coach voice. "I've got two hungry kids who need to go and a long drive ahead of us. Get out of the way and I won't call the cops."

"Freedom of expression, brother. We can stay here aaall night." The speaker was a young man in a skinny suit with a bushy beard. The protestors linked arms and made a U around Jane and the family.

"This is ridiculous." Jane turned around. She grabbed a boy by each hand and dragged them behind her as she busted through the two skinniest arms. She stepped over the loungers in front of the door and pushed her way into the restaurant.

"This had better be worth it." The father passed Jane and turned his eyes to the menu. The mom and the two boys went around the corner to find the bathrooms.

"Of course it's worth it!" Jake Crawford appeared in front of the register. "I guarantee the burger with the Roly-Poly bun will be the best you've ever had, or it's on the house. Hey! You know what? It's on the house anyway! Whatever you want, it's yours."

"It's the least you can do. What's with those jerks outside?"

Jake forced his face into a somber expression. "They are anti-freedom communists who care more about cows than the rights of people to eat food that makes them happy. It's a crime. Or it should be a crime. The least I can do is feed you."

The dad ordered several combo meals and then took a seat to wait for his wife and kids.

"And for you? Whatever you want, Jane the Brave. You faced down the enemy and brought me customers. Your order is my command."

"What are you doing here?"

"This is my domain. My castle. I defend it to the death."

Jane leaned to look behind Jake. He had a full crew cooking up orders. She turned and looked into the restaurant. The family she had escorted inside sat together, and a skinny teenager in a Roly Burger golf shirt sat alone playing on his phone. "This is a pretty sorry dinner hour. Has the whole day been like this?"

"It's been worse. You have to help us. Stay here with me until closing, okay?"

Jane eyed the clock on the wall. There were four more hours till closing. "Why?"

"Because we still have one news van in the driveway. Eventually the evening news will update the situation. When they poke their camera in the window, I want them to see a pretty girl eating a Roly Burger. Please?"

Jane licked her lips. This could work in her favor. "I can stay until six-thirty. That's over an hour, but if I do, I need a favor."

"I don't know. Can't you make it any longer?"

"Absolutely not. I have class tonight. You've got an hour and a half or nothing What do you say?" Jane folded her arms across her chest in an attempt to look stern.

"What's the favor? Maybe it's not worth a mere hour and a half of Jane Adler's precious time."

"I need you to come with me to the Medical Examiner's office first thing tomorrow morning."

"Your first thing or mine?"

"Don't worry, the Medical Examiner's office isn't open by *my* first thing in the morning. Yours will do."

Jake stuck out his hand. Jane shook it.

"It's a deal then, Janey, but I'm going to do my best to make you forget about your class tonight."

"Good luck with that." Jane settled into a booth by the front window where she'd be in plain sight of any news cameras. "If I'm going to sit here for the next hour I would love to be able to read the newspaper."

"Next hour-and-a-half."

"Yes, that's what I meant."

"As you wish." Jake bowed deeply and went back into the kitchen.

Jane watched the protestors relax outside. One of them smoked what Jane assumed was a clove cigarette. It seemed at odds with the Harm No Bodies philosophy of Help. Eventually Jake brought her a tray full of food and a newspaper.

Jake moved to hover around the windows, watching for news cameras.

Jane opened the newspaper to the business section. She found what she was looking for on page three, a tiny paragraph near the bottom. Headline: Yo-Heaven Corp Expansion Stymied by Crawford Family Deaths.

According to Jim Needles of the Oregon Journal, The Yo-Heaven Corporation and the acting head of the Crawford Family Restaurant Corporation were both aggravated by delays in the planned transformation from Roly Burger to Yo-Heaven. Jane turned her head back to Jake. He seemed to want to keep his restaurant open at all costs. Would he have killed his parents to save the store?

Before she could completely dismiss the idea as impossible, her phone rang. Caller ID said it was Sam.

A wave of anger rolled off Jane. She took a deep breath before she answered. "Yes?"

"Hey, so, yeah. The landlord wants your junk cleaned out of the apartment."

"Great!" Relief spread across Jane's tense shoulders.

"By like, tonight, yeah?"

"Excuse me?"

"So, he's um, unloading your stuff tomorrow morning. He's got a dumpster. So if you want it back you need to get it tonight."

"Slow down. What do you mean? How can I get it? He changed the locks. And it's furniture. How do I get furniture in my rabbit?"

"You know what, Jane? I don't need this. I totally didn't have to call you. I'm trying to help."

"Okay." Jane took another deep breath. She did need help and Sam drove a pickup truck. If she could keep herself together, keep it friendly, she might be able to salvage something.

"Let's just take it one step at a time, okay? How can I get in to get my stuff?"

"Do you know anyone who picks locks?"

Jane glanced up at Jake. She'd bet money he could do it. "Not offhand."

"Then call the landlord, Jane. Do I have to do everything for you?"

Jane took a drink from her soda so that she wouldn't blurt out what she was really thinking. "May I have his number?"

"Yeah, um, about that. I wasn't supposed to have a roommate in that small apartment, you know? So, um, calling him isn't a good idea."

Jane bit her lip. When she tasted the first coppery hint of blood she stopped. She prayed silently for the strength to be gracious. "Sam...I really want to get my stuff. Thank you for calling me." It hurt to say it, but it was said and she thanked God she did it. "But I really don't know what to do now. I don't want to be involved in a breaking and entering situation."

"Then get there first thing in the morning to collect your stuff when he opens the apartment up."

"Sam...would you come too? I am not supposed to live there then I am not supposed to have stuff there. Would you come and help me get it?" Jane crumpled a napkin in her fist, squeezing it until her knuckles went white.

There was a pause on the other end.

"Yeah...I could do that."

Jane's mouth dropped. Sam agreed too easily.

"But I'd need gas money. It's a long ways from here to there."

Jane squeezed her napkin harder. Sam wanted money. It made sense. "How much will you need?"

"Three hundred dollars."

Jane inhaled sharply. She did not have three hundred dollars to spare, but she forced herself to agree. "Take the truck, okay, Sam? So I have something to carry the furniture in."

"Yeah, sure. Whatever. Be there at seven."

"Of course. Seven o'clock tomorrow."

Sam hung up.

Jane stared at her tray of food, her stomach in a knot of anger and frustration. She'd be there to get her furniture, if she gave up all of her time and money. She stared at her phone. She wanted to call Isaac, but she didn't want to be *that girl* whose life was always a mess of drama. She checked the time on her phone. She still had a long hour left before she was free to leave.

CHAPTER 13

TUESDAY MORNING, FIRST THING, Jane stood in the parking lot of her old apartment building, shivering in the early morning mist. She stared at the warped vinyl siding, irritated with Sam.

Of course Sam was late. Jane had almost anticipated that. But the landlord wasn't there yet either. She recognized the few cars in the parking lot as her old neighbors.

Jane was about to give up when she heard someone pulling into the parking lot. She turned and saw Sam in the muddy, lifted, Toyota. Sam had been having fun recently, if the amount of mud caked on the off-roading truck was any indication. As muddy as it was, at least she had brought the pickup.

Sam joined Jane at the foot of the stairs to their apartment. "The landlord's not here yet." Jane looked at her watch.

"Not a prob."

A short, skinny, young man with a shaven head and a black hoodie joined the girls. "Hey." He tipped his chin to Jane.

"Oh...hi." Jane turned back to Sam. "Thanks for bringing help. How long do you think we have to wait to get in?"

Sam laughed. She pointed at the door to their old place. "How's now?"

Jane turned to the door. The bald guy had already gotten it opened.

"Let's get your stuff and go."

Jane was torn. This was obviously breaking and entering. It was probably stealing as well, but if the landlord was coming to dump it all, it must be no big deal. She ran up the steps and followed Sam into the apartment.

The lights were off. Jane flipped the switch a few times to no avail. She shivered. It was as cold in the apartment as it was outside. The apartment smelled stale, like dust and old appliances. She stared at the gray carpet. Had it smelled like that the whole time she had lived there?

The bald guy lifted her futon mattress off the frame. Sam pulled down the curtains with a crack. The screws from the flimsy curtain rod left small holes in the sheetrock.

"Hey, Jane, did you bring cash?" Sam rolled the curtains into a messy ball and tossed them to the door.

The bald guy laid the futon mattress on the floor. He folded the futon frame and lifted it on his shoulders.

Jane had a sinking feeling in her stomach. She was pretty sure the landlord wasn't coming.

"Yeah." Jane pulled her phone out of her pocket and toyed with the keys. "I did bring cash. How about I give it to you after we get my stuff stored?"

The bald guy was already outside putting her bed frame in the back of the pickup. She stared at him from the window. How did a little guy like that get so strong?

"How about when we all get back in the truck? It's on empty and I need gas before I can take your stuff."

Jane's miniature safe was sitting in the middle of the floor. It had been hidden under the futon before. "I'll get your gas, no problem, but I'll pay you the cash when we get my stuff stored." She picked up the box and cradled it in her arms. She scanned the room. She wanted the small box and her bed. She wouldn't feel like a thief if that was all she took.

The bald guy came back up and grabbed the mattress. He began to drag it to the door. In an effort to save it from the asphalt, Jane set her box on the breakfast bar and picked up the other end.

"I'm Jane." The mattress, though heavy, wasn't as bad as she had expected.

"Hey."

They hefted the mattress on top of the bed frame in the back of the muddy truck.

"Looks like rain." Jane had a smear of dirt across her chest from leaning over the muddy truck bed.

"We'd better get your stuff put away fast." The bald guy still didn't introduce himself. As soon as he had balanced the mattress on the bed frame he hoofed it back up the stairs.

Jane followed him. Where was she going to take her stuff? She couldn't keep it at the Crawfords' house.

She grabbed her ever ready phone and called her friend Sarah at Harvest.

"Hey, Jane! Whassup?"

"I need a huge favor. How much stuff are you allowed to have on campus?"

"I dunno. What do you mean?"

Jane stood at the breakfast bar in the small, cold, apartment. She traced the company logo on her lock box. "I mean, like, do you guys have storage there or something?"

"Not really. What do you need to store?"

"I finally got my stuff from the apartment and I need a place for my futon. I think everything else can come to the room I have, but it's already got a bed."

"Oh that! That's no biggy." Sarah mumbled something away from the receiver. "We've got a really empty common room we can put it in."

"You can? The school won't mind?" Jane let out a sign of relief.

"Nah. Lila and Holly keep a mini fridge and a PlayStation out there, but there's nowhere to sit. We'd all love to have your futon for a while."

"Great! Great, great, great!" Jane tapped her toes. It was a long drive to the school, but she was buying the gas so Sam had better not complain.

"Hey, if you can get here in an hour you can catch Mr. Daniels before he leaves again."

"Isaac is there?" The news kept getting better and better.

"*Isaac* is here." Sarah's sing-song voice didn't ruin Jane's good mood.

"Well then, I'll get there in an hour."

Jane ended the call.

As soon as all of Jane's limited belongings had been stuffed into a black trash bag she was ready to go. Jane grabbed her lock box on her way out.

The bald guy had the screen.

"Let's leave right now. I've got to ride with you guys, okay?"

Sam frowned. "That'll be cozy."

Jane didn't respond. She ran down the steps and climbed into the truck with the lock box on her lap. Sam took shotgun. She had shoved the trash bag into a free spot in the truck bed.

Jane bought their gas with her emergency credit card. The freedom of having her safety net back made her heart soar.

When they arrived at Harvest the bald guy toted all of the furniture up to the common room for Jane. Sam dumped the trash bag on the sidewalk in front of the dorm building.

"Cash, Jane?"

"Yes, just a sec. Are you splitting it with your friend?"

"None of your business, is it?"

"No, of course not." Jane dug the envelope of cash she had made up for Sam out of her purse. Before she handed it over she took out the gas money.

"Three hundred dollars?" Sam took the envelope from her.

"Minus what I just put in your tank."

"Excuse me?" Sam gripped the envelope in her hand, her eyebrows pulled down.

"You said you needed money for gas. I filled your tank with my card so I took it out of the cash." Jane's heart was racing again. Confrontation did that to her. Her cheeks were hot. Sam had spent most of a year's rent on whatever it was she spent money on. Jane wasn't going to let her clean out the rest of her hard-earned money.

Someone put a hand on the small of Jane's back.

She jumped.

"Sorry," Isaac said, "didn't mean to surprise you." He didn't remove his hand.

Jane's heart slowed to normal. A smile crept onto her previously angry face. "Isaac, this is Sam, the roommate I told you about."

"Ah." Isaac used his "professor" voice. "Did I tell you yet that I talked to my dad, the judge? He thinks you have at least a small claims case on this."

Sam sniffed. "Whatever. She's got her stuff."

"And you seem to have her money." There was a tone in Isaac's voice now that Jane hadn't heard yet. It was serious. It also reminded her how little she knew him.

"We made a deal, a'ight?" Sam flipped her stringy brown ponytail over her shoulder.

"Like the deal where Jane paid you half of the rent so she could have a home?"

Before Sam could respond the bald guy was at her side. "What's going on?"

Sam nodded her head in Isaac's direction. "Someone's got a problem with our deal."

"Oh yeah?" The bald guy cracked his knuckles.

In her peripheral vision, Jane saw her classmates gathering. She closed her eyes and prayed for wisdom and calm.

"What's the big deal? We moved her and she paid for gas." The bald guy was looking over Isaac's shoulder.

Jane turned and saw the pastor of Harvest Bible Church, who was also the administrator of the school, standing in the front door.

Sam's face flushed red. "Let's just get out of here."

"Do we still have a problem?" The bald guy's eyes darted to the crowd gathering to his left.

"Yes, we do still have a problem. Jane paid for the gas and gave Sam an envelope of money. Jane is really nice, but you and I can agree that since Sam spent all of Jane's rent money, Jane doesn't owe Sam anything for bringing her stuff here."

The bald guy looked at Sam. He snorted. "Idiot." He snatched the envelope from Sam's fist and tossed it at Jane's feet. Then he grabbed Sam and dragged her back to the truck, muttering to her under his breath.

The crowd of students laughed a little and dispersed in a ripple of horseplay.

Isaac stooped down to pick up the envelope. "You are a very, very nice person, Jane."

"Mr. Daniels? Jane? I'd like to see you in my office." The serious, pastoral voice of Pastor Barnes echoed in the tree-lined driveway.

"Yes, sir." Jane hated that tone of voice. Officious and doom-ridden. Nothing good could come from a meeting in Pastor Barnes's office that started with that tone of voice.

Isaac cocked an eyebrow at Jane. He took her hand and held it all the way into the office.

Once in the office she dropped Isaac's hand and laced her fingers together.

"Take a seat, please." Pastor Barnes's voice was quieter, but just as low and serious. "Word has reached me, as administrator for Harvest School of the Bible, that there may be…inappropriate flirtation going on between the two of you."

"How do you define flirtation, sir?" Isaac asked.

Jane's mouth popped open. Isaac had his own pastoral voice.

"May I remind you of your contract? This goes for both of you. Instructors at this Bible school are strictly forbidden from dating students."

Jane twisted her mouth. This wasn't like Pastor Barnes. Sure, he was as straight-laced as physically possible, but he didn't usually glower and boom like this. Whoever complained must have been important.

"Have you called us into the office for flirtation or dating?"

Had Isaac inherited his official tones from his father the judge?

"Flirtation is in direct conflict with the spirit of the rules, *Mr.* Daniels. It is never appropriate for an adult instructor to instigate a romantic relationship with one of our teenage students."

Jane cleared her throat. "I will be twenty-one in April."

Pastor Barnes stared at Jane for a moment. "That's right. You are a *non-traditional* student for this school."

Isaac smiled at Jane with a sparkle in his eyes. "Pastor Barnes, I'm only a year older than she is. How can our getting to know each other be against the spirit of the rule?"

"Age is beside the point. When you accepted admittance to Harvest School of the Bible, young lady, you agreed to abide by the rules. You, in fact, agreed not to date at all while you lived on this campus. It's a time-honored tradition at Harvest."

"Ah." Isaac drew out the word with satisfaction. "If you recall, Jane doesn't live on campus."

Pastor Barnes stood up. "Let's not get cocky, Isaac. You signed a form stating you would not date students while you were our guest lecturer. Your conduct has been noted by several people and I have received complaints. End it now. Do you understand?"

Jane's jaw tightened. Two years. For two years she had abided by the rules of this little school, though she was a part-time, off-campus student. Graduation, if you could call it that, considering what she had recently learned about their loose curriculum standards, was just three months away.

A wave of guilt washed over her. For two years she had been building relationships with the staff of the school and the church in hopes of having their future support as a missionary—both prayer support and financial, if possible. Had she thrown all of that away by accepting a date with Isaac? By having a conversation—a class related conversation—about a hurting family in need? She looked at the ground.

"Yes, sir," she said quietly. "I understand."

"You are both excused."

Jane walked back out to the parking lot without looking at Isaac.

Sam and the bald guy were long gone.

Jane picked up her trash bag of personal effects.

Personal effects.

She checked her watch. If she left for the Crawfords' right this moment she would make it back in time to pick up Jake for their trip to the medical examiner's office. She worked her jaw back and forth in an effort to keep from crying. At least she had the cash. She could pay for a taxi home. She patted her pocket but the reassuring crinkle of the envelope full of cash was missing.

"Hey, it's okay, Jane. Don't let Barnes bother you."

Jane looked up at Isaac. His eyebrows were lifted in a warm, reassuring, way.

"You didn't happen to see what I did with that envelope, did you?"

He held it out to her with a smile.

Jane tried to take it nonchalantly.

"I see your ride is gone. Can I give you a lift?"

"Is that allowed?" Jane looked back at the church building.

"It's carpooling. It's the right thing to do."

Jane had a fair amount of certainty in her heart that it was not the right thing to do, but it would save her the expense of a taxi.

"You're not going to get kicked out of Bible school for letting me drive you home. Don't worry."

"What about you?" Jane asked as she clicked her seatbelt. "Could they dismiss you?"

"I hope not." Isaac pulled onto the open highway that led back to town. "I kind of need this job."

"I totally get it." Jane stared at the passing fields of hops and wheat. The freshly planted earth was black with fertilizer and rain while the old vines were still brown from their winter. "So…you're only twenty-two? How did you get this gig?"

"My PhD advisor over at Western hooked me up."

"And how did you get a PhD advisor at your age?"

"Home-schooling, of course. I finished everything early." Isaac dropped one hand from the steering wheel and let it rest next to Jane's. "But I'm not weird or antisocial."

"Of course not."

"What about you? Where did you go to school?"

"Presbyterian Prep." Jane let her fingers slowly connect with his until they were holding hands again. "But I'm not an elitist snob."

"Obviously not."

"So…about Saturday."

"Yeah." Isaac didn't sound happy.

"We'd better put that off." Jane looked at their fingers and smiled.

"Reschedule?"

"Indeed."

"When's graduation?" Isaac squeezed her hand.

"May 24th."

"Are you free May 25th?"

"As it happens, Mr. Daniels, I am free May 25th."

"Then it's a date."

Jane turned on the radio. *Dancing on the Minefields* was playing. The minefields analogy seemed entirely too appropriate.

Once they hit town Jane directed Isaac to her old apartment so she could collect her Rabbit.

"What's this?" Isaac appraised the car, with his head tilted.

"It's a Rabbit. A Volkswagen."

"Ha, ha. What's wrong with your tire?" He knelt down next her car and stuck a finger into a tire that looked very flat.

"What?" Jane dropped down to take a closer look.

"Someone slashed your tire."

Jane poked her finger into the deep gash. She pictured her mom saying, 'I told you so.' Getting a roommate from Craigslist had been a very bad idea. She checked the time on her phone. The morning had sped by. It was almost two hours later than she had wanted to leave for the Medical Examiner's.

"I bet I can guess who did it." Jane's stomach turned at the thought.

"My first thought is your old roommate."

"My thought exactly." Jane stood up and scanned the parking lot for people who might have seen something. She and Isaac were alone.

"That's just my first thought. My second thought is: how many people know you were the one who found the bodies?"

"Bob and Pamela?"

"Yeah. How many people know you found them, or know that you are involved with the family?"

"I don't know. The family. Some folks with the restaurant business. Who knows how far the word has spread." Jane itched to put her spare tire on and get moving. She just needed Isaac to tell her how.

"Have you run across anything you shouldn't have? Any info that could make you unsafe?"

"Not yet, but I'm supposed to go to the ME's today and pick up their personal effects and the autopsy report with Jake. Do you think someone wants to keep us from seeing the report?"

"Who knows you are picking it up?"

"Jake and Marjory know we are going for the personal effects, but they'd hardly try and stop me, especially since Marjory is the one who told me to go. But I did talk about it last night at dinner...maybe the protestors at Roly Burger, or the staff heard me."

Jane explained the situation at the restaurant the night before and how the employees and the protesters could have listened in on her conversation with Jake.

"I hate to sound paranoid. Call it the result of growing up with a legal family, but this could have been an attempt to keep you from finding out how the Crawfords died."

Jane swallowed hard. "Or, it could have just been a mad ex-roommate who wanted to get even with me for not giving her the cash."

"Yeah." Isaac kicked a tire. "That's most likely."

"So what do I do now? I hate to admit it, but I've never been in this position before. Do I have to make a police report?" Jane asked.

"Well," Isaac paused in thought, "we don't have any evidence to indicate who might have done this. If I've learned anything from *The Judge*, it's that you need evidence. Do you have a spare?"

"Yes. I hate to sound like a helpless female, but could you help me change it? I'm in kind of a hurry."

"Of course." Isaac got to work on the tire.

"So, no police?"

"What would we tell them?"

"I suppose I shouldn't call and tell them that I let some guy I've never met before, who may in fact be a neo-Nazi, break into an apartment I have no legal right to be in to collect things that the landlord technically owns and that I then refused to pay him so he slashed my tire."

"Agreed, you can't call them and say that. This spare is in sorry shape." Isaac shoved the flat tire into the back of the Rabbit. "I'd like to follow you back to your place, just to be sure you make it."

Jane looked at the small wheel on the back of her car. "Thanks. I wouldn't mind that at all."

They connected again at the front door of the Crawford house.

"You know, my parents live just a couple of blocks away." He patted the pocket of his button-down shirt. "Do you have a pen?"

"There's one inside." Jane opened the heavy front door and led Isaac into the kitchen.

She opened the drawer of the kitchen desk and rummaged for a pen and paper.

"Coach?!" The voice that said this was vaguely familiar, with a panicked note at the end of the drawn-out word.

"Phoebe?" Isaac responded with a matching note of surprise.

Jane jerked herself up to see what was going on and knocked her head on the cupboard.

"Crawford. Phoebe Crawford. How did I not put this together?"

"You know each other?" Jane rubbed the sore spot on top of her head.

"From soccer camp." Phoebe made her way into the kitchen, her hips swinging. Her tall, curvy form was wrapped in a pair of tight, skinny jeans and a t-shirt with a deep v-cut neckline.

Isaac met her in the middle of the kitchen. He offered her an awkward side hug. "How are you holding up? I am so sorry about your parents."

Phoebe slung both her arms around Isaac's neck and squeezed him. "Oh, Coach, I'm a complete wreck."

Isaac hit his hip on the granite counter with a thud, as he disentangled himself from Phoebe's arms. "Is there anything I can do for you?"

The golf pencil Jane had found slipped through her fingers. Phoebe. Eighteen year-old college freshman. Soccer star. Grieving orphan. That definitely topped slashed tires and a promise not to flirt or date for two more months.

"I really need to get out of this house. What are you doing? Will you go run some drills with me?" Phoebe lowered her eyes and then looked up at him again, through her long, thickly mascara-ed eyelashes.

Isaac caught Jane's eye. He shook his head. "I can't kiddo. I've got a project to take care of, but if there is something else I can do to help later you can let Jane know. She knows how to get a hold of me. I mean, if there is anything that we can do to help, we will."

Jane's mouth quivered into a half smile. He said 'we.'

"Did you find a pen?"

Jane held out the pencil and a scrap of paper.

Isaac wrote a note and folded it in half. "I've go to run."

Jane followed him to the door.

He leaned down to kiss her cheek goodbye but stopped. "Ah. Sorry. Rules, right?"

"Yes, right."

He waved and ran down the many concrete steps to his car.

Jane shut the door. She needed to have a conversation with Phoebe.

CHAPTER 14

JANE PRAYED FOR WISDOM as she walked down the hall, back to the kitchen. The family needed Phoebe, and as much as Jane would have liked to ignore the existence of the beautiful, athletic young woman who had just smeared herself all over Isaac, she had to try to convince her to stay.

Jane went straight to the coffee pot. "Can I pour you a cup?"

"Are you sleeping with Coach *and* Jake?"

"What?" Jane swung around to face Phoebe, the coffee sloshing over her feet.

"Because that hardly seems fair. Jake's my brother, so it makes the most sense for you to stick with him and leave Coach for me."

Jane set the coffee pot on the counter and counted to fifteen. She dropped the dishcloth from the sink into the puddle of coffee. While she swished the dishcloth back and forth on the floor with her foot, she prayed again for wisdom. With all of her heart she wanted to slap Phoebe across the face.

"It was nice of you to bring him by though, knowing that I'd need someone to comfort me during this trying time. To be honest, I had completely forgotten about him, But whooo—he's cute right? And fit. You should see him in a tank top."

"I'm not sleeping with anyone, Phoebe." Jane's jaw hurt from clenching it.

"Jake won't stand that for long, I imagine." Phoebe took an apple out of the bowl. She turned it over in her hand, the kitchen lights making its waxed red skin shine. She took a bite.

The crunch seemed to echo in the kitchen. "He is paying your room and board, Jane. You should show your gratitude."

Jane dropped to the ground. She mopped up the coffee with firm, angry strokes. Nothing good could come of this conversation. She repeated it to herself again. Nothing good could come from this conversation. She stood up and wrung the sopping rag out in the sink.

"I'm glad you came." It was hard to pull out the words, and they felt like a lie, but for better or worse, it seemed like Phoebe needed her aunt and brother as much as they needed her. It was right, even if it wasn't comfortable, for her to be back at the house. "Are you planning on staying through the funeral? Maybe afterward as well? At least for a while?"

Phoebe crunched her apple again. "Depends. Is it a double funeral?"

"Of course." *Now*, Jane wondered, *why would her staying depend on that?*

Phoebe chewed on her apple for a while. "Then, no. I wouldn't go to a funeral for my mother if my inheritance depended on it."

The sound of sock feet padding into the kitchen made Jane turn around.

"That's because you are a big, fat, brat," Jake said. He pulled a stool up to the kitchen island. "Did you stand me up, Jane, or is it earlier than I think?"

"I was delayed this morning." Jane turned on the water to rinse her dishcloth. She had forgotten the personal effects again.

"She was out with Coach." Phoebe set her half-eaten apple on the counter and rolled it back and forth. "They came in together this morning, but don't worry. Jane says she's not sleeping with him either."

"Good." Jake laid his head on his arms. He was dressed in his boxer shorts and sweat socks. His arms and back were covered in goose pimples. "Coffee? Please?" Jake sat up again. "Who is this 'Coach'?"

"From summer soccer camp." Phoebe rolled the apple to her brother. He rolled it back. The apple left a sticky trail on the black granite every time it rolled.

"Name?" Jake said.

Phoebe shrugged. "How should I know? He's just some camp coach, but he does look fine in a tank top. And his calves? Yummy. The boy runs, that much is obvious."

"Jane? Enlighten me. What specimen did you drag into my lair this morning?"

Jane rubbed her eyes, exhausted already. "Isaac Daniels. My teacher."

Jake looked unimpressed.

"Ahh!" Jane remembered what Isaac had mentioned earlier, about where his parents lived. That should put things in perspective. "His dad is your neighbor, Judge Daniels."

"That puts a different spin on things." Jake sat up, and stretched his arms, his skinny, bare chest exposed.

"Neighbor like they have money?" Phoebe crunched her apple again.

"Neighbor like those weird Daniels kids who didn't go to school. I think you could do better, Jane. You've got a pretty face, a nice figure. You could definitely do better than that weirdo Daniels kid."

Jane let her dishrag fall into the sink with a wet plop. "Just get dressed, Jake. Your aunt wants the stuff from the Medical Examiner's office ASAP."

"Yes, ma'am." Jake laid his head back on the counter.

Phoebe tossed her half-eaten apple in the sink. "I don't care if he is weird. You can bring Coach back here any time you want."

CHAPTER 15

JAKE DROVE HIS PARENTS' JAG to the Medical Examiner's office.

The supple leather interior was immaculate, and, Jane had to admit, incredibly comfortable.

"You've got to forgive Phoebe. She's off her meds." Jake stared straight ahead, a look of serious concentration creasing his forehead.

"What meds?"

"For her 'she's crazy' disorder." Jake gunned his engine to make it through a yellow. "It runs in the family."

"Can you be a little more specific?"

"Can I? I suppose I can be honest with Jane Adler, humble but righteous house-cleaner. Phoebe is bi-polar. She's a brat when she's medicated. When she's off her meds she's a crazy brat."

"How crazy, Jake?"

"She just said she hated our dead mother. Is that crazy enough?" Jake cranked the wheel and made a fast, wide left turn.

"Yeah. I'd say so." Jane watched the suburbs fly past. Was Phoebe crazy enough to kill? "So, Jake…do you think your parents were murdered?"

"Of course. Rich middle-aged Americans of average health don't just up and die. Not first thing in the morning. Maybe on the tennis court, or after a long day at work, but not first thing in the morning."

"I'm sorry, Jake. I really am." Jane cracked her window to let in some fresh air, but the road noise was too much. She closed it again, willing to suffer the close atmosphere of the luxury car for the sake of the conversation. "Are you scared?"

"Never." Jake slammed his brakes at a stop sign.

"Even though there is a murderer loose?"

"There's always a murderer loose, isn't there? If all the murderers were contained there wouldn't be any murdered people. I can't be scared every day, can I? So I'm not scared ever. It saves energy." Jake took a curve too fast, throwing Jane into her door.

"Who do you think did it?" Jane's stomach was roiling from the driving. The conversation didn't help either.

"Fitch."

"Fitch? In buildings and maintenance?"

"Yes. That Fitch. He never ordered my new equipment. He's clearly out to get us." Jake stopped the car in the middle of the quiet road. "Who do you think did it?"

Jane squeezed the handle of her door. "Shouldn't you be driving?"

"Sure. Why not." He started the car back up, but drove more slowly.

"Jake, why aren't you grieving? I'm concerned for you."

"Didn't I say it earlier? Crazy runs in the family." Jake merged onto a busy road. They were getting closer to the Medical Examiner's office.

Jane exhaled slowly. "It's okay to be scared and sad right now. Do you realize that? No one expects you to be strong or funny, or brave."

Jake slammed the brakes again, this time at a red light. "Leave it, Jane. Okay? No one cares what the housekeeper thinks."

Jane left it. She rode the rest of the way to the ME's office in silence.

When they arrived at the office Jane followed Jake inside the building. The receptionist with the big glasses sat at her desk, alone again.

Jake buzzed the button three times.

The receptionist glared at him for a moment. She turned back to the machine.

Jake buzzed the button again.

"Jake." Jane kept her voice low.

The lady stood up at the pass through in the bullet proof glass. "Yes?"

"You have my dead parents' stuff." Jake hit the buzzer one more time.

"Name?"

"Robert and Pamela Crawford of the hamburger empire. I am Jacob Terwilliger Crawford, Esquire. *Not* at your service."

"May I see your ID?"

Jane inched her way back to the door. As long as Jake was in this mood, she didn't want to be seen with him.

Jake handed his ID over.

"Just one moment." The receptionist left the room.

"Jake...I'm sorry." Jane kept her distance.

"Sorry that I'm crazy, or an orphan, or that you are a lemon-sucking prune-faced church girl who needs to get some action?"

Jane took a deep breath. "I'm sorry that I was rude. I'm sorry that I overstepped my...boundaries."

"Yeah. Whatever."

The receptionist returned with a parcel wrapped in clear plastic as though it had just come from the dry cleaners. She pushed it through the opening in her glass wall.

"Jake, can you get the autopsy report?" Jane stepped a little closer so she could ask in her quietest voice.

Jake grabbed his package. He turned around and gave Jane a withering look, his thin, blond eyebrows drawn together. "No."

She watched him exit the office. Before she followed him she tried the receptionist. "May I have the copy of the autopsy report?"

"You're the housekeeper, right?"

"Yes, ma'am."

"Then I'm sorry, miss. You can't." The receptionist sat down at her desk again.

Jane heard the engine of the Jag start up. She ran out to catch it.

Jake let her get in.

"I thought we wanted to get the report." Jane buckled herself in. She didn't dare make eye contact.

"*You* wanted to get the report." Jake tore out of the parking lot.

"It would be good to know what happened." A wave of nausea rolled over her as he whipped around a turn.

"Why? It won't bring them back." Jake spoke in a low rumble.

Jane snuck a glance at Jake. His shoulders were stiff and his jaw was tense. "No, you're right. It won't."

She sunk down in the leather seat. So was her service to this family really going to just be cleaning and cooking? Was she not going to be able to solve the murders of Bob and Pamela after all?

Jake dropped Jane off at his house, but immediately pulled away again, driving off with his parents' personal effects. At the very least, Jane had been hoping to go through them with him, to help him process his loss…and see what clues might be hidden in their clothes.

She let herself into the house by the door to the mudroom. There weren't many things left on the funeral to-do list. A rest before her next client's house sounded like a dream come true, but on her way to the third floor bedroom she called her temporary home, she stopped.

She had dusted and tidied in Bob and Pamela's room since the accident, but she hadn't purposefully searched for clues to what had happened that morning. The police had, but they hadn't told her what they had found, of course. Would there be anything left to find now?

She wandered down the hallway to their bedroom. It wouldn't hurt to take a look.

The room smelled empty. It was a weird, hollow smell, similar to her apartment this morning, but without the layer of old appliance. It was the smell of a closet full of winter clothes the first time you open it in the late fall.

She sat down on the small, round stool in front of Pamela's mirrored dressing table and pulled open a drawer. Nothing but small make-up compacts. Jane shut it and pulled open the drawer below it. This one was full of carefully organized costume jewelry. Small dishes held rings, and chains were laid out lengthwise in a velvet box with long compartments.

She tried the drawers on the other side, but nothing looked important. Just the every day things a middle-aged lady needed to get ready in the morning. Jane tried the bedside table on Bob's side of the bed.

She hadn't known which side was his, before she had found him dead.

The image of the paramedics pulling him off the bed flashed in her mind. She had to sit down and steady herself. She didn't want to make finding bodies a habit. It was terribly uncomfortable. The drawer next to Bob's side held a notebook and a pen. It was deep enough to keep extra pillows in, but that was all it had.

She took the notebook out and opened it. The pages were blank. She rubbed her fingertips across them but couldn't feel the indentations of previous writing. It appeared to be completely unused.

Jane crawled across the king-sized bed and pulled open the drawer next to it. It was chock full. Paperback novels, handkerchiefs, several colorful sports watches, hand lotion, a crochet hook, a pair of nail clippers. Jane knelt on the bed, leaning over the drawer and pawed through it trying to figure out what all else was there. This was exactly the opposite of the dressing table. Unorganized and unimportant—the last stuff Pamela held in her hands before she went to bed.

Jane found a crumpled picture of Phoebe tucked in the mess. She looked about twelve years old. At some point in time Pamela had reminisced, holding a picture of her daughter in her hands, right before she went to sleep. A little sob welled up and stuck at the back of Jane's throat.

Then the bed shook.

Jane rocked forward and steadied herself on the side table.

"I am so sorry." Jake grabbed Jane around the waist and pulled her to himself. He wrapped his arms around her, resting his head on her shoulder. "I am so sorry I was a jerk. So, so sorry." He wept as he held her.

They were both on their knees on Bob and Pamela's bed. Jane held Jake and let him cry.

Jake's weeping subsided. He lifted his head off Jane's shoulders. His eyes were round and red.

She wiped his tears away with her thumb. Her face was hot, and Jake was inches away, his breath sweet like minty toothpaste.

He leaned in and kissed her.

Jane pushed him away. Her hands were sweating and she could hear her heart beat in her ears. "Jake, no. I'm sorry."

He stared at her with his big, sad eyes. "No?"

Jane scooted backwards on her knees until she reached the edge. Then she stood up. He looked so small, kneeling on the bed, that she sat down again, but on the edge of the bed, a couple of feet away from him. "I'm sorry."

He flopped back on to his father's pillow, his eyes closed. "No one else on Earth would say no to me, right now."

"You're probably right, but I don't kiss boys I don't love, and I am not in love with you." She bit her lower lip, sure she meant what she said, but also, just a little unsure.

"What are you doing in here?"

"I'm looking for anything that can help me understand what happened to your parents." Jane shut the side table drawer.

"Are you having any luck?" Jake asked.

"No."

"Me, neither."

"Why didn't you want the autopsy report?"

"Because they are my parents, not a science experiment. I don't want to read about them getting cut up and looked at." Jake rolled over and leaned up on his elbow. "I could really love you, you know."

"Maybe you could, but you don't yet, so you don't need to try." Jane walked over to the highboy dresser and sifted through a stack of papers on top. "How did your mom feel about the businesses closing?"

"She didn't like it."

"Why not?"

"All that change at their age? No way. She liked status quo—especially since she had pretty good status. What if the new business venture had failed?"

"But everyone loves Yo-Heaven. Why would it fail?" The stack of papers all seemed to be school-related, soccer meet schedules, class schedules.

"That trendy locavore stuff? Lots of veggies and fruit and yogurt for lots of money? The Roly Burger crowd were not going to like it."

"What's going to happen to Roly Burger now?" Jane opened the top drawer of the dresser. Pamela's underwear. She shifted through the silky garments, all of which she had washed and folded many times.

"I can't decide."

"Is it up to you?" Jane found a travel wallet, the kind that hides under the waistband of your clothes, in the underwear drawer. It felt stiff.

"I can't tell. I keep thinking if I wait long enough everything will go back to normal." Jake's voice broke on the word *normal.*

Jane turned back to him, the wallet in her hand. He was watching her with his big blue eyes. She needed to finish what she was doing before the temptation to go back and let him kiss her overwhelmed her.

He lifted an eyebrow at her.

She looked away. The zipper on the wallet stuck as she tried to open it.

"What is that?" Jake asked.

"Travel wallet. It's probably got old papers in it." Jane pulled out a sheet of printer paper and unfolded it to reveal a travel itinerary. The ink was bright and fresh. "Was your mom planning a trip?"

CHAPTER 16

"I DON'T KNOW." Jake lay back on the bed and covered his eyes with his arm. "I don't want to think about my parents right now."

Jane sat on the edge of the bed. "I think you need to start thinking about them."

"I thought about it last night. For real. It was awful." Jake's voice was serious, for the first time since he had come down the stairs without his shirt on the week before. Possibly for the first time since she had met him. There was a weak sound to it, the bravado stripped away.

"Yeah." Jane patted his knee. "I could tell." She pulled her hand away and set the itinerary on the bed. "You needed that. You'll probably do more of it—the grieving, I mean."

Jake inhaled deeply, his chest rising. Then he sat up. "So what did you find?"

"A travel itinerary in your mom's wallet waist pouch thingy. You know, the one you hide under your clothes when you travel?"

"I hate those, but mom always made us wear them. Where were they going?"

Jane read the paper, her face puckering. "Your mom and your aunt were going to Switzerland for a month. Did you know that?"

"No."

"Do they have business in Switzerland? Or family?"

"No."

"Do they ski? Is there any reason at all for your mom and aunt to go to Switzerland in March?" Jane followed the travel dates with her finger as she read it, trying to figure out exactly how long they were traveling.

"No, they don't ski. It's not a mystery Jane. Mom and Marjory like Europe. They go all the time. At least once a year." Jake leaned over the paper.

Jane was aware of how close he was, but the heated moment had passed. He wasn't interested in her, not really. He had just been overwrought, and wanted to escape his emotions. And as for her…she looked up from the paper to watch his face. No, she wasn't interested either. His face was familiar from too many years of school together. She knew him for a player and a jerk. Yes, when he kissed her she had been…moved. But that was all. The moment had passed, for both of them.

"Can we at least ask your aunt about it?" Jane left her finger under the departure information. They were meant to leave early in the morning, the day Pamela had died.

"You can. I wouldn't though. Aunt Marjory is completely overwhelmed right now. She's trying to run the business even though it is not her job, and no one is listening to her. She's on a warpath, and I want to keep out of her way."

"I kind of thought she had mellowed."

"Around the house maybe, but I'd watch out. My aunt is under a lot of pressure and she is about ready to blow. Personally, I don't want to be around when it happens."

"Can you tell me anything more about what she is trying to accomplish with the business?" Jane stood up again. She wanted to search more of the room while they talked. She hadn't even touched the closet or the bathroom.

"She wants to follow through with dad's plans, but she wants to wait until the investigations are over and the estate is settled. I guess the board is trying to get it done immediately instead."

"Why does she think she has the authority to slow things down?" Jane searched the drawers of the dresser one at a time, but she only found the clothes she expected to find.

"She has a pretty big stake in the company. As big as mom's was, but not as big as mom and dad's together. With them gone she thinks she gets to be the decision maker, but it's still up in the air. The lawyers tell me they aren't able to make the final call yet."

"Have you been talking to the lawyers?" Jane opened the closet. The clothes were organized by type and color. No surprise to Jane, as she had organized them. Nothing seemed to be out of place. The closet was small, as the house was built before walk-in closets were in fashion. There was a shelf above the closet rod, lined with boxes. Jane knew they were supposed to be full of hats and shoes that were stored during their off-seasons. She turned to Jake. He was watching her dig around in his parents' stuff. Maybe she didn't need to pull down all of the boxes. "Marjory had a lot to gain by your parents' deaths. If she killed them, why would she do it the day she was supposed to go on vacation?"

"I don't think Aunt Marjory killed them. She really loved my parents."

"But she could have done it. What time was the plane leaving?"

"At 8 am."

"So your mom and aunt would have had to be there at six, right? Your parents would have expected your aunt to be at the house first thing in the morning, right?" Jane didn't like where her train of thought was headed, but Marjory, who seemed to have mellowed recently, had both a motive and access to Bob and Pamela.

"No, not at all. I told you, mom and Marjory went to Europe together all of the time. They met at the airport. Marjory always took a taxi and dad always drove mom. If Aunt Marjory had shown up at the house they would have been shocked."

"Are you sure, Jake? That's how they always did it?"

"Yes. Always. Two trips a year, at least. Sometimes more, except last year. They only went once last year. This would have been their first trip since dad's heart attack."

"But...if she was going to kill them both it wouldn't really matter how they usually traveled. She still could have come here and done it."

"If she was going to kill them, why plan a trip?" Jake walked to the master bathroom and began to dig around in the cupboards.

"Alibi? Maybe she did it so we could ask 'If she was going to kill them, why plan a trip?'" Jane shut the closet door.

"How well do you know my Aunt Marjory?"

"Not at all." Jane joined Jake in the bathroom. A silver tray on the tile counter held their daily medicines. She picked up a translucent brown bottle and read the label.

"Aunt Marjory is cheap. Yes, she's rich. Yes, she travels, but she's cheap. Did you notice they were flying economy? They were taking an early flight? She would not have spent money on tickets if she wasn't going to take the trip. In my opinion, if she had wanted to kill them she would have planned a trip by herself and after she did the deed she would have taken her flight. That would have been an alibi."

Jane pondered. It might have been an alibi, or it might have made her look guilty. Hard to say. She didn't know what questions the police might have asked Marjory. She didn't know if Marjory's prints had been found in the bedroom, and not having seen the autopsy report, she didn't know what the real cause of the deaths had been.

There were several prescriptions on the silver tray. She read each one with care, though she didn't know what most of them were for.

She put down the bottle she had just read with a huff. She just didn't know enough to know what to look for. Then she frowned at herself in the mirror. The bottle she had just replaced wasn't as full as it should have been. The other tall, fat bottles had been, she thought, just a bit heavier. According to the label Pamela had been one month into a three-month supply. She picked it up again. She tilted it side to side. She shook it a little. The pills in the bottle just didn't seem to go up far enough. *Kal Potassium 99.*

Jane picked up another bottle about the same size. She read the label—also a three month supply of once-a-day pills. She opened the lids of the two bottles. The second bottle was definitely fuller and the pills were smaller, as well. She shut both bottles and held them up again. The Kal Potassium pills were about two millimeters lower than the other, smaller pills. Where had Pamela's missing potassium supplements gone?

"Jake, look at this." She passed the two bottles over.

"Yeah?" Jake turned the bottles around in his hand. "What am I looking at?"

"There aren't as many potassium pills as there should be, are there?"

Jake sucked a breath through his teeth. "Maybe? I can't tell."

"Do they both look normal to you?"

Jake nodded.

"Do you think they would both look normal to the crime scene investigators?"

"Yes. They look the same to me. Plus, this was never a crime scene." Jake set the bottles on the counter. He turned back to the drawer he had been searching.

"I thought you mentioned there was an ongoing investigation."

"You're right. I did say that. There is an open case, I think. Just waiting for the results on the blood work though. That's what Marjory told me. Do you remember if they had turned the house into a crime scene?"

"I—oh Jake, I'm sorry. I don't know! I had to leave and when I came back it was two days later and everything seemed normal."

"I think everyone has been working under the assumption that the deaths were natural." Jake flipped through a small spiral bound book that he had pulled from a drawer.

Jane stared at the two bottles of pills. "Do you think the deaths were natural?"

"No, I don't." Jake slipped the notebook into the back pocket of his jeans. "So, what happened to my mom's pills?"

"Good question. And what would have happened if, say, she had been given an overdose of those pills?" Jane picked up both bottles.

"Time for Google, Jane?"

"Yes, I'd say it's time for Google."

Jane and Jake raced down the stairs to Bob's office. Jake grabbed a seat in the leather and wood swivel desk chair. Jane leaned over the side and watched as he typed.

Overdose Potassium Chloride pulled up pages of material. They started with Wikipedia.

"Lethal injection?" Jake's voice was low.

"That's bad," Jane whispered. The drug, prescribed for Pamela's deficiency, was also the acting agent in Dr. Kevorkian's death machine. "That's really, really bad. But are enough pills missing to kill her?"

Jake shook his head. "I don't know. Let me keep reading."

"What we want to know though, is are there enough missing to kill both of them?"

"Wait." Jake held up his hand. "With dad's heart issues and meds, it would only have taken a little bit to kill him. But I can't tell how mom would have reacted to an overdose."

Jane continued to read over his shoulder. "190 grams? It says the lethal dose is 190 grams. These pills are only 99 milligrams each."

"School me—how many would you have to use to kill someone then?"

"Like, the whole bottle." Jane's heart sank. The missing pills were weird, but not lethal.

Jake rocked back in the chair. "I have to say, Jane, I don't mind that someone didn't break into the house and kill my parents' with prescription supplements."

Jane stroked the top of Jake's sandy-blond head. "I know. I don't blame you. Maybe it was just natural deaths."

"What do you remember from the morning? Anything at all?"

Jane closed her eyes. She remembered Bob's naked, hairy shoulder. She remembered the thud of his body as the paramedics dropped it on the floor. She remembered the sound of the cell phone, and the paramedics saying, "coroner," and "bruising." She could remember the horrible, awful bits.

"Jane? Anything important at all?"

"I don't know. They had to call a coroner because it wasn't normal for them both to be so young and dead at the same time. Then there was the paramedic who noticed bruises on your mom's wrists. Why did your mom have bruises on her wrists?"

"Handcuffs? Leather ropes? What kind of stuff did you find hiding in their closet?"

"Jake. Please."

"I don't know. No reason, I guess. I don't live here. I do now, but I didn't two weeks ago. It could have been anything."

Jane rolled her wrists. No, it couldn't. Wrists don't get banged up and bruised in everyday life. "The autopsy report wouldn't say anything about Potassium Chloride until after the blood work comes back, but it would talk about bruising. Could we please get it?"

Jake nodded. "I don't want to, but maybe we'd better do it."

CHAPTER 17

MID-MORNING WEDNESDAY JANE'S PHONE JANGLED. She was having a quick doze after her early morning work. Yesterday's hunt for clues had turned up nothing further, as Jake had had an emergency social call and didn't immediately run to get the autopsy report. The call was from Isaac, inviting her out tire shopping. Romantic? Maybe not, but certainly more fun then replacing her spare on her own.

She dug through her closet for something remotely cute to wear. It was a bust. She'd stick with what she already had on and do something with her hair instead. She stared at herself in the mirror. Nope. It was already in a ponytail and there wasn't much more she could do with her straight hair. Braids, maybe, but she wanted to look young and hip, not young and in grade school.

She added a little lip-gloss to her make-up free face before she left her room. She went straight to the front room, but waiting there for Isaac made her feel desperate. She went into the kitchen. She didn't want to start cleaning something and make herself look like she didn't care about his time, but she didn't want to be waiting by the door either. She checked the coffee pot. It was still half-full so she dug around for a travel mug and filled it up. She thought about pouring it back into the pot and re-enacting the "pour the coffee" moment over and over again until he arrived, but there was a knock on the door, so she didn't have to.

She ran to answer it.

Isaac stood at the door, a smile on his face, and a small bouquet of daffodils in his hand. "I picked these on the way out.

My mom might kill me, but I thought after the day you had, you could use them."

"Thank you." Jane took the flowers. She smiled up at Isaac. "Whatever you do, don't tell your mom you picked them for me! I don't want her to hate me before we meet."

"Neither do I. Are you ready?"

Jane grabbed her coat and purse from the closet. "Lead the way."

They both climbed into her Rabbit, leaving Isaac's car parked at the curb.

"So how are things with the Crawfords?"

"We found some interesting information yesterday." Her face flushed. Did she tell him that Jake kissed her or not? She didn't know what he would think about it. She hadn't liked it. She had made him stop. But then, there was that brief moment when he was so sad that she almost wanted to kiss him again, but it had been nothing.

It had either been nothing or it had been a good reason to move out.

"Like what?"

"We found a travel itinerary. Pamela had a trip planned with Marjory, her sister-in-law. They should have left the morning I found them."

"Was that the first you had heard of it?"

"Yeah, it was."

"Seems odd. Wouldn't you have needed to know her schedule?"

"No, not with Bob working from home." The tire shop seemed miles away.

"I assume Marjory hasn't said anything to you about it."

"No, but I was thinking it might have been related to the deaths. Don't you think so? I mean, it just seems like too many coincidences all together. Do you think Marjory killed them and planned to get away?"

"She didn't leave," Isaac said.

"That does punch a hole in my idea." Jane drummed her fingers on the steering wheel.

"Does Jake think she had anything to do with it?"

"No. Not that he tells me, at least."

"So...speaking of Jake, how is he grieving?" Isaac gave her a sidelong glance. "Have you been able to find a way to serve him?"

Now was the moment. Her heart was in her throat, but she had to tell him. "He's not doing well, I don't think. Last night he finally seemed to have a real emotional experience. That seemed good."

"That is good. It means he feels safe with you, and he should. You are pretty great."

"Yeah..." She didn't know where to start. It wasn't really Isaac's business. He didn't need to know. She went back and forth on it. If Isaac was one of her girl friends, she would tell him. If he was her boyfriend she would tell him, but he was neither. He was someone she'd maybe like to have for her boyfriend.

Where did that put him on the "tell" list?

"Do you want to talk it through? I've got some solid grief counseling classes under my belt." He grinned at her again.

Jane took a deep breath and then plunged in. "So he was crying really hard and I gave him a hug and he kissed me but I told him to stop and he didn't do it again." She got it all out in one breath, staring straight ahead.

Isaac was silent.

"I wasn't expecting it. I mean, I've known Jake since forever and he's never shown any interest in me. I don't believe he's interested now. He was just acting out."

Isaac was still silent.

"Anyway, I put my foot down and made it absolutely clear that that was unacceptable and inappropriate." As she tried to clear herself of wrong doing she was very glad she hadn't mentioned being alone and on a bed at the time of the kiss.

"What a jerk."

"Yeah. That's kind of been his M. O. since his parents died. He definitely needs counseling." Jane steeled herself for the worst, and then turned to look at Isaac. His face looked sad.

"Is Phoebe staying there now?" Isaac asked.

"She is, and Marjory. And I'm on the third floor in the old servants' bedrooms."

"Good. But if he should do anything—try anything like that again—you know you could call me if you needed help, right?"

"Thanks." She let out a breath that she had been holding. It was okay. He didn't think she was responsible for the kiss.

At the tire shop Isaac let Jane fumble her way around, picking a tire and paying for it. The shop strongly encouraged her to buy all four, or at least two. Not knowing exactly how she was going to pay off her slowly mounting credit card bill, she refused.

The drive back to the Crawford house was equally silent. Jane turned on the radio. If the drive to the tire shop had felt like miles, the drive back felt eternal.

She pulled around back and parked in her usual spot. While she was turning off her car, Isaac got out, and opened her door for her.

She kept her eye on Isaac as she got out, but he looked distracted, his eyes darting from her to the house.

"Would you mind if I come in with you?" Isaac was looking toward the house, not at her as he spoke.

"Not at all. Come on in." She let him in through the mudroom door, wondering if it was late enough to offer him lunch.

They stepped through into the kitchen where Jake was sitting, in his boxers yet again, eating a bowl of cereal. Isaac joined him at the island.

"Jake."

"Daniels."

Jane hovered in the door.

Isaac leaned forward. "About Jane."

"She's a good girl, that one." Jake slurped a spoonful of cereal. A bit of milk dribbled down his chin.

"She's a really great girl, and you need to leave her alone."

"What's this?" Jake let his spoon fall into his bowl. Droplets of milk splashed onto the black counter.

"I know things are rough right now." Isaac bobbed on the balls of his feet, like a boxer. "But that's no reason to be a jerk."

"What's his problem?" Jake looked past Isaac.

Jane cringed and shook her head. "Hey, Isaac, can I fix you some lunch?"

"My problem is that you need to keep your hands off of Jane."

"Oh. I see. Is she yours then? You, like, own her or something? You met her like yesterday and now she's yours? Sure. Why not? You can have her. She doesn't like to have fun anyway." The look on Jake's face was a mixture of boredom and superiority, and yet, Jane thought she saw pain in his eyes.

"She's a lady. Don't forget it." Isaac rocked back onto his heels. He crossed his arms on his chest, and for the first time Jane noticed his thick, muscled arms. Phoebe had said he looked good in a tank top—she wasn't exaggerating.

"I won't, *Coach*. She made it perfectly clear to me that she is a lady and I am nothing but a big, dumb boy. Why you know about it now, well, I can guess why. But it doesn't matter, does it? I've been firmly, resolutely, and completely rejected."

Isaac gritted his teeth, his jaw flexing. "I'm glad to hear that you know it."

"Walk out with me, Isaac, okay?" Jane led Isaac outside. "What was that about?"

"I've known that kid for a long time and I don't trust him. When I brought you home yesterday and realized where you were staying, I wasn't comfortable with it."

"You shouldn't have let him know that I told you about the kiss. He's in a really bad place right now. What if he won't trust me anymore?"

"What if he tries something worse? I couldn't live with myself. He had to know you have someone looking out for you."

Jane pursed her lips. She was surprised to find that protective jealousy was a bit ugly. Flattering, but not attractive. "I understand what you're saying."

"I'm sorry you're mad at me, but I'm not sorry I did it. Just remember you can call me, anytime, okay?" He raised his eyebrow, hope written on his face.

Jane nodded. She was melting. He was looking out for her, after two long years of mostly looking out for herself. "I really wish you hadn't said anything, but thank you for the thought behind it."

"See you in class tonight?"

"Yes, Mr. Daniels. I'll see you in class tonight."

Isaac grinned, then strode down to the street, to his car.

Jane stared at the big house. Go back in and face Jake or let him cool off first? She decided to get in her car and drive to her next client.

Jane felt like she had scrubbed every inch of the Laurelhurst neighborhood into hygienic submission before she finally got back to Jake. He was waiting in the office with the autopsy report. Jane's shoulders ached from scrubbing the stained grout in the tile surround of a new client's garden tub. She rolled them back and forth in an attempt to stretch the tight muscles.

The oiled leather furniture gave the room the dignified aroma a hundred-year-old mansion deserved. A light breeze blew fresh spring air in through the opened window, rustling the papers on the desk.

"Cute boyfriend. Kind of tough, but kind of smart at the same time."

"I just met him. He's hardly my boyfriend."

"Well he and *I* didn't just meet, and I'd bet money that he *thinks* he's your boyfriend."

"He doesn't. Just forget about it."

"Why did you tattle on me?" Jake's eyes still had a look of pain in them. That moment when he'd cried and kissed her had been his first sincere moment with her.

"I'm sorry. I really am. I didn't say anything bad, I promise. It's just, that I *am* interested in him. I really didn't know if I should say anything or not, but if it had come out in some other way, that I had been kissing you, it could have been worse."

"Were you afraid *I* would tell on you? For shame. You can trust me." His eyes sparked with humor again, the hurt look mostly gone.

From the way his face relaxed, she guessed Jake had only been scared someone else knew he had been crying.

Jake stuck his hand out.

She shook it, half expecting him to pull her in for another taboo kiss, but he was as good as his word.

"Do you have the autopsy report?" Jane asked when their moment was over.

"Here it is. Are you ready?" Jake sat cross-legged in front of Jane. He held the report in front of him like a menu. "For bruising: Pamela Crawford has one bruised wrist that looked consistent with finger tips, like someone had held her real hard. She also had a bruise on her shoulder, cause unknown." Jake cleared his throat and turned to the next page. "Robert Crawford had bruising and burns on his chest from trying to electrify him back to life, plus bruising on his collar bone, cause: unknown."

"That's not what it says," Jane said.

"It is a highly accurate paraphrase."

"Okay, so they have some bruising. What else does it say?"

"The medical examiner says the bruising is consistent with a light altercation between two adults, quite possibly, I am adding myself, these same two adults."

"Or those two adults and a third, unknown person." Jane leaned forward, resting on her elbows to stretch her back.

"Yes, of course. It is always possible that there was a third person in the room the night before, getting into a light altercation with my parents." Jake rustled his papers in an officious manner.

"What about the cause of death?"

"Now here is the suspicious part. The reason, I am sure, for the continued investigation."

Jane sat up.

"They both died of cardiac arrest. Heart attacks. Their hearts stopped."

"Is that all?"

"That's all it takes."

"Nothing more? The lady at the desk at the M. E.'s office said it would say that, but doesn't it say anything else?"

"I suppose something could come up when the lab reports are back." Jake laid the papers on the floor. "But they'll be buried and memorialized long before that. She said it would be at least two weeks more."

"Do you think the 'light altercation' could have caused a heart attack?" Jane reached for the papers. Jake's paraphrase might have left out something important.

"You knew them. Dad was a recovering burger-a-holic and mom, while a fine figure of a woman, huffed and puffed climbing the stairs. I would guess for two people not used to 'light altercations' it could have given them a heart attack."

Jane read while Jake spoke. He was back in his mood again—erratic and sarcastic. Whatever serious, grown-up personality he had found while they searched the bedroom had been tucked safely away, but as far as she could tell from the M. E.'s report, his paraphrase had been accurate.

"I know if I had seen them in a 'light altercation' *I* would have had a heart attack."

Jane smiled, though not with her heart. "Me too. I can't imagine them fighting, much less using force against each other. Bruising each other? It's unbelievable."

"Suing each other, I could see. But bruising? About as likely as a slap fight, hair pulling, or kung fu. More likely mom fell and he dragged her up, bruising her wrist and she pushed him out of the way or something like that." Jake leaned back against the big, old walnut desk.

"But where would she have fallen?"

"Bathtub? If she fell in the bathtub, it would have been slippery. She might have needed help up. He might have bruised her wrists while he was helping her. I don't know. Is it more likely that there was a third man in there having a push fight with them?"

"No. It's not more likely." Jane stood up and stretched her legs. "The trouble is, no one who had a motive had any access to your parents. I am beginning to think it really was just a tragic coincidence."

"But it wasn't. By no stretch."

"Wouldn't it be better if it had been?" Jane shut the window.

"That's like asking wouldn't it be better if Bob Dole had been the President. It's not what was, so it doesn't matter." Jake stood up too. He picked up several papers that had blown to the floor.

"I feel that way too, but I have nothing solid to pin my suspicions on."

"Nothing solid? Ask yourself this: Why did Fitch refuse to order new restaurant equipment for me?"

Jane's heart sank. If Jake was going to revert to nonsense as a way to deal with the tragedy again then she'd have to continue her hunt for the killer on her own. He was no use to her if he wouldn't be serious. "If you figure out the answer to that one, let me know. I've got to go study for a while. I'm pretty behind on my school work." Jane left Jake sorting the papers on his father's desk. She was honest at least, and once in her room she took out the articles that Isaac had sent the class off with and settled in for some study time.

Several hours later, Jane woke up, the staple from the photocopies pressed into her forehead. She sat up, rubbing at the spot. Bleary-eyed, she patted her bed for her phone. When she found it, she pressed it at random with her thumbs to wake it up. When she finally managed to unlock it, she checked the time. Ten pm. Class was out.

She flopped back on her bed. She couldn't remember a thing she had been reading, but she was intensely aware that she had parted with Isaac more than a little annoyed with him, and then skipped his class.

She crossed her arms over her head and yawned. She'd have to find a way to let him know she hadn't missed it on purpose, because of the thing with Jake. She tried to focus on how she might do that without seeming forward, or breaking the law from Pastor Barnes. Before she had any solid idea, she had drifted back to sleep, to dream of punctured tires, dead friends, and little rats chewing their way through her homework.

Traci Tyne Hilton

CHAPTER 18

JANE STOOD IN FRONT OF THE HOT STOVE on Thursday morning trying to put the perfect crisp on a batch of hash browns. She wanted to put a feast in front of Marjory, get her happy and comfortable, and then ask her a few questions about Switzerland and the corporation. It wasn't just an excuse to put off planning her own future, she told herself. She was helping solve the crime.

The potatoes were soggy on the outside, raw on the inside, and sticking to the pan. Jane gave up on them. She checked the oven. The frozen quiche seemed to be doing fine.

Marjory, dressed in a business suit with full make-up and hair, like always, stood in the doorway between the kitchen and the dining room. "It smells heavenly in here."

"Thanks. Why don't you sit down? Breakfast is almost ready."

"Save it for the kids, Jane. I don't have any time this morning."

Jane tried to keep her smile in place. "Are you sure? Not even a little?"

"I'll take a cup of coffee with me, but I need to shut myself in the office. I'm swamped with work."

Jane decided to plunge right in, before her few seconds with Marjory vanished. "What you need is a vacation."

"I needed a vacation before Bob and Pamela passed. Now I need a personal assistant, and a vacation." Marjory filled a mug with coffee.

"Will you have time to get away after the funeral?"

"If only I could. I don't dare leave until probate is over and the estate is settled."

"How long could that take?" A bitter, burning smell hit Jane. She dug into the potatoes with her spatula trying to turn them.

"I can't say for sure, but the lawyer indicated it could be up to a year." Marjory frowned at the stove. "You need to take that off of the heat."

Jane moved the pan. "Who is in charge while you all are waiting for probate?"

"You really aren't a cook, are you?" Marjory stared at the pan of potatoes. "Didn't you ever work in your father's kitchen?"

"Of course I did, but we deep fried those potatoes." Was Marjory avoiding her questions?

"Ah yes, that's right. We do deep fry them. Well, I don't yet know who will be in charge after the estate is settled. It's a private company so Jake and Phoebe will each own half of the lion's share. They'll have to make a lot of decisions about the future of the company."

"Are they ready for that?" Jane stirred her potatoes around, trying to look casual.

"No. Not at all. I'm trying to hold the ship together for them until then. One good thing about probate: it gives them a year to learn about the business."

"And when you are done schooling them you'll really be ready for a vacation." Jane turned and smiled at Marjory, hoping her look came off as sympathetic.

"I will." Marjory looked at her watch. "The worst part about all of this is that Pam needed a break too. We were headed off together." Marjory's voice cracked. "She had invited me back to her favorite little Swiss village for some R and R." Marjory shaded her eyes with her hand. "Next time I have a break, I won't get to have it with my best friend."

Jane pulled a paper towel off the roll by the stove and handed it to Marjory.

Marjory held it under her eyes. "Thank you. I need to keep it together until the funeral." She dabbed with the towel to mop up the tears that were beginning to smudge her mascara. "And I need to pull myself together for the business meeting. The board wants to run away with the business before Jake and Phoebe

have a chance to make any decisions. I can't let that happen."
Marjory looked up at Jane with a grim face. She folded her paper
towel into quarters and slid it into the pocket of her suit jacket.
"Thank you for thinking of a nice breakfast, Jane. We'll have to
try again another morning." Marjory wrapped her hands around
her mug and left.

Marjory didn't seem to relish running the business. Jane
thought it was impossible that she would have killed her best
friend for any reason, much less to get control of a business she
didn't like running.

Jane dumped her potato mess in the scrap bucket. She
considered taking it out to the compost when there was a knock
at the back door. Killing two birds with one stone, she grabbed
the scraps and went to the door.

She opened it to find Isaac on the other side of the screen
with a sheepish grin on his face.

"Want to play hooky with me?"

Jane looked from Isaac to the scraps. "I can't."

Isaac opened the screen and took the bucket of scraps. He
walked beside her to the compost. "I missed you yesterday, but I
don't blame you for not wanting to see me. I kind of
overstepped."

Jane gave him a bit of a smile. "Agreed. You kind of
overstepped, but I didn't mean to miss class. I fell asleep reading
the sociology report on teen suicide in resource-poor-
communities that you sent us home with."

"I agree. Very dull paper." Isaac tipped the scrap bucket,
letting the potatoes, et al, spill into the compost bin.

"It's not that. It wasn't a thriller, but I was just exhausted.
It's been a rough couple of weeks." Jane took the scrap bucket
back from him and headed to the house.

"That's why I thought it might be a good idea to play
hooky together. I skip class, you take a day off. We do
something relaxing. Just hang out. Get to know each other. No
pressure, no murder solving, no discussions of your future
plans."

"No illicit flirting?" Jane nudged him with her elbow.

"I'll do what I can, but I am only human." Isaac sprinted
ahead of her and opened the screen door. "We could go to the

park and kick a ball around. You do play soccer, right? It's a prep school staple."

"I played field hockey. Don't kill me."

"Kick the ball around?" Phoebe was in the mudroom in her very short, very thin nightgown. Her tall, curvy figure displayed in detail. "I'm game." She smiled at Isaac, cute dimples popping out in her cheeks.

Isaac put his arm through Jane's. "Sorry," he said to Phoebe. "This is one on one practice. Jane is in desperate need of help."

Phoebe yawned, and stretched so that her nighty pulled a little tighter and got a little shorter.

Isaac kept his face on Jane. "I've got a ball in my car. Get your tennies."

Phoebe scowled and slumped out of the mudroom.

Jane wanted to apologize for Phoebe's inappropriate clothes, but kept her mouth shut. He was ignoring it, so she would too. "You know what? Let's do it. I can play hooky for an hour anyway."

"Perfect." Isaac dropped her arm and pushed her towards the house. "Go get your shoes."

"Why don't you follow me, just in case." She nodded towards the door Phoebe had just exited.

"Yeah. That's a good idea."

As Jane passed the office she heard Marjory in deep conversation. The other voice sounded familiar, so she paused by the door. It was Vargas, the same man who had been at the abrupt meeting the week before. She held her finger to her lips to keep Isaac quiet.

"You believe we can make Wally agree to this?" Marjory asked.

Wally Walker. Jean knew she had known that unnamed man at the last meeting. He was Wally Walker, the head of franchising.

"If you can keep Fitch out of things, I believe between the two of us we can make Walker see that patience is a virtue."

"Don't talk in riddles. I don't have time for it. Will Wally agree to wait on the sale or not?"

"Yes, he will, but I am serious about Fitch. He's not on the board and he has no business at these meetings. I don't care if he agrees with you."

Isaac frowned at Jane. "Eavesdropping?" His voice was a low whisper.

Jane repeated the international sign for "hush" and nodded *yes.* There seemed to be more than just paperwork keeping Marjory away from breakfast.

"I only invited the people who were on the minutes at the last meeting. Fitch is nothing to me, but if Bob wanted him involved, I thought I had better as well."

"Bob?" Vargas laughed. "It wasn't Bob's idea to involve Fitch. It was Pamela's. He was her protégé while Bob was recovering. I never got the impression that Bob appreciated it."

"Neither here nor there. If keeping Fitch out of the meetings is all you need me to do, I'll do it. All I want is to wait until the estate is settled. Sign nothing, agree to nothing, change nothing, until then."

Jane tiptoed past the door with new questions on her mind. What future job had Pamela been grooming Fitch for, and did it have anything to do with the murders?

Up in her room, she posed the question to Isaac.

"How should I know? I know less than nothing about corporations, small, large, or otherwise."

"What if Fitch hated the job he was being groomed for and so he killed Pamela?" Jane was on her knees digging through the stuff she had shoved into the small closet. She looked to Isaac for his answer.

"Wouldn't it have been easier to just quit?" Isaac scratched his chin.

"In this economy? If he was unstable for any reason he could have seen murder as an easier option than finding a new job."

"Before you make wild leaps, ask yourself this question: What job in the restaurant industry could have been so horrible that he would rather kill two people than perform it?"

Jane rocked back on her heels, a pair of cross trainers in her hand. "There is that. I suppose someone who managed several locations had already done everything humiliating and disgusting at that point. There's no job worse than cleaning the public restrooms after the little league team comes to celebrate their season."

"So we can agree it wasn't Fitch, and we can go play soccer. Right?"
Jane looked back at her closet, her shoes resting on her knees. "We can agree that if it was Fitch it wasn't because his new job was awful. And yes, we can go kick the ball around the park. I make no promises that it will look anything like this game you call 'soccer.'"

CHAPTER 19

IT WAS FRIDAY, the day after what had been a very fun, if not exactly flirtation free, hour of soccer in the park, and the day before Jane and Isaac would have had their date had it not been against school policy. If she could muster the energy, she thought she might like to dress up just a little for school.

A hot shower had loosened her shoulders and relaxed her back, not completely but at least she was more comfortable. She stood, towel wrapped, in front of her closet, disturbed by the state of her clothes. Bleach stained house cleaning clothes and church dresses. That was all. Nothing in between. She felt the need for a pair of skinny jeans and a…she scrunched her mouth. She couldn't imagine what kind of shirts were considered cute and "in" right now, but whatever they were she wished she had one. After her lean winter the closest jeans she had to skinny were pretty baggy still. She didn't even want to look at her shoes. Two choices. Bleach stained converse or the black buckled Mary Jane style flats she'd been wearing since she was a sophomore at prep school. She grabbed a vintage Roly Burger t-shirt from one of her dad's promo events in years past. It wasn't too bleach speckled yet.

And what did it matter? It really wasn't a date, after all. Just school like any other day. She threw a light sweater over it and called it good. Not stylish, but good.

At school Jane settled into her seat, in the clothes she had settled on. Settled. The word had a depressing sound to it, like a dirt mound sinking into the ground after a heavy rain. How badly had she settled?

It wasn't like she had *settled* on Harvest School of the Bible. She had graduated high school with high honors. Her parents had given her carte blanche to pick a school. This one, this little school with its missions focused Bible program, was the one she had felt called to. *Had felt*. Past tense. When, exactly had her feeling changed? Or was the problem that it had always just been a feeling, and nothing more? Had she truly been called or had she merely made an adolescent, emotional decision?

Jane crossed her arms on her desk and laid her head down, stretching her neck. With only three months left until "graduation," if you could call it that, the "feeling" of being called to Harvest hardly mattered. She certainly wasn't going to quit this close to the finish line.

Isaac stood at the front of the class shuffling his papers. After exchanging a brief, rueful smile, she avoided making eye contact, and he seemed to avoid her as well. Whoever had been telling tales to Pastor Barnes needed to get the message that she and Isaac were trying to be above reproach.

Or were they?

Graduation was coming. Last year's graduation had been fun. She had started at Harvest a year after her high school graduation so that she could have a stash of money saved up to allow her to work less as she went to school.

Still, though she had started the program as a part time student, only taking the night classes, she had had plenty of her friends from high school with her. The graduation ceremony had been emotional, knowing that several of her friends were leaving straight from the ceremony to short-term overseas missions. She sat up and looked around the room. Her fellow students this year were not her friends the way they had been the year before. Even though she had grown up with some of them. Was it because they were so frivolous or was it really because her attitude had changed over time?

Would she have been better off to do one of the short term missions with her real friends?

Isaac began his lecture. His microphone crackled and Jane sat up.

He caught her eye, and despite her internal moaning she felt a smile creep across her face. Her heart fluttered, against her better instincts.

No, she was glad she hadn't gone on a mission this year. Not exactly because she had met Isaac, rather, because meeting Isaac had pointed out an important flaw in her character. She felt like she ought to have been lost in thought over how to serve the grieving and seemingly unsaved Crawford family, leading them to Christ, helping them during their time of crisis, figuring out who was behind the murders. But what was she doing instead? Moping. Decrying her current life situation because she was sad that she didn't have anything cute to wear for Isaac. Clearly she wasn't mature enough to serve overseas yet.

The smile disappeared. If she wasn't mature enough to go overseas yet, what was she going to do after graduation?

Class dragged on forever.

At the end of class—Isaac had not given them a mid-way break—Sarah grabbed Jane by the elbow. "Your futon has become the center of female social life here on campus. Come enjoy it with us."

Jane allowed herself to be pulled away, but gave a fleeting glance in Isaac's direction. He was engaged in conversation with three of the more studious boys in class.

In the girls dorm community area Sarah settled Jane on the futon with a mug of herbal tea and a fleece blanky. As Sarah had promised, most of the forty girls who lived in the dorm were lounging with them.

"Spill." Sarah leaned against Jane's knees with her own cup of tea.

"I assume you don't mean literally." Jane blew on the top of her cup to cool the hot liquid.

"What is going on with you two?" Mina asked. She lay on her stomach on the indoor-outdoor carpeted floor painting her nails. "We know he likes you, so, like Sarah said, spill. Are you and *Mr.* Daniels an item or not?"

Jane took a drink of her tea.

"Come on, Ice Queen, we demand to know!" Trinity, one of the youngest at the school squealed as she spoke.

"Ice Queen?" Jane rested her cup on her knee. Moments ago, sitting at her desk, she had felt like a twelve-year-old, but now she might as well be forty.

"Too cool for school, Ice Queen. Too cool for boys. Just plain Jane, the Ice Queen."

"Plain, I can understand, but since when have I been icy?"

"This is the first time you've ever sat in the lounge, Ice Queen." Mina finished her nails off with polka dots.

"No it's not. What are you talking about? I—" Jane stopped, mid-defense. She was about to say she hung out in the communal room all the time, except that it had been last year, with the other class. She had stayed here past curfew most nights, last year. Mina was right. This was the first time all year she had sat in the lounge to hang out with the girls. "Sorry. I didn't mean to be cold."

"Forgiven. Now, tell us what is going on with you and that handsome devil who teaches our class." Mina sat up. She waved her hands back and forth in front of her to dry.

"Nothing." Jane took another drink, heat rising to her cheeks.

"Because of Pastor Barnes?" Trinity asked.

Jane chewed on her bottom lip. If these girls had been last year's girls they would have known everything by now. "Yes, because of Pastor Barnes. There are rules against instructors dating students."

"Not fair!" Trinity cried. "Totes not fair, like, really, really totes not fair. He is so into you."

Jane's smile came back. She couldn't help it. He *was* into her. So much so that the other kids noticed.

"So what are we going to do about this grave injustice, my friends?" Sarah asked.

The girls began to giggle, all of them at once.

"Oh no." Jane didn't like the sound of the giggles.

"We have a surprise for you, Jane." Sarah stood up and motioned to Mina.

Mina stood up, and fluttered a long, thin scarf out in front of her. "Stand, Jane."

Jane did not stand. She did not like the looks of that scarf, but Trinity and Sarah and a couple of other girls dragged her off the futon, with minimal tea spillage.

Mina wrapped the scarf around her head.

"You are coming with us." Sarah used her most ominous voice, the effect slightly ruined by the sheer volume of giggling.

Jane allowed them to lead her away. She had done something similar to a student last year. A girl who was in love with a quiet, shy boy who sat at the front of the class. Jane had helped sneak her friend into the boys' dorm hall so that the love-struck kids could have a little bit of privacy to "talk" about their feelings. It had worked. Jane had received an invitation to their upcoming wedding shortly before she was evicted, but where were these girls taking *her*?

They were outside. They walked so far that Jane was certain they had left the school grounds. It was cold, and Jane knew it was very dark.

And then it was warm, and smokey. The crackle of a fire filled the air. Sarah had taken her to the fire pit. Then she helped Jane sit down on a log.

The secret fire pit. Jane remembered it well.

Sarah pulled the scarf off and ran.

Jane was completely alone. She leaned forward and stared into the fire. Last year, when she had taken the time to make friends with the other students, they had come to the secret fire pit in the woods. She missed them. Part time school had been a bad idea.

She could hear footsteps crunching on the forest floor, and then Isaac sat down on the log next to her. He sat close, his arm warming hers.

"The guys told me there was a student out here who needed some advice."

"They were right." Jane leaned her head over on his shoulder. "What was I thinking, Isaac?"

"I think you were probably thinking about using your life to grow God's kingdom."

"Yes, I was, but my idea was bad. I should have done everything differently." Jane kept her eyes fixed on the crackling flames.

"Maybe, but isn't that true for all of us? We never know what the best idea really is until after we've done something." Isaac wrapped his arm around her shoulder.

"What a shame. I can't go back now and make the right decision." Jane leaned forward and picked up a stick. She poked into the fire with the green wood, sending sparks into the night air.

"But you can use this experience to help you make the next decision."

"I don't know what the next decision is anymore." Jane poked the fire again. The larger log rolled off the burning pile. The fire dimmed with the loss of contact, but the white coals glowed.

"I have an idea, but it's going to sound really stupid, and you probably aren't going to like it."

Jane doubted it would be a stupid idea. Isaac, in their short acquaintance, had never sounded stupid, but from the serious set of his mouth, she thought she might not like what he had to say.

"Never mind." Isaac tossed the stick he had been toying with onto the fire.

"You've got to tell me now. It's only fair." Jane cracked the thin bark of her stick with her fingernail and began to peel away at it.

"This is going to be a really long spring." Isaac lifted the hem of her sweater. He let the thin knit fabric fall between his fingers.

"Isaac, I didn't ask the boys to bring you here to counsel me." Jane peeled another long, thin, strand of bark off of her stick. "I'm just moping right now. I swear my life—and I—aren't usually this dramatic. Everything will calm down after the funeral."

"I figured you didn't ask for counseling." Isaac smiled at her "And I wasn't talking about drama. Your drama isn't your fault."

Jane let the strips of bark fall into the fire. They lay on the coals, sweating and curling in the heat. They were too green to burn. "Then what do you mean?"

He gave her sweater hem a tug. "I don't want to wait until May to take you out." His smile looked a little embarrassed.

Jane leaned into his shoulder. "That's not stupid, and I *do* like it."

"That wasn't the part you wouldn't like." He let the sweater fall from his fingers. Then he picked up her hand. "So, Harvest."

Jane's heart sank. "Yes?"

"You've earned a lot of credits here."

"Yes. I have." Jane looked down at her hand in his. She was surprised again, by how rough his hands were. Not at all what she would have expected for a career student.

"Remember how badly you don't want to go on short-term missions?"

"How could I forget?" Jane said.

"Do you remember what you said not so long ago about how you don't need my class?"

Jane's hand went cold in his. "Yes."

"You have a lot of credits, probably more than you know. You could drop my class. You'd still get your certificate, and then, you know…"

Jane slipped her hand out of his.

"I knew you would hate it. Never mind." Isaac tipped her chin up with his knuckle so she had to make eye contact.

"I know I should be flattered." Jane stared into his eyes—those beautiful hazel eyes.

"Just forget about it, Jane. I'm sorry."

"What difference will a few months make…to us?" Jane had difficulty getting the words out. On the one hand, he wanted to date her now, and in her heart, she agreed. She didn't want to wait twelve weeks either, when she knew—what did she know?

She dropped her eyes. All she could say for sure was that she really *could* love him, if she had the chance. On the other hand, he wanted her to drop out of college for him, and that was completely out of the question. She lifted her eyes to his again. She was too old to let her feelings for a boy she just met direct her decisions.

"You should transfer to university, Jane. You are so smart." His eyes were mesmerizing, ringed in thick black eyelashes. "You could take the credits you have now and transfer. My one class wouldn't make any difference at all."

Transfer. University. Hazel eyes. Her head was swimming. She had avoided boys for two years. Studiously avoided them. University wasn't waiting, the mission field was.

He was so close now that she could feel his warm breath in the frosty air. "Just think about it?" His voice was low and quiet. One hand was on the back of her neck, his fingers laced though her long, straight hair.

Jane found herself nodding, against her better judgment.

She closed her eyes and he kissed her, with firm, gentle lips. It was just a moment, and then he hovered away from her lips, ever so slightly. She leaned in and found his lips again. Her whole body trembled.

Isaac pulled away again, just a few inches. "I shouldn't have done that." His nose bumped hers as he spoke. "I'm sorry."

Jane bit her lip. She shouldn't have done it either, but she was glad she had. "I can't promise anything, but I'll think about it. I just don't know."

"Please forget I said it. I was impatient. You are worth the wait."

"How do you feel about the mission field? I mean truly feel."

"It is very, very far away." Isaac smiled while he said it. "It's going to take me at least another year to finish my PhD. Maybe two." His fingers were still entwined in her hair. "If you were to be on the mission field while I was here I would say it was very far away."

Jane nodded, her chin trembling. It was a non-answer and she knew it.

For a long moment all that could be heard was the rustling of the leaves above them and the crackling of the dying fire.

"It was just an idea." Isaac turned to the fire, pulling her into the crook of his arm.

Jane rested her head against his shoulder. Night air that enveloped her smelled of moist earth, campfire smoke, and Isaac's crisp, button down shirt. She stared at the flames, breathing deeply, trying to memorize everything about the moment.

Transferring to university was just an idea. An idea just like everyone else's idea for her life.

The troubling thing was, when Isaac said it, she liked the idea.

Oh Lord, she prayed in her heart, *help me stay true to your plan, and be only guided by your Holy Spirit*. She listened, but no leading whisper responded with the answer to her unspoken questions.

"How do you kids put out these fires?" Isaac asked.

Jane straightened up, pulling herself away from his arm that held her. "Last year we kept a bucket of water, but I don't see it." She walked around the fire looking for the bucket her old friends had kept handy. She found a shovel. "I guess we just bury it."

"Good thing it's been raining." Isaac took the shovel from Jane. He turned the dying fire over onto itself. He buried the still glowing embers under shovelfuls of damp earth. When he had finished he stood next to the ring of rocks with his shovel balanced on the pile of earth. "Did I ruin this, Jane?"

The night was dark without the fire, but she could still see the whisper of steam from the wet soil. "No. You didn't ruin it." She watched the steam slowly fade away. The fire was banked, for now. "We were supposed to put it out. Those are the rules."

Isaac held her hand as they walked out of the little woods behind the school, but as the chapel came into sight, he dropped it. He paused by the door to the girls' dorm, where she needed to collect her things. "I'll see you on Monday? For class?" He smiled, his brows lifted, looking hopeful.

Jane nodded. She didn't want him to know how close she was to tears, and her voice would betray her if she tried to speak.

Isaac quickly looked around. Then he kissed her on the cheek, lingering close to her ear. "Until May, Jane. I can wait until May." He left before she could say anything.

Jane watched him walk to his car, his steps light and happy, but they would be, because he didn't have to choose between his plans for the future and what was beginning to feel a lot like love.

CHAPTER 20

SUNDAY CAME, BUT THE SUN WAS NOWHERE TO BE SEEN. Jane pulled her comforter over her head. She had managed to clean all Saturday without interruption. She especially didn't stop to think about the fireside conversation, at least not too much.

She squeezed her eyes shut. She had thought about the fireside conversation the whole day, nonstop. She thought about dropping out of school while she made breakfast for Jake. She thought about dropping out of school while washing her laundry. She thought about eloping with Isaac while she went grocery shopping, even though that hadn't been one of her options.

She wanted nothing more than to stay in bed all day, but it wasn't happening. Not at the Crawford house. The next best thing to hiding under her blankets all day was driving far, far away. Heading back to Harvest for church in the little school chapel fit the bill perfectly. She got ready for church in a haze, but attempted to pull herself together so she wouldn't die in a fiery car wreck on the way there.

She hadn't anticipated seeing Isaac. She had no reason to think he would attend services at the school where he taught night classes part-time, but when he sat next to her on the old wooden pew she felt waves of relief wash over her, as though in fact, she had only come to Harvest to see him after all.

When Pastor Barnes took his place at the podium Jane was painfully aware of how close Isaac was sitting next to her. The chapel was packed with students and the couple of dozen families that also called Harvest their church home, but it was obvious that Isaac was sitting close to Jane, and that he was glad about it.

He put his arm around the back of the pew and leaned over to whisper to her. "Glad you came today. I really didn't expect to see you. Hoped I would of course, or I wouldn't have come."

"Me, too." Jane gave him a half smile. From behind her she could hear Trinity and Mina whispering, probably about them.

Pastor Barnes began a sermon that was sure to be unpopular with the fresh-from-the-nest eighteen-year-olds who made up his school. It must have been an annual tradition because Jane remembered it as basically the same last year. "Honor Your Parents Even though You Don't Live with Them Anymore."

Jane tuned it out and commenced exchanging a lengthy string of notes with Isaac. It felt scandalous, but he had started it with questions about how the Crawfords were doing.

Suspicious death. Jane scratched on her bulletin. *Don't know how to prove it.*

Do you have to? Isaac responded. *Aren't the police looking into it?*

The autopsy report didn't indicate they were. Jane felt Pastor Barnes's eyes on her as she scribbled 'indicate.'

What did it say?

Maybe small fight. Heart attacks. Should I keep looking into this? It was much easier talking about the deaths with Isaac than about her future, or their future.

You pray. I'll pray. God knows. Isaac's answer was a bit theology-student for her. She wanted his personal opinion on it, as time was running out. She wasn't sure what her role in the Crawford household would be after the funeral.

I won't stop praying. Jane passed the note.

Wait—listen to this. Isaac passed the note, and then nodded at the pastor.

Jane frowned. What was Pastor Barnes saying that was so important?

"The gift our parents give us is grace—and you know it, you remember your teenage years, if your parents are giving you anything at all right now, it's a gift of grace—that gift of grace is their wisdom."

The congregation chuckled in response.

"We're all adults here, some of us young adults, some of us young adults at heart," the congregation responded with another little laugh, "and we don't technically have to obey our parents any longer."

A young male voice popped out an "Amen," followed by more chuckling.

"Obedience isn't the only way to honor our parents. Our parents are offering us their wisdom. Wisdom gleaned from years of hard experience and bad mistakes. If we are so lucky as to still have parents—"

Jane's heart hurt for Jake and Phoebe at those words. They were so young to be facing the world without their parents.

"If we are so *blessed* as to still have our parents, we should listen to them. Don't just nod and smile, but listen. Open your hearts and your ears. When they give you advice, and so long as it doesn't contradict God's word, consider taking it."

While the bulk of the congregation fidgeted at these words, Isaac nodded along with the sermon like the old folks in the room. It must have been the home-schooled-relates-well-to-adults thing he had going.

Jane felt awkward. She hadn't been listening to her parents lately, and wasn't planning on it. She wanted to honor them though, and listening did sound easier than obeying.

Isaac passed her another note. *The answer, maybe? What do your parents say you should do?*

Jane knew exactly what her parents said she should do. She folded the note in half and tucked it between the pages of her Bible.

Around the closing song, Jane found herself holding hands with Isaac. She gave his hand a squeeze before they stood up, and then made a quick exit. She didn't want to face Pastor Barnes after their obvious flirting during his service.

She made her way back to her temporary home, determined to bury the nagging issue of listening to her parents under a whole load of housework and murder solving.

CHAPTER 21

BY MONDAY MORNING Jane had thoroughly put aside the honoring-her-parents issue. She was immersed in housework. The funeral was just five days away now. Jane had finished the last of the extra tasks on her list, only to be thrown a whole new litany of tasks.

"All of the silver, Jane. We need it all for the reception. Even if we don't use it, it is heirloom and we want it out with the buffet. See me immediately when you finish the silver." Marjory hadn't looked up from her computer as she spoke.

Jane had stationed herself in the mudroom. The first batch of the silver service was laid out on the marble counter next to the utility sink. She hadn't polished silver in at least a year. Each piece took twice as long as she anticipated. While she worked she plotted the paper she would write for Isaac's class. Now, more then ever, she was determined not to shirk her class work. For this paper, she thought a review of her weeks of practical experience tied to pertinent articles in the journals would do. If she could spend a couple of hours at the school library, she should have a top-notch piece to turn in.

Jane set an elaborate salad spoon covered in deeply carved grapes on the "polished" side of the counter.

She could hear voices in the kitchen, but had been trying to ignore them as she worked. She could tell that Phoebe and Jake were arguing. Their voices had risen in anger, and now couldn't be ignored.

"You need to stop saying that you hate mom. It looks bad," Jake said.

"It's the truth and I don't care who knows. You don't even know how awful she was."

"Pheebs, I know more than you think, but you can't keep saying it, okay? It will get out."

"What if it does? The truth shall set us free. It said so in that one movie and they said it at Prez Prep, too."

"It's from the Bible, Phoebe. It means Jesus, not your irrational hate for your mother."

"If you had seen what I saw, you wouldn't say it was irrational."

"What you saw, when? What could you have seen to make you so mad? You don't even live here." Jake's voice faded away a little, as though he had stepped out of the room.

"That's *why* I don't live here. She was hateful."

"You'll regret this, someday, when you realize that she's never coming back. When you realize you can't make up from whatever fight you two had. Then you'll wish that the whole city hadn't heard you say you hate mom." Jake's voice rose again. He was yelling, and close to the mudroom door.

"I didn't use to *hate* mom."

"Not until she locked you up."

"She didn't lock me up. I went because I needed to." Phoebe's voice was closer now as well. Jane hoped they wouldn't come into the mudroom. She just wanted to finish the silver and get out.

"They did everything for you, Phoebe. You can't go around saying you hated them."

"I never said I hated *them*, Jake, and don't forget it. Dad was a saint."

"No, he wasn't. He was difficult. He was overbearing. He ruled mom to within an inch of her life. Why else would she and Aunt Marjy spend so much time in Europe?"

"Because mom was the most selfish person on Earth. You know it's true."

"I don't know anything." Jane barely heard the last line, as Jake's voice dropped to a whisper. She could tell he was still near her door though.

"I left because I needed help, Jake, and I needed help because mom was a monster. I didn't know it then, but I do now."

"Phoebe...Phoebe. I will give you five thousand dollars if you promise to stop saying you hate mom. Keep whatever you think you know to yourself, and the money is yours."

Jane gasped. What did Jake and Phoebe know that was worth five thousand dollars?

The door popped open. "Jeeze, Jane, didn't anyone ever teach you not to eavesdrop?"

"I'm just working, I swear." Jane kept her eyes on the silver.

Jake pulled the door shut. "Phoebe spent a month at the hospital—inpatient therapy to deal with the family-crazy thing she has going, and now she thinks she's a martyr."

Jane rubbed the grape leaves on the cake sever. She nodded.

"I need her to keep her crazy to herself until the loss of our parents stops being a news item. You understand, don't you?"

Jane nodded again. What could she say? She was embarrassed for Jake. She had assumed he had been exaggerating just how badly imbalanced his sister was, but from the sounds of the fight, she had serious issues. "Is there anything I can do to help?"

"Force-feed her her pills? I swear she's fine when she's medicated and working out. Soccer has always been great medicine for her, but this stress has really rocked her. After the funeral I'm going to see if she might like to go back to the facility, just to rest."

Jane tried to keep the shock off her face. Mental illness was foreign to her—more than foreign. She was trained in counter-culture outreach, not in mental illness.

Jake chewed on his lip. "I hate to say this, but I think you should know. Rich people tend toward crazy. It's the inbreeding. I'd stick with the upper-middle class, if I were you." His joke sounded forced.

Jane moved the cake server to the polished pile. "What do you think she saw, Jake? Could she have seen your parents fighting the night before they died?"

"She could have seen anything, I suppose."

"She really hates her mom right now. If she saw the fight she might think your mom was responsible for their deaths."

"It sounds like that's what Phoebe thinks, but I couldn't tell you why."

"I heard you offer her money to stay silent. Don't you think it would be a better investment to pay her to go to a counselor? A professional could help her work out what she saw, help her understand it, and feel better about it."

"It'll take more than a week to work that out. I'll buy a week of silence, and then she can get the help she needs. Don't let it worry your pretty little head." Jake let himself out the back door before she could reply.

One question nagged at Jane as she scrubbed polish into the handle of a silver serving tray. *What if Phoebe wasn't crazy? What if she really did see something?*

CHAPTER 22

JANE RUBBED HER POLISH-COVERED RAG across the rounded belly of the hundred-year-old silver coffee pot. *Carafe? Pot?* She couldn't decide. She had put this one off to the last. After an hour of polishing silver, her arms were sore, and so was her head.

Would she consider Phoebe crazy under normal circumstances? It was hard to say with so little information about how her issues presented. She was bi-polar. That wasn't easy, sure, but crazy? It seemed a little harsh. In a world where every third person was medicated for a neurosis and on some spectrum or other, how crazy was crazy?

Jane turned the pot to rub polish into the finely detailed handle. These days you had to be more than just bi-polar to be crazy. That was clearly a word Jake used to torment his sister. Cruel, yes, but of a piece with his normal, which wasn't so normal, M. O. He hadn't come clean with his own issues, but he had said crazy ran in the family, so at the very least, she figured Jake struggled with anxiety issues, if not being bi-polar himself. He had certainly been manic since his parents died.

Someone needed to keep an eye on him, just to make sure he was okay. If he was in some kind of manic phase, when it passed, his depression could be very deep. She didn't want to be the one stuck with the job, but she made a mental note to talk to Marjory just so she could be sure that someone else who cared would pay attention to how he was dealing.

Her phone jangled into life with the ring tone she had set up for her parents, so she set her half-polished coffee *carafe? pot?* on the counter.

"Hey, darling," her mom crooned.

"Hi, mama." Jane spoke into the Bluetooth that she kept around her ear while she worked.

"We saw the funeral announcement in today's paper." Jane's mom's voice had warm, sympathetic undertones.

"Are you back from vacation already?" Jane rubbed the polish off the round belly of the pot. The spring sunshine from the opposite window glinted off the shiny surface.

"Didn't we tell you, sweetie? We didn't go on the cruise after all. Your dad came down with shingles. It's been awful for the last three weeks."

Jane scrunched up her mouth, glad that her mom couldn't see her. It would have been nice, back on that night she had come to the Crawfords' home in desperation, to know that her parents could have helped her after all. "That's awful, mom. How's he feeling now?"

"So-so. Not perfect. But he's good enough to come up to the funeral."

"Oh!" Jane stopped mid-rub. They were really coming, so she'd have to find a way to explain her new living situation that didn't sound as horrible as the truth without lying. "When are you coming?"

"We'd like to spend a little time with you, sweetie. It feels like we haven't even heard from you since Christmas, so we'll be flying in on Wednesday."

Jane rubbed the pot hard. Wednesday. What was she going to do with her parents?

"We're going to get a suite by the airport. Don't worry about trying to fit us into your little place. In fact, if you need a mini-vacation, come stay with us. We'll make sure we have room for you."

Jane put her rag down and pressed her hand over her eyes. It was meant to be a comforting move, but the polish on her hands made contact with her eye. The burning pain went straight to the top of her head and sent shivers up and down her arms. Her eye responded with a flood of tears. She opened her mouth to speak to her mom and a groan came out.

"What's that, Janey?"

Jane gulped a breath. She wiped the tears away with her hand, but it was still polishy and only aggravated the situation.

She hopped away from the silver and wiped her hand up and down her apron. She wiped her eye again, with the back of her hand. It must have been psychosomatic this time, because it hurt as bad as the first two hits and she was sure she hadn't been polishing silver with the back of her hand.

"Did I lose you, Jane?" her mom asked.

Jane grabbed a towel from the hooks above the sink. She soaked it under the faucet and pressed it to her eye. She was trying to respond to her mom, but it wasn't happening.

"Okay Janey, I think I lost you. I'll email you with our flight info. If you can't make it to the airport, just call us and I'll give you our hotel info. Love you, baby. Wish you had called to tell us about Bob and Pam."

Jane's mom ended the call.

Jane sat down with the rag pressed to her eye. The thought of escaping to her parents' suite at a posh hotel by the airport was like a fresh spring breeze, despite the burning eyes. By hook or crook, she was going to do it.

The compress did nothing for Jane's burning eye. She needed to flush it out. She headed back upstairs to her bedroom to search for saline drops.

Marjory stopped her at the second floor landing. "Oh, Jane. Good. I have another list for you. Come down to the office with me."

"Just one moment." Jane managed a hoarse whisper. She blinked hard trying to keep her eye watering.

"What's wrong with your eye? You haven't been using drugs, have you?"

"No!" Jane's hackles went up. As though she would use drugs at all, much less at an employer's house. "Polish in my eye." Jane choked the words out. The burning in her eye made her want to sob instead of talk.

"How did you manage that? Really, Jane. I expect better. You need to be in top form. We have the funeral to get through this week. Be in my office, ASAP."

"Yes, ma'am." Jane ran up the rest of the steps.

In her room, she dug through her bathroom caddy. She found the soothing drops and breathed a prayer of thanks. She risked taking too long and sat on the edge of her bed, letting the drops of saline trickle into her eye to wash it clean and soothe it.

When her parents arrived in town, she could lay her whole dilemma at their feet and they could help her solve it. The whole works: school, housing, boy troubles. Maybe they'd even have an idea about who had killed Bob and Pamela.

No. Jane thought better of asking them that. She didn't want them to think she had gone completely off her rocker.

She sat on her bed until a sense of guilt washed over her. Marjory was waiting.

The mirror showed that her eye was still bloodshot, but the pain was gone, so Jane made her way back downstairs to the office.

Marjory handed her a yellow folder marked 'memorial.' "We'll be using the ballroom upstairs for the memorial. You've got it looking all right, but the floors need to be deep cleaned and polished. You'll also need to rent chairs and tables." Marjory handed her a stack of papers held together with an alligator clip. "I've got the flowers ordered, just call them and confirm delivery. Do the same thing with the food. The numbers are all in there."

"Yes, ma'am." A fleeting vision of herself on a plane to Phoenix, that afternoon, tempted Jane.

"Make a note: I want the floors done by Wednesday. They need to be cleaned, polished, dry, and ready to set up."

Jane nodded. She could agree all she wanted but she really had no idea if she could make it happen.

"They need to be cleaned, polished and ready to go because you need to get the chairs ordered so that they can be set up by Wednesday."

Jane licked her lips. That sounded suspiciously like work that would interfere with her class, and her parents' arrival. "Isn't the funeral on Saturday?"

"Yes, it is. That's why you need the bones in place by Wednesday. Flowers will come late Friday and the caterers will be there on Saturday. Call Jake if you have any questions."

Jane rolled her head to stretch her neck. Tension had built up in her spine while Marjory gave directions and that last bit was about to make her snap. "Will Jake have any idea what is going on?"

"Jake will have the credit card. Jake is the next of kin. Make him have an idea what is going on."

Jane rolled her head the opposite direction to work out the knots that Marjory was putting into her person. However, since Marjory had brought Jake into the conversation, it seemed as though this would be good a time to discuss her concerns for him. "I think grief has hit Jake pretty hard. I'm kind of worried about him. Do you think this is a good idea?"

"Yes. He can't keep moping around. He needs something to do to keep him out of trouble. You saw what went on at his restaurant the other day. He's impossible right now."

"I don't know that I can make him do any of this." Jane fluttered her stack of papers, like a bird who tries to make himself look bigger by puffing up his feathers.

Marjory looked up from her computer screen, a severe frown creasing her face. "You are to do all of this, Jane, not him, but if you have any questions you can call him. It will give him a little control over things. He's just a boy." Marjory shook her head sadly. "He's just a boy. I wouldn't ask him to do all of this."

Jane looked at the papers in her hands. That was the real trouble with Jake. He was just a boy and couldn't do all of this. It didn't matter that they were the same age, had gone to the same school, and had both come from families with means. Jake had not yet grown up.

"Yes, ma'am."

Marjory nodded towards the door, dismissing Jane.

Jane went straight back to the mudroom. She had to finish the carafe or pot or whatever that thing was and then put it all away again. She'd set herself up at the kitchen desk to do her calling.

Jane's legs burned from her many trips up and down the stairs to stash the silver collection in the ballroom where Marjory instructed her to store it until the reception. Now she had her papers spread across the kitchen desk, the small television turned on to drown out the quiet of the empty house, and a sandwich made to tide her over. If she could make heads or tails of the paperwork before lunch was over she could get to her next client with a clear conscience.

The first floor company she called laughed at her when she asked them if they could get it all done by Wednesday, but the second company on the list booked her in. She was getting voice mail for the chairs and tables so she stopped, just for a moment, to eat.

The local news had moved from the weather report to the HLP protestors. Jane turned the sound up.

"Activity surrounding local hamburger giant 'Roly Burger' has increased overnight," the reporter said. "Help has organized non-violent sit-ins at three locations, but a fourth location has been vandalized. Dirk van Nuyens is on the scene. Dirk?"

The TV moved to a location of Roly Burger that Jane couldn't place. The camera panned from painted-over windows to Dirk. "The local head of HLP has decried the vandalism as unconscionable, but local restaurateur, Jake Crawford, doesn't buy it. Jake?"

Dirk put the microphone under Jake's mouth.

Jane groaned.

"The graffiti," Jake said, "is clearly biological in nature, hearts, livers, all of that. It is a shame and a blemish on an organization that claims to care about people. Our family is in the midst of great grief right now. We fully intend on honoring my father's wishes, but when tragedy strikes, as it has stricken our family, putting his plans into action takes time. To hit us right now, when we are the weakest, is beneath them."

"Thank you, Jake. What are the family plans now?"

"We haven't even had the funeral yet, Dirk. We will take care that the city knows everything it needs to know, as it happens."

"Thank you, Jake. Back to you, Anna."

The television switched back to Anna at the news desk. "Rose of Sharon, the head of the local chapter of Help has issued a statement to the effect that so long as the plans for the Roly Burger conversion are delayed her organization will continue to 'help' consumers make wise decisions regarding their bodies. Whether this includes more vandalism, or just peaceful protest, we will have to see."

Jane looked at her tuna sandwich. Rose of Sharon would hate her for it, but the news report made her want a cheeseburger.

HLP seemed to thrive on publicity, and the deaths of Bob and Pamela had given their current campaign much more television time than it would usually have garnered. It seemed to Jane that this was at least a small motive to do away with the Crawfords, but what evidence could she gather to make a case for her hunch?

She took a bite of her sandwich. Like all of her other hunches, this one suffered from a sad lack of physical evidence.

Perhaps she should have a burger for lunch after all.

The nearest Roly Burger was just around the corner from the Crawfords' home. Jane was glad to see that its location on a busy intersection had drawn a few protestors. She parked her Rabbit far from the front door so she would have to walk past as many protestors as possible on her way to lunch.

As she hoped, she was stopped mid-parking lot by a short, young woman with thick dreadlocks and a peasant blouse. "You wouldn't do this to your body, would you?" The protester held up a flier with a picture of diseased arteries on it. They looked an awful lot like the spray paint she had seen in the news video.

"I might order a salad." Jane smiled at the protestor.

"You can't get a salad here." The protestor waved the flier again.

"Sure I can. They have several options including smoked salmon, apple and bacon, and vegan legume salad. Tons of healthy options inside."

The protestor rattled her paper at Jane. "You kill the world when you kill yourself with this food."

Jane walked past her. She was hoping to engage someone a little more coherent.

A thin man with a thick beard stopped her next. "Hey there." He smiled down at her. "You don't really want to do this, do you?"

"It's a free country," Jane said.

"It is, that's true, but come on, you know. When you eat this stuff you aren't free. You're just a slave to the calories." The protestor handed her a leaflet.

"You must really care about people to come out here like this." Jane spoke in a matter-of-fact tone of voice.

"I do, man. When you look around and see how badly this world is hurting, you're like, willing to do anything to help." The protester gestured towards the road packed with cars.

"That's totally how I feel too, but I can't help thinking that hamburgers aren't the worst of society's ills. Isn't there something more urgent to help with?"

The protestor leaned forward and opened her flier for her. "See that boy?" he said, pointing to a picture of a very obese kid about ten years old. "We had his mom's permission to use his image and story. Dead at eleven years old. Heart attack. How much more serious does it get?"

Jane frowned. "Did this kid ever eat at a Roly Burger?" she looked up at the protester. He had tears in his eyes. "And wasn't it his mom's job to make sure he ate well?"

"She was ignorant. She didn't know. That's what we're here for, you know? People need to *know* before they enter the restaurant. How can they be expected to make great choices if they don't know?"

"Have you ever met Rose of Sharon? I see her on TV all the time. She's super passionate, isn't she?"

The protestor's face lit up. "She's a-maaa-zing. Really amazing. She has given her whole life for this cause. Do you know how many times she's been arrested? Amazing."

"Wow. She's been arrested for her protests, huh? I bet she's really angry at the people who own places like this." Jane attempted to keep a nonchalant tone of voice, but the word 'arrest' had sent shivers up her arms. She was on alert now. She had to get this guy to give up what he knew about Rose of Sharon's arrests.

The protester leaned in closer. "Very angry, and don't mess with Rose of Sharon when she's angry."

"Does Rose of Sharon ever get violent?" Jane whispered.

"There's no telling what she is capable of." The protestor was at her elbow now. He turned, and out of social instinct, Jane turned with him. Two other protesters joined them and walked her back to her car. "Go home, sweetie. Eat organic."

It wasn't until Jane was in her seat, revving her engine, that she noticed the news cameras. Was there any chance at all that what the protestor had said had been recorded?

CHAPTER 23

BACK AT HARVEST, after having made at least initial contact with several potential vendors, Jane just stared at Isaac. His voice rose and fell as he told the story of a family he had known at a homeless shelter where he had volunteered. His passion for his work was palpable. He leaned forward, listening intently as students asked him questions. As much as Jane secretly wished it, he didn't stare forlornly at her, fumbling with his pages, searching for words.

As Isaac described a late night meeting with the homeless father, how they had talked about the man's dashed plans and hopeless dreams for his children, Jane tried to picture Isaac as a professor. Why was he so intent on getting a PhD when what he really loved was helping people? Jane twirled her pen through her fingers. Isaac would be happy on the mission field—it was as obvious as the raw emotion on his face.

He moved on to cold statistics—measurable effects of prayer and faith on a family's security. Jane pictured him in a cold dark Ural mountain tent, helping an oppressed family find faith. She would be stitching intricate embroidery at the feet of a grandmother, telling generations of women about Jesus. A wave of peace washed over her. She stopped twirling her pen.

The only fly in the ointment was his seminary education. Could she get access to a closed country with a husband who had a M div? But that wasn't her problem to sort out, was it? God could handle the details.

Isaac closed class early. He walked straight to Jane and sat on the edge of her desk. "Holding up?" he asked.

"Yeah." She tilted her head and smiled up at him.

"You looked like you were barely staying awake tonight." His smile had a hint of concern.

"I was distracted. There was a terribly handsome man standing at the front of class." Jane looked down at her fingers and then up again, quickly.

Mina snorted.

Isaac cleared his throat.

"Mr. Daniels, how are we supposed to do your practical application assignment? We live on campus." Mina's voice had a whiny, nasal tone.

"I've worked that out with Pastor Barnes. He'll charter a bus and take you all into Portland to work at some of the shelters. It will be much later in the term."

"Ew." Mina rolled her eyes.

"Jane...." Isaac cleared his voice again.

"Yeah. Sorry about that. It just came out." Jane looked at her fingers again. Mina was her best guess as to who had turned them in for inappropriate behavior. There was a good chance Isaac would be called back to the office for another talking to.

"No, not that." He blushed a little. "I saw the funeral notice in the paper. I just wanted to let you know that my parents are going. I'm going too, so you might meet my family."

Jane bit her lip. "Oh?"

Isaac lowered his voice. "I wanted you to know in advance. I haven't said anything, I mean I may have mentioned that I met someone great, but I didn't tell them who. If you don't want me to introduce you, I won't."

Did she? Didn't she? She spun the thought around. She swallowed. "I'd love to meet them." She counted back the days trying to remember how long ago she had met Isaac. Not long enough to be meeting his parents.

"It's just, they're neighbors, you know? And friends. They wanted to go. I don't want to make you feel uncomfortable. You hardly know me."

Mina's snickering carried over the low murmur of voices that filled the room.

Jane turned toward the sound. Pastor Barnes stood in the doorway, his black brows pulled together, a deep crease cut between his eyes. He eyes bored into Jane. He caught her eye and nodded toward the door.

She flipped her head back to Isaac, but he had turned and was talking to Sarah.

Jane stood, her knees shaking. She joined the pastor in the hall. He closed the door to the classroom.

"Jane, I am not just the Pastor of Harvest Church. I am the administrator of this school. I am responsible for the spiritual growth of the young men and women who come here."

Jane looked at her feet. Mina had worked fast.

"I cannot have our rules flouted."

"Yes, sir." Jane's face burned with shame. She hadn't just broken the rules, she had thought of herself as above them. Her stomach was sick with misery.

"Every now and again, when I feel a student has the potential to be successful, I allow part time status. I allowed you part time status because I believed you were a serious student."

"I am. I swear I am." She still couldn't look up at him. Not with all of her recent thoughts on the value of the school racing through her brain. She had been a serious student. The school had changed, not her.

"I have two choices, Jane. And I need you to help me decide the wisest course of action."

She nodded. She knew this was going to be one of those impossible choices that Christians like to pose. The right answer was always "Die to Self."

"If I suspend Mr. Daniels for his behavior eighty-five students will miss out, not only on this night class you are a part of, but also the other two classes he is teaching here this term."

Jane's eyes filled with tears. She knew what was coming and she hated it.

"If I suspend Mr. Daniels he is without a job for the term. He is without a reference from this school. You might not know this, Jane, but I report to his thesis advisor. If he is suspended for inappropriate behavior, they will know why."

"But he hasn't acted inappropriately." Jane lifted her head and stared at the Pastor. "It would be wrong to tell them he did." Her voice rose.

"I know about the fire, Jane."

"That wasn't his fault. Or mine. He was tricked into coming out there." Jane crossed her arms. Pastor Barnes struck her as a small man. Small in stature and small in grace.

"You were seen, Jane. No one tricked him into behaving the way he did."

The warmth of his arm around her. The kiss. Her face flushed with the memory. "The alternative is to punish me in some way. I understand." Despite the waves of shame that rolled over Jane, she didn't turn away from Pastor Barnes' stern face. "That's what you had better do." With great effort she kept her voice from quivering.

"We've counted up your credits, Jane. We'll allow you to collect your certificate with the rest of the students in May, but we can't allow you to finish this course." His black eyes flashed—with humor?

Jane stopped, her mouth parted. Humor? She even detected a bit of a smile on his face. "Sir?" she said.

"Isaac is a good teacher, Jane, but we have rules and until the board tells us otherwise, we have to abide by them, no matter how hard it is." His face softened, the humor in his eyes mixed with a fatherly, gentle smile. "I think you understand me?"

She thought she did as well. "Yes, sir." She looked over her shoulder through the small rectangular window in the door to the classroom. Isaac was still sitting on her desk, but a crowd of students had gathered around him.

"We'll see you at graduation." Pastor Barnes looked into the classroom. "I think it is best if you go home now."

"Can't I say goodbye first?" Jane searched the room for Sarah.

"Yes, of course." Pastor Barnes looked at his watch. "I've got to get home. Leslie is waiting. He didn't hurry away. "A Pastor needs a good wife, Jane. A man doesn't meet the right one everyday." Pastor smiled at her again, but didn't wait for her to respond.

Jane watched Isaac talk with the students for a while before she entered the room. She had just been expelled from Bible school, sort of. *He had better be worth it.*

Jane kept the radio off as she drove home. Had her conversation with Pastor Barnes really just taken place? She rolled the words over and over again in her mind. What exactly had just occurred?

She was being disciplined for inappropriate behavior. The school had chosen to discipline her, rather than Isaac, because it was inconvenient for them to find a new teacher.

She was being allowed to collect her certificate with the other students, but did she want to? The idea of reaching across the pulpit to shake Pastor Barnes' hand and collect her certificate repulsed her. If she read his underlying message correctly, she was being expelled from class because she could be a "good wife" for Isaac. Was this really, as past students were prone to say, "Harvest Bridal School"?

Jane slammed her brakes at a four way stop light. She was alone at the intersection so she just sat there for a moment. Self-sacrifice was the ideal she held highest. Give up a university education to pursue a ministry education. Give up the comforts of a life and home in the States to serve overseas. Give up the intimate setting of dorm life at a small school so she could earn her own way through—owing nothing to no one.

A pang shot through her. How stupidly proud and self-righteous it all sounded. She dropped her head and banged it on the steering wheel. She had always been very proud of her humility, but her humility had failed to get her what she was aiming for—perfection. One attractive male dropped into the mix, when the end was near, and she had been unable to keep up her defenses.

She could say it was stress from the murders, stress from her housing situation, stress from living in the same house as Jake, but when it came down to brass tacks, she had decided she was above the rules at Harvest.

As Pastor Barnes had made abundantly clear, she was not. The rules were being applied to her very directly.

A car pulled up behind Jane at the light. As she crossed the intersection the car behind her flashed its lights. Then her phone bleeped that a text had come in. The road was dark and long—the nearest building in the long stretch of farmland was at least a mile up. She didn't pull over to check her text.

The car behind her kept close on her tail. It flashed its lights at her again. Jane gritted her teeth. She gripped the wheel until her knuckles hurt. She pulled to the right so the impatient car could pass, but it didn't.

The car pulled up next to her, keeping pace. The dome light in the car next to her flicked on, catching her eye. It was Isaac. He waved at her and mouthed something. She frowned and mouthed back, "What?"

He motioned to the side of the road.

Jane pulled over. Her heart leapt to her throat. It was just Isaac. It wasn't like Pam and Bob's killer had just pulled her over.

Isaac pulled over and parked. He walked up to the passenger side of her car and knocked.

Jane kept her grip on the wheel. She squeezed her eyes shut and prayed. She had choice words for Isaac, if she opened the door. Words she might live to regret, no matter how good they would feel right now.

When her heart slowed down to almost-normal she reached across the seat and unlocked the door.

Isaac climbed into the passenger seat. He didn't say anything at first, just reached for her hand.

She let him.

"I am so sorry."

Jane bit back the words she was thinking. She wanted to hate him for getting her kicked out of school, but she knew it wasn't entirely his fault.

"Pastor Barnes talked to me after you left. I think they made a very bad decision."

Jane looked at her hand in his. "I broke the rules."

"So did I. Kicking you out of school was completely unfair, but he did say you would still get your certificate, so that's good."

Jane shrugged. The piece of paper that Glenda the secretary had so recently revealed to be meaningless. "I don't care about the piece of paper."

Isaac lifted his eyebrow and gave Jane a hopeful smile. "You know, now it's not against the rules…"

Jane pulled her hand away.

"Sorry. Bad timing." Isaac reached for the door handle. "It will be okay, Jane. You'll still get to the mission field, even though you can't finish this class."

"I really don't want to talk about this right now." Jane stared out the front window of her car.

"Are you sure? I've got all night. Or we could go somewhere, Starbucks or wherever."

"I just got expelled from *Bible school*, Isaac. I was expelled for inappropriate behavior because it was more convenient for them than disciplining you would have been. *I don't want to talk about it right now.*" Jane's jaw was so tight that spitting the words out sent a spasm of pain to her head.

"Okay. We won't talk about it right now." Isaac opened the car door. "But when you are ready, you know where to find me."

"Yes." Jane turned to him. "You'll still be teaching your class." A little voice in the back of her mind told her she wasn't being fair, but she squelched it.

Isaac lingered in the door for a moment before he shut it. He kept close to her car the whole drive back to town.

Back at the Crawfords' house Jane slammed her car door shut. She let herself into the mudroom and slammed that door shut too. She stomped her way up the back stairs to the servants' quarters she called home and slammed her bedroom door shut. Isaac was like a stalker, following her home, making her break the rules, getting her kicked out of school and being happy about it.

Maybe he had killed the Crawfords. From the way Jake talked, Isaac had been an outsider in the neighborhood, a kid the other kids didn't like. Jane kicked her shoes off. They landed by the closet with a thud. He was obsessed with religion. On the one hand this was a good thing, but it did tend to be a quality psychopaths had in common with regular old believers. He was awfully young to be in a PhD program, and high intellect seemed to be another quirk of the successful serial killer.

Did he, or did he not like hamburgers? She couldn't remember.

He had access, since he had every reason to be in the neighborhood whenever he wanted to be. He had motive, what with being picked on—ooh! And Phoebe seemed to hold him in high regard. Maybe she had seduced him and convinced him to kill her parents for her.

Jane flopped down on her bed.

It could also be that Isaac was a really nice, really smart boy who loved Jesus, liked her, and honestly didn't see the big deal about not having to take the last class at Harvest.

Or he could be a killer.

Jane rolled over. She squeezed her pillow to her chest. Of course, Pastor Barnes had taken time to personally remind her of the school rules, so whether Isaac was a killer or not, she had only gotten what was coming to her.

She pressed the pillow against her face, biting at the side of her cheeks. Getting kicked out of Bible school for kissing the teacher was a sure sign that she wasn't ready for the big time yet, no matter how badly she wished she was.

CHAPTER 24

A RUSTLING NOISE WOKE JANE. She rolled over in her bed towards the noise and blinked her eyes to clear them.

Jake was sitting on the floor, reading the newspaper. "Good morning." He didn't look up.

Jane pulled the blanket over her head.

"Have you read this article, the one by that putz Needles?" Jake shook the paper, making it rustle loudly again. "Well, of course you wouldn't have, since it's this morning's paper and you are still in bed. Why are you still in bed, Jane?"

Jane pulled her blanket down just far enough to read her clock. It said *6:30*.

"Aren't you usually up way before this? I went downstairs and there wasn't even any coffee yet."

Jane pulled the blanket back over her head again.

"Needles thinks he's done some sort of exposé. He's got Phoebe's time at the center in here, and that one time when I had to spend the night in juvee—which, by the way, was not at all my fault."

Jane slumped forward and stared at Jake. "Why are you in my room? Why?"

"Why does Needles say 'the Crawford Family Corporation which employs over a hundred people in the Portland area is on the cusp of bankruptcy'? It's not true, for one thing, and it's irritating for another. Do you think Rose of Sharon fed him lines? Because I do."

Jane pressed the heel of her hand against her forehead. "Jake. Please leave my room."

"I think Rose of Sharon may have been behind my parents' deaths, don't you? Who else has as many reasons to destroy us?"

"Jake—I just want some privacy to get dressed. Give me five minutes and I will be downstairs making your coffee and solving your problems, I promise."

Before Jake could respond, the sound of a motor filled the room.

Jane dropped her head into her hands. Whatever it was it sounded like it was right outside her door, and that couldn't be a good thing.

"It's the floor cleaners!" Jake shouted over the noise. "They called me last night so I set them up to come first thing."

The floors. Called Jake. Whatever. She tried to care, but the machine was already going so what did it matter? So long as they were done stripping and waxing the floors in time for the tables and chairs it didn't matter to her.

When she joined Jake in the kitchen the coffee pot was already brewing.

"Aunty did it," Jake said.

He sat in his usual stool at the kitchen island. "Now that you have granted us the privilege of your company, do you care to share your opinion on the Needles article?"

Jane found a mug and filled it with hot coffee. "You say he dragged up your sister's medical history?"

"Yes, he did."

"And your own history?" Jane took a drink. It burned her tongue.

"Yes, and I'm deeply insulted by his insinuations. I was out after curfew. Period."

Jane nodded. *It's always the small infractions that come back to bite us.* "And what does he say about the bankruptcy?"

"Needles claims that our business is on the brink of ruin. Do you know what that could do to our upcoming sale thingy, Jane? Put the kibosh on it, that's what."

"Help me see this straight." Jane took the seat next to Jake. "Were your parents converting the restaurants, selling the restaurants, merging the restaurants or what?"

"Your guess is as good as mine."

"That's not true, Jake. Every now and then you let slip that you are aware of what is going on and capable of understanding it."

Jake spun his coffee mug on the counter. "He was buying. He was buying the name Yo-Heaven and converting his restaurants. If we smell like failures, we won't get the loans we need to make that happen."

"I knew you knew what was going on." Jane drummed her fingers on her mug. It had to cool a little before she could drink more. "What does Needles have against the Crawford family?"

"It's about the newspaper sales and the awards from his peers. He wants to uncover something big so he can sell papers and win awards. We are the unlucky victims."

"You have to call your lawyer, I guess. Sue him for slandering your business."

"That would be stupid. I expect better of you, being Isaac's girl."

Jane felt her face turn red. She moved away so he wouldn't see her blush.

"Trouble in paradise?"

Jane opened the freezer. The blast of cold air cooled her cheeks. She pulled out a box of microwave breakfast sandwiches.

"Always more fish in the sea. Hey, are those for me?"

"Sure." Jane put three sandwiches on a plate and tossed them in the microwave. "Do you want me to talk to Marjory about the lawyer?"

"It's kind of complicated. Look at it this way: If I sue Needles and win he has to retract his misstatements and stuff. But then the lawsuit would be news, and the retractment itself would repeat the items in question."

Jane watched the plate of sausage and egg biscuits spin. She was doing her best to care about what Jake was saying, but it was hard.

"For Phoebe's sake, if nothing else, I don't want these things repeated. Can you imagine what would happen if it went viral and then someone overheard her say she hated mom? It could end in a murder trial."

"But if you don't sue, he could just as well keep saying these things over and over again. At least if you sue you are defending yourself."

"We'd be defending ourselves over the issue of our business solvency. We couldn't deny that Phoebe spent time in the loony bin."

"You need to stop calling her crazy and saying things like 'loony bin.'" The microwave beeped. Jane took the plate out. She set it in the middle of the kitchen island, but didn't take one.

"If you can't laugh at your hardships…" Jake popped the cellophane wrapper on one of the sandwiches.

"It's not your hardship."

"Ah. There is that." Jake took a big bite of the steaming sandwich.

"If you are concerned about the business reputation you need to have the Roly Burger lawyer sue Needles. If you are concerned about Phoebe's reputation you have to start being respectful. Spending time in rehab doesn't have the stigma it used to."

"It wasn't rehab, Jane. It was a mental health institution. Tell me that doesn't have a stigma."

"How you all react to the news getting leaked is how the city will react. If you have respect for your sister, so will the city. Period."

Jake put the rest of the sandwich in his mouth.

While he chewed, Jane bit an apple. The sweet, juicy flesh was like ashes in her mouth. How was she going to tell her parents she had been kicked out of school?

"I've just got to keep Phoebe quiet until summer when she can go off on her soccer tour thing."

"How do you plan on doing that?" Jane managed to swallow her apple, but didn't take another bite.

"If you're done with that weird Daniels kid already, she seemed pretty in to him. I could maybe make something happen there. Having a new boy to toy with could distract her from wishful thoughts of matricide."

Blood rushed out of Jane's head. She leaned back on the counter.

"You are done with him, aren't you?"

"I don't know." She wasn't. She knew she wasn't. Unless he was the killer, of course.

"If you could decide, it would help the family. We're all in this together, after all."

"How well did your parents know the Daniels family?"

"Not too well. Never even appeared before the old judge in court." Jake popped open another bagged sandwich.

"Did you see a lot of Isaac growing up? I mean, I know you didn't like him, but did you see him much?"

"Sure. Don't you remember him from the company picnics?" Jake stuffed most of the sandwich in his mouth, but had to bite off a small part to make it fit.

"No." Jane grimaced as Jake chewed like a cow.

He swallowed most of it before he spoke again. "Sure you do. Weird kid. Glasses. Spiky hair. Always playing his Gameboy. Didn't even have a DS, poor sap."

Immediately Jane pictured the weird, spikey-haired kid who hung around the peripheral of the Roly Burger family picnics. "That wasn't Isaac, was it?"

"Of course it was. Mom made me bring him to have someone to play with. She and Isaac's mom were in a golf foursome together."

Jane closed her eyes and tried to remember everything she could about the weird spikey-haired kid with the wire-rim glasses. He hadn't seemed miserable at the company picnics, just distracted. "But wait, Jake, if that was Isaac how come he didn't recognize Phoebe when he was her coach?"

"Would you have recognized her? She used to be so fat."

Jane closed her mouth. Phoebe had been a very fat kid. She could see not recognizing her now if the last you had seen of her was when she was still a chubby butterball.

"For the record, Jane, I did not torment Isaac so that he went crazy and murdered my parents. He didn't like playing with me anymore than I liked him. If you recall, I stopped bringing him to the parties around the same time you got really good looking."

"So you don't think he is a likely suspect?"

"He doesn't have the kahunas, to be frank. He'd never even play tackle football with the rest of us."

Jane took another bite of her apple. Isaac was her least likely suspect, which came as a relief.

"Unless keeping him on your suspect list means I can use him to distract Phoebe. Please say I can use him to distract Phoebe."

"Honestly, I don't think he is interested in being a distraction for your sister." Isaac was interested in *her*, and now that she was conveniently out of school he could date her.

Jane coughed on her apple. It was convenient, wasn't it? Had Pastor Barnes suggested this alternative to Isaac before he spoke with her? Had the two men high-fived when they came up with a great solution that could give them everything they wanted? Happy school, happy Isaac, happy Jane? If either man thought that taking the full blame for the kissing incident made her happy, they were fools. *Jesus took the full blame, you know.* She shoved the thought aside. It clearly wasn't the same. Isaac had kissed *her*, after all. The rule was meant to prevent the men in position of authority from violating the students. Jane stared down at the apple in her hand. *The snake told me to eat it.*

Fine. It didn't matter why or how, she had to accept her own role. She hadn't needed to hold his hand at church, or pass notes, or kiss him by the fireside. She deserved a good, solid, punishment for breaking a clear rule, despite having been warned once.

"Earth to Jane."

"What?" she snapped at him.

"Is there any more orange juice? I'm parched."

Jane threw her apple in the garbage can. "I guess you'll have to walk all the way around the kitchen island and open the refrigerator door to find out. Good luck with that." Jane stormed out of the kitchen and ran all the way back to her room.

An idea had occurred to her while she fumed downstairs. She had earned disciplinary action, but that didn't necessarily mean she had to be kicked out of school.

She got Glenda from the Harvest School of the Bible of the phone. "What classes are going on this term that *Mr. Daniels* isn't teaching?"

"Oh, Jane, don't go making more trouble for yourself."

"Please, humor me." Jane took a seat on the edge of her bed.

"Mornings on Monday, Wednesday, and Friday the kids are taking New Testament Survey and Tuesday and Thursday mornings they have Jesus and the Law of Moses."

"Who's teaching?"

"Pastor Barnes is doing the Jesus class, and Simcox is doing the New Testament Survey."

"Can I please talk to Pastor Barnes? Is he free?"

"He is, but you've already had Jesus and the Law."

"Nope, I didn't. Last year you all offered Jesus in the Minor Prophets. May I *please* talk to Pastor?"

"But, honey, you already have all of your Old Testament credits."

"Is there a better time to call back?"

"Isaac is such a nice kid, Jane. I don't know why you are doing this."

Jane gritted her teeth and kicked the edge of the bed. "I didn't come to Harvest to meet a man." She took a deep breath. "May I please speak to the pastor?"

"Hold a moment. I'll transfer you." Glenda's voice sounded tired.

"Pastor Barnes speaking."

"Pastor, this is Jane Adler, please listen to my idea and consider it."

"Slow down. What do you need?"

"I am so sorry, and so ashamed of my bad decision. I appreciate that you want to let me walk with the class anyway, but I just can't be kicked out. Please."

"Jane, we've been over this already. I thought you would like the solution."

"But I don't, Pastor. I was thinking...obviously the right thing to do would be to get kicked out of Isaac's class. But I'd really like to take your class. I haven't taken it yet, and I can rearrange my schedule to be there in the mornings. Can't I please?"

"You understand what this means, right? You would be an active student this term and would have to abide by the school rules until graduation."

"Of course, of course. That's what I want to do. Can't I, please?"

"I appreciate that you are taking your studies here seriously, and your repentance sure sounds sincere to me, but you are a couple of weeks behind on my class. Think you can catch up?"

"Yes, sir. I can." A weight of shame floated away. Jane let out a slow sigh.

"Then I will see you in two hours for class."

"Thank you, Pastor Barnes, from the bottom of my heart."

Jane ended the call and her phone rang immediately. "Yes?"

"Hey! How are you holding up?" It was Isaac.

"I feel much better this morning, thanks."

"That is very, very good to hear. So, I was thinking, I'm in Portland all day today. Want to get some lunch together? I could show you around the seminary and try and convince you to transfer here."

Jane's arms tingled. Her guilt was vanishing. Isaac wanted to spend the afternoon together, what could be better?

"It could be like a new first date."

Date. "Ah, well, there's a kink in the plan," Jane said. "I sort of am taking a different class at Harvest now. So, you know, no dating for me until I finish."

"Oh."

"I had to do it. I..." She searched for the word. Failing made her miserable? She hated losing? She was ashamed to tell her parents she got kicked out? It sounded suspiciously like pride. Had she chosen pride over Isaac? "Well, anyway, it's only until May. If I can't wait until May to go have lunch then I have a serious self-control problem."

"Yeah." Isaac's voice registered chagrin. "I don't blame you, you know."

"That's a relief, because May 25th still looks free."

"Then put my name on it, okay?"

"All right, but I think I'll see you Saturday, at the funeral."

"Okay. I'll see you at the funeral."

Jane hung up. She set her phone on the side table and stared at it. There was always a cost, whether you were doing the right thing or the wrong thing. She just wished she knew which one she had done.

Rearranging her schedule went off without a hitch, though she wondered how long her clients would stay flexible for her. Class went off without a hitch as well. Plenty of whispers and snide comments from her classmates, but she would take that over failure any day.

CHAPTER 25

THE HOT SHOWER WASHED away some of Jane's tension Wednesday afternoon. Her Tuesday client had been flexible enough to let her come on Wednesday, but it was a backbreaking day of work. Every piece of upholstery in the fifteen room home had needed steam cleaned. Whether as a punishment to herself or just because, Jane didn't know. She just let the hot shower drum against her aching shoulders.

Back in her bedroom, she had a message waiting on her phone. "Hey, Janey, this is mom. We're waiting outside of your apartment, but it looks like you are at work. We're going to get going now—dad wants to stop and see the old restaurants. Call us when you are back in."

Mom. Jane vaguely remembered that today was the day they were coming up for the funeral. She shivered. She had to call them back, but she didn't have to like it. She pressed send with a shaking finger.

"Hey, Mom!"

"Sweetie! We're outside of Hazelton at the first restaurant. How was work? Or was it school this morning?"

"Work. It was hard! I'm exhausted."

"We're headed back up to town to see the second restaurant. Want to meet us there for a late lunch?"

"Dad remembers he sold out, right?"

"Of course, silly. We heard rumors about the switch to healthy food. I think he just wants to say goodbye one more time."

"That sounds good. I'll meet you at the second restaurant."

"That's the one in town, remember? On Fourth and Mill?"

"Of course I remember, Mom. That's the one I worked at."

"See you in about twenty minutes, okay?"

"Okay, love you." Jane hung up. In twenty minutes she had to tell her parents exactly how badly her life had fallen apart in the last two weeks. She'd have to let them buy lunch first.

It didn't take even ten minutes to get to Fourth and Mill. Jane sat in her little car, waiting for her parents, and watching the protestors. She hadn't known they'd be here, but they seemed to be hitting all the Portland locations, so she wasn't surprised either.

This group of protestors looked rowdy. She counted four faux-hawks and one real set of liberty spikes. There were two pit-bulls on leashes and one Doberman on a chain. She tried to count the children in the group, but they were moving around too much: shinnying up and down the flag pole, climbing in, under, and around the outdoor seating.

More unnerving than the dogs or the children was the leader. Rose of Sharon was present and representing. She stood on the curb in front of the drive-through menu with a bullhorn. Jane cracked her window open to have a listen.

"Two-four-six-eight: don't put a burger on your plate! Two-four-six-eight: don't put a burger on your plate!"

Jane rated the cheer a D-minus for lack of originality or emotional punch. Rose of Sharon seemed to be losing her sting.

Jane decided to chat her up before her parents arrived. She sauntered over to Rose of Sharon, offering a mild smile. "Hey there."

Rose of Sharon put down her bullhorn. "For your own sake, don't do it. Don't get a burger for lunch today."

"But they have such good, roly-poly buns."

"And so will you, if you eat this garbage. You look like a smart kid. Do you really want to destroy your body?"

"Well, no, not this afternoon anyway."

"Then sit down with us or eat somewhere else." She put the bullhorn back to her mouth and aimed some more cheers out to the street.

Jane was disappointed. She had hoped for a little more passion from the leader of the Human Liberation Party.

The man with the liberty spikes joined her. "Don't be a slave to the calories, sister. Set your body free."

Jane looked him up and down. Body ink. Piercing. That lean, hungry look of the dedicated punk. "But isn't life about more than the body?"

"Your body is your instrument. Love it so it can make beautiful music."

Rose of Sharon kept chanting in her bullhorn, but she nodded approval at the spiky guy.

"All things in moderation, right?" Jane said. She wanted to think of the right thing to draw Rose of Sharon out. Something that would make her confess to murder, if she happened to be the murderer.

"Moderation is for people who don't care about life."

The punk annoyed Jane. She turned away from him and watched the street with Rose of Sharon.

"How much must you hate Bob Crawford, right?" Jane said.

"Who?" The punk asked.

Rose of Sharon dropped her bullhorn. "Bob Crawford died. I can't help but feel guilty. If only I had been able to get through to him sooner."

"And Pamela too, right? Poor old girl." Jane shook her head in exaggerated sadness.

"Yes, that poor woman." Rose of Sharon bowed her head.

"You aren't mad at them for the restaurant thing?" Jane raised an eyebrow at Rose of Sharon.

Rose of Sharon rested her bullhorn on her hip. "I was mad for years, but when the plans to convert the restaurants to Yo-Heavens were made public, all was forgiven. What a huge, beautiful thing to do for the city." A car pulled into the parking lot so Rose of Sharon lifted her bullhorn again. "Save yourselves while you still can!"

Jane squinted in the distance. Still no sign of her parents. "If all was forgiven, why are you protesting?"

"It's what Bob would have wanted. He never would have wanted these houses of death to stay open like this. They should be shuttered and draped in black in mourning for Bob, Pamela, and everyone who has died of obesity-related disease."

"But I mean, surely it has just been delayed, right? The plans will still go through if they were what the owners wanted."

"But how long? How long will this city have to wait?" Rose of Sharon lifted her bullhorn again and began her chanting.

Jane was forced to admit that Rose of Sharon didn't sound guilty of murder. The Doberman growled at her as she let herself into the restaurant, but Jane ignored him. She was down another suspect and she didn't like it.

Moments later Jane's parents joined her. Her father was red-faced and his jaw was working back and forth. Her mom was holding onto his arm and patting it. She looked tanner and blonder than when Jane had last seen her. They both looked rumpled like they had just gotten off of the plane.

"What is going on out there?" Jane's father asked.

"That's HLP, you remember them? They've been at this since the deaths were reported in the news."

"It's absolutely ridiculous. That parking lot is private property. Why don't the police get them out of here?"

"You've been living in Arizona too long, Dad. This is Portland, remember?"

"Stan, relax. You don't own this restaurant anymore. It doesn't make a lick of difference what the protestors do. They could torch the place and you'd still be fine."

"You say that, Nance, but I know how hard this whole transition thing is going to be. The company needs as much income before then as they can get. What does that woman out there want? The whole city on welfare? This town needs jobs!"

"Jane, just order some lunch for us all, will you? Come with me, Stan, you need to sit down."

"Okay, Mom. I'll get the food."

Nancy handed Jane her wallet. "Just get me a salad, okay?"

That would make Rose of Sharon happy. Jane ordered two salads and the biggest burger she could find for her dad. When the order was up she carried it to her parents. Nancy was leaning across the table whispering to Stan, her blond, bobbed hair falling in front of her face. Stan was still fuming. He sputtered a few sentences only to be quieted by a word from his wife.

"So tell us everything, Jane," her mom said, a smile plastered to her face.

Where to start?

"How's that roommate of yours? Samantha, was it?"

Jane bit her lip. It was now or never. "Well…I ran into a little trouble with her. See, it turns out she was kind of rotten."

Stan lowered his eyebrows. "How so?"

"You aren't going to like this, guys. And I should have told you before."

Jane's mom set her folk full of salad back on the plastic bowl.

"See, she stopped paying rent and we got evicted."

"Oh no!" Nancy reached across the table for Jane's hand.

"So, I, um, well, Marjory is staying at the Crawford house and they offered to let me be live-in help. It's not permanent but I'm saving a lot of money on rent."

"The Crawfords are good people. Aren't they good, Stanley?" Nancy said.

Stan nodded. "Why didn't you move to campus?"

"Well, you know, Dad, I can't be going back and forth from Harvest to the houses I clean everyday."

"Who is staying at the Crawfords' house with you?" Her father's tone was serious.

"Marjory, Phoebe and Jake."

"How long do you plan on living there?"

"I know I want to see them through the funeral, but I can't say after that. Marjory will go home, I'm sure. And Jake and Phoebe will have to go back to school eventually. I guess whenever they all clear out I'll have to as well."

"You need to have a plan in place. You can't just wait around or you'll get stuck again like you did last time."

"I won't, Dad, I promise." Jane stuck her straw in her mouth. She wanted to tell her dad she had things under control and that he didn't need to freak out. "I've got to see them through the funeral anyway, and with that and school and my other clients I just haven't had a chance."

"You raised a hard worker, Stan. Don't get down on her now just because she is working hard. Is there anything you need to tell us about school, Jane?"

Jane sputtered on her soda. "Fine. It's fine. I'm taking a day class this term."

"Why?" Her dad spat the word out. "Why on earth is that woman still out there?" He was fixated on Rose of Sharon out his window.

"Let it go, Stan."

"I will not let it go." Stan stood up, pushing his chair into the chair behind it with a clank. "I'm going to have a word with her.

Jane watched in horror as her father stormed out to Rose of Sharon.

Torn between burying her head and chasing her dad, Jane stared at him, unable to move. He was quickly surrounded by several mohawked men, but his wild, swinging gestures kept them an arm's distance away.

Jane's mom was just standing up when they heard the wail of police sirens. Nancy pressed her hand to the window. "Thank the Lord. It looks like the cops are going to clear those hippies out."

Jane pressed her hand to her forehead. She wanted to stay as far away from the protestors as she could.

"Should we go get your father?"

Jane peered out the window. The protesters had joined Rose of Sharon on the curb. "No, but I wish he'd come in here." Her father stood apart from the protestor, his arms crossed on his chest.

Two cops went straight to him. At first it looked like a calm conversation, as though maybe they were asking him what he had seen, but as Jane watched them talk, her father's face turned beet red. Then he had his arms up.

"Jane I think we need to get out there."

"I don't know. I—" Before she could finish her thought her mom was outside. She ran straight to the officer and grabbed his elbow. She tugged at it like a kid trying to get the attention of her mom while she was on the phone.

Jane pressed her nose to the window. The officer jerked away from Jane's mom and yelled, his mouth a huge black hole in his face. The protestors seemed to be singing.

For the first time, Jane noticed the TV news van.

Jane watched as a camera trained in on the picture of her parents being put into the back of a police car. Jane turned her head away. Was there someone in the restaurant who could help them? She ran back to the manager's office, an instinct from the days her father had owned the restaurant. "Hey! We need help out in the parking lot!"

A man in a gray suit sat at the desk. He turned slowly to her.

"Fitch?"

"Jane? What are you doing back here?"

"I think my parents just got arrested in the parking lot! Come help!" Jane ran back out before Fitch could respond, but she was too late, the police car was already pulling out of the parking lot.

Jane held her side, panting. "What happened?" she hollered towards the protestors.

"Justice!" they shouted in unison.

Fitch was at her side. "Jane, what just happened here?"

"I don't know. One minute I was having lunch, the next minute my parents were in the back of a police car. Where is the restaurant manager?"

"He's at a manager's meeting with his shift leaders. I'm pitching in and looking over some requisitions at the same time. Tell me again: Why did your parents get arrested?"

"I don't know." Jane scanned the row of protestors. They were stamping their feet and cheering. She approached at the outer edge of the group. "Hey." She attempted to sound cool. "So, like, what just happened?"

"That crazy man with fat on his breath just came out here yelling at us. He was like, threatening our freedom. It was so rad, because the cops just came, and arrested them, like that." The protestor snapped his fingers.

"Who called the police?"

The protestor shrugged. "Got me, man."

A skinny blonde with a half-shaven head leaned over. "It was the universe, man." She grinned from ear to ear.

Jane stared at the crowd. She couldn't see anyone still holding a phone. She marched over to Rose of Sharon. "What were those two arrested for?"

"Assault." Rose of Sharon looked grim. "And step back, if you don't want more of the same."

"Assault?"

"That's right. His hands came in very close proximity to my person. I've learned from hard experience that that is assault."

"Did you call the police?"

"No, I did not." The bullhorn hung by a strap from Rose of Sharon's wrist. Her body was less rigid, more relaxed, as though the arrest had satisfied her.

"Did you make the charge?"

"Absolutely. Are you kidding? That arrest is gold to me."

"But who called them in the first place?"

"Universal justice. I don't ask questions." Rose of Sharon put the bullhorn to her lips and began a rousing rendition of "I like to eat apples and bananas."

Jane stepped back and looked at the restaurant. Rose of Sharon had made the complaint, no matter who had called the cops. But what could she do now? How did she find out where her parents had been taken? She looked for Fitch, but he was gone.

Her appetite had fled with her parents, so she got in her car and drove. She thought she remembered a police station not too far away. She wasn't wrong.

Jane's parents were tucked away somewhere in the police station and she was given a cup of brackish coffee and told to wait. The chairs in the waiting area were hard and plastic, but remarkably clean. Jane kept her eyes on the bronze bust of an old police dog on a pedestal in the middle of the room. She had never been in a police station before and the cleanliness, the dog bust, and the general air of calm were disconcerting. Airy Celtic music was playing quietly over a sound system and the smell reminded her very much of the hand soap in the bathroom of the last airplane she had been on. It was labeled "calm" and really did calm her down when she held her hand to her nose and breathed deeply.

Her Styrofoam cup of coffee did not calm her down.

Jane knew her parents had lawyers, but she didn't know what to do to help them. They would call the lawyer themselves. She could call Isaac, but what could he do? He could make her feel better anyway. At least being arrested couldn't hurt her parents' career—one benefit of retirement that she was sure they hadn't anticipated enjoying.

She dialed Isaac. While she sat with the ringing phone a short, balding man in a red windbreaker joined her in the room. He had come from the interior of the police station and paused by the dog head to type something on his phone.

Isaac didn't answer. She hung up. There was something about "My parents were arrested, I'm at the police station" that didn't make her want to leave a message, but she didn't want to be alone either. While the windbreaker man continued to type she called Jake. The phone rang, and rang. The man in the windbreaker looked familiar.

"This is Jake."

"Hey, this is Jane. I've got a serious problem."

"What's up?" Jake sounded bored."

"I'm at the police station. We were having lunch at Roly Burger and my parents got arrested."

"Nuh-uh." His interest seemed to have been piqued.

"Yes, seriously. The protestors were out and my dad was talking to them and he got arrested for assault."

"Crazy. What are you going to do?"

"I don't know. Just wait I guess. They have a lawyer...or they used to. What do you think I should do?"

"Rose of Sharon was at the Fourth and Mill location, right?"

"Yes, that's right."

"Fitch was supposed to be there all day today. Don't you find that interesting?"

"I guess not."

"Fitch was all up in my mom's business and now she's dead. Your parents had lunch with him, and now they are arrested. I find that far more than just interesting."

Jane closed her eyes. Jake was exhausting, but she'd play along with him, for a moment. "Do you think that when Fitch saw his previous employer engaging with the protestors he saw the chance to get revenge?"

"Very likely."

"Have you thought of what he might have wanted revenge for?"

"How about years of humiliation? You used to work at your dad's restaurant. There's not a lot of dignity in fast food."

"But that's not a good reason to kill your parents." Jane tried to keep her voice low. She remembered where she had seen the windbreaker man. He was the one in front of the news camera at the restaurant during the arrest.

"No, he had to have another reason for that. I am close to figuring it out. You take care of your parents, okay? I'll pin down Fitch's motive. I think we can have this problem solved before the funeral."

"Okay, Jake. Call me when you nail down the motive." She hung up, feeling sad for Jake.

The man in the windbreaker smiled at her. "I couldn't help over hearing your phone conversation."

"No comment."

"No problem. I just wanted to ask, you're with the couple from the burger place, right?"

Jane nodded, her spine shivered. She didn't want to say anything to the news guy.

"Relax, okay? I saw everything and have film to prove it. I talked to the cops and they aren't going to book your parents in."

"But didn't Rose of Sharon press charges?"

"She and I had a chat on my way over." He grinned. "Ever heard of power of the press?"

Jane narrowed her eyes and nodded.

"Nothing your dad did consisted of assault, and I have the whole thing on film. I merely reminded Rose of the fact that she likes my cameras, and she had a change of heart about your parents' assault charges."

"But why? I mean, why did you step in like that?"

The newsman shrugged. "It was the right thing to do. There was no reason for your parents to go through that. If it had been my parents I would have wanted someone to step in."

"Thank you." Jane didn't know what to say. It seemed like an unnaturally kind thing to do. She wondered, just a bit, if he had done it to earn a new favor.

"Just sit tight, they'll be back out soon." He handed her a business card. "If you do have a comment, just give me a ring, okay?"

Jane stuffed the card in her pocket. "Sure." Always a price. The newsperson left.

When her parents were finally released, her father was fuming.

"Now, it wasn't so bad, Stan. We were in and out, no charges." Nancy's voice cracked, though she was trying to be soothing.

"Come on, Jane. We're going straight back to the hotel."

"What about the car, hon?"

Jane's stomach turned. Dad couldn't go back to the restaurant while the protestors were still there. "Let me and my friend get your car for you, Dad."

"Later, Jane. You need to come back with us. We have a lot of talking to do."

"Stanley, can't this wait? We promised we'd wait until after the funeral."

"Absolutely not."

Jane knew that tone of voice. It was the one that had sent her to Presbyterian Prep when she had really wanted to stay in school with her friends. It was the tone of voice that had said if she wanted to go to Harvest she'd have to figure it out for herself.

Stanley's ire only seemed to rise as they drove back to the hotel room, so that by the time they arrived he was steaming.

"The problem with this town is they don't have any common sense. I'm not leaving you here to fend for yourself any longer, Jane."

"But, Dad!"

"But Dad nothing. You just sit there and listen."

"Mom, what's he talking about?"

"Shh, just listen to your father."

"We've talked this over, Jane. You have two choices, and you know it: pick a university or go on a short-term mission."

Jane's mind whirled. Of course she only had two choices, but why were they talking about it now?

"You know that you don't want to do any more short-term missions. You made that clear two years ago when you started at Harvest."

"But things have changed, Dad."

"Not that much. You haven't applied with any short-term agencies and you haven't done any fundraising."

"It's only March. I still have time."

"Have you changed your mind about short-term trips?" Jane's mom sat next to her at the little table in the hotel suite. "Because if you have maybe we should let you tell us about it."

"She hasn't."

"You don't know that. Let her talk."

"Fine. Talk."

"It's just that I don't know yet what I'm supposed to do."

"This dilly-dallying is ridiculous. Do you realize how many college credits you graduated high school with? Or how many you have earned here? One more year of school and you could have a useful degree. Would you really rather head off with another group of teenagers to lead Vacation Bible School in Spanish?"

"I said that I don't know!"

"I know. I know you. You would hate that. You want all or nothing. Your college fund is untouched and your GPA is impeccable. You need to come home with us right after the funeral and start the application process."

"But Dad, I'm not done at Harvest yet!"

"That is not what Pastor Barnes said."

"What?" Jane felt faint.

"He called us two days ago to explain that you had been expelled and why."

Jane buried her face in her hands. Her shoulders shook, but she didn't make any noise, or feel any tears. She was completely mortified.

Nancy began to rub her back. "It's okay, love, everyone makes mistakes. Pastor Barnes said your credits will transfer just fine."

Jane tried to straighten up, but couldn't. "I am so sorry. I didn't plan on it, or mean to, or anything." Her shoulders kept shaking.

"Calm down, love," Nancy said, her hand still rubbing small circles on Jane's back. "It is a very silly rule at a very silly school. Just come home with us. You'll love university. You are so smart."

Jane groaned.

"It doesn't matter how silly the rules are, young woman, we expect you to follow them. It is utterly ridiculous for you to think that you could go into a dangerous country unprotected when you can't even follow the rules at Harvest."

Jane's breath was ragged but she tried to speak around it. "I-I spoke with Pastor Barnes. I'm not kicked out. I'm taking a different class."

"Over my dead body. They just want your tuition money."

Jane stood up. "Dad, I hardly know what to say. I mean, I, I," she stumbled over her words. "I guess the point is that I am twenty years old and I am staying in Portland."

Stan went silent. He stared at her, his face getting redder.

"That's enough for now, Stanley," Nancy said. "We've all had a very stressful day."

Tears filled Jane's eyes. She needed to get out of the hotel.

She pushed the door open, but her father stalled her with a word. 'Listen to reason, Jane."

Listen.

She had the terrible feeling that her good character truly was the result of pride: she could work harder, sacrifice better, do more than anyone else she knew, but could she listen? Could she really listen to her parents in an honoring way?

Not this afternoon.

"We'll talk when you've cooled down." Jane pulled the door shut behind her and ran down the hall. Her parents were overreacting because of the arrest, because they had had a twisted version of events at the school, and because they were just overacting. When they had cooled down she would listen to whatever they had to say.

CHAPTER 26

THURSDAY AND FRIDAY CAME AND WENT in a flurry of class, housecleaning, and vendors setting up for the funeral. All of the tables and chairs arrived, followed by linens and candles. A woman who claimed to be a stager hired by Jake showed up and pulled things from all over the house into the ballroom. It looked like the set up for a very sad wedding.

After the funeral, it would all be over. Everyone would move out of the big house and she would have to admit the deaths of Bob and Pamela were just a sad coincidence. Marjory would not want to keep Jane on full time with room and board in an empty house, so Jane's life would turn from the social, if bewildering, life of taking care of Jake to one of scrubbing drudgery and school again.

The one bright spot was that date with Isaac waiting for her on May 25th, but that seemed very, very far away.

Jane hadn't spoken to her parents yet. She didn't answer their calls. She texted once just to say "Hey" but didn't give them any details about her schedule. As she hadn't had a free minute to herself since their fight, it wasn't hard to avoid them.

But the day of the funeral had come and she would be seeing them soon. She'd also be seeing Isaac, and his parents. And her parents would be seeing the boy that got her temporarily kicked out of Bible school. Her stomach was a hard knot. She worked to keep God front and center in her mind. Wasn't it just two weeks ago that she had been cleaning the banisters and reciting the beatitudes? *Blessed are the poor in spirit for they shall inherit the earth?*

She had been using hard work as a substitute for a humble spirit, in the hopes that she could inherit the earth the old fashioned way: as a missionary.

A for effort. That had been her motto.

She pulled her hair back into a tight bun. Today she needed to blend in, disappear into the crowd. She didn't want to be noticed as she served. The funeral was for the family and friends of her departed boss, not for her to try and chalk up more 'Ain't Jane Great' points.

The bright sun baked the black asphalt. Little waves of evaporation shone above the parking lot of Pioneer Presbyterian Church, erasing the night's rainfall. Fumes from hundreds of cars idling as the cortege slowly filed out of the parking lot tickled Jane's nostrils. Family, employees, media, and the curious swarmed the stairs of the church, attempting to make their way back to their own cars. There weren't nearly enough chairs in the Crawford ballroom to seat everyone.

Jane put her hand to her brow and scanned the crowd for her parents. Marjory, Jake, and Phoebe were in the limousine at the head of the cortege. The hearse with the two urns and all of the flowers from the service followed behind. Jane needed to scoot around back where she had hidden her car outside of the traffic pattern, so she could beat everyone back home, but first, she wanted to find her parents and make sure they were okay. She had worked every second of the day since their argument and it was eating away at her. She wanted to apologize. She wanted a chance to listen to them, or at least, considering the tightly packed schedule she faced from this moment until the vendors would haul away the tables and chairs, she wanted to tell them that she *would* listen to them soon.

She spotted the silver head of her father by a large rhododendron bush and hurried to join them.

Her dad gave her a quick hug. "How are you holding up?"

"Just barely. There are so many details to the day. I've got to try and get back to the house before the family and guests arrive. I hid my car in the staff parking lot behind the funeral home. Do you want to ride with me?"

Her parents exchanged a look. "No," her mom said. "You've got work to do. We'll just meet you there. If we don't connect during the reception, call the cell, okay?"

"Sure thing." Jane barely nodded goodbye before she ran to her car. She had the sinking feeling that they hadn't changed their minds in the last two days. She exhaled a puff of exasperation.

Back at the house, two of Marjory's nephews were directing traffic as cars parked up and down the narrow, tree-lined road.

Inside, the caterers were dragging steaming chafers up three flights of stairs and lighting Sterno cans. Jane moved from table to table, checking the linen for wrinkles and the place settings for spots. The reception was a four-course dinner, not unlike a wedding feast. A trio of strings played hymns in the corner. Apparently Jake had hired them. She prayed a silent thanksgiving that he hadn't ordered a DJ and a dance floor.

A grove of silk ficus trees with twinkle lights surrounded a lectern where the pastor would give a prayer and share some more words while guests ate. The whole shebang was expected to take two hours. Jane wanted to apologize to Bob and Pamela. She was overcome with nerves and anxiety rather than grief.

The janitorial smell of the fresh floor wax and lit Sterno cans brought tears to her eyes. It felt disrespectful, but there was nothing she could do to make it right. As she straightened the napkins on the table in front of her she wondered what food paired best with Sterno fumes.

As the activity of the caterers slowed down, the room began to fill with guests. Jane watched from a corner. The pastor and the grieving family entered first, with the funeral director close behind. The funeral director stood by the door to the ballroom, directing people to the tables as they entered. It was only a matter of moments before the flood of guests became too many for him to greet.

A very old gentleman with a walker staggered toward the table. Jane went to help him find a comfortable seat. She nodded at the funeral director who mouthed, "Thank you."

She spotted her father and mother at a table with several of their business friends. She scanned the room again for Isaac.

He wasn't hard to find. Phoebe, in a long maroon dress with short sleeves and a plunging neckline, was draped on his arm, her head resting on his shoulder. His face leaned toward hers, talking. The two of them stood in conversation with an older couple, perhaps Isaac's parents.

Jake and Marjory sat at a table near the lectern with the pastor who had performed the funeral and a few other people Jane had seen with the family.

She didn't want to watch Phoebe entrap Isaac, but she couldn't help it. Her eyes were drawn back to where the pair had been standing. Isaac had taken a seat at the table and was leaning over his plate with a look of concentration on his face as he listened to an older man. Phoebe was gone.

She enjoyed a moment of relief before she went back to watching the tables fill up. So far all seemed to be going well in the kitchen, with the temporary sound system, the outmoded facilities, and with the parking. She was about to join Isaac when her phone rang. "Yes?"

"Hi, Jane? This is Stefan. I'm helping park cars? We've got a little problem down here." Stefan didn't sound like he knew where his head was, much less what he was doing with the cars.

"I'll be right down." Jane took the back stairs and sprinted across the main floor to the front door.

Stefan was over six feet tall, but built along the lines of Abraham Lincoln, more or less. He had his long arms full trying to hold onto a shorter man. They were practically wrestling right at the curbside. The shorter man's dirty jeans and high tops didn't fit in with Stefan's black suit and orange traffic vest.

"What's going on here?" Jane shaded her eyes with her hands. The sun had begun its afternoon descent.

"I caught this guy trying to break into that car back there." He gestured towards the Crawfords' back driveway.

"What were you doing way in the back?"

"I followed him."

The man in the dirty jeans was remarkably silent. And bald.

"Do I know you?" Jane asked. He looked an awful lot like Sam's bald friend.

The bald guy in the dirty jeans spat.

"We're having a private family reception here. What do you need?" Jane crossed her arms over her chest.

"I must have the wrong house."

"Yeah, you must."

"Jane, he ripped up the top of that Rabbit back there. He had a knife."

"Stefan! Are you okay?" The blood rushed to Jane's head. Of course he was the same man, but what was Stefan, no more than sixteen-years-old, doing wrestling with an armed man?

"Yeah, yeah, Mark got the knife from him and I'm just holding him." Stefan nodded to the other kid Jake had talked into helping park the cars.

"Thought it was my car. So sorry, man." The bald guy in the dirty jeans muttered, not making eye contact.

"Did you call the police, Stefan?"

"Not yet, hands kind of full." He held the bald guy with one arm around his neck and his other hand gripping a beefy, tattooed arm.

"I called 'em," Mark hollered, running back from where Jane had parked her car. "I left the knife on the ground where it fell and I took a bunch of pictures. The cops said they will be here in a second."

Jane dialed her dad's cell phone while Mark updated her. "Hey, Dad?" she said when he answered. "I really need you out front as fast as you can get here."

"On my way! Just hang on the line."

Jane set her phone to speaker. "Can you keep holding him?"

"Yeah sure." Beads of sweat had broken out of Stefan's forehead, but he looked happy to be holding the perp.

"What did I ever do to Sam?" Jane asked the bald guy.

"You promised her that money," he said.

Jane swallowed. "So you're going to keep vandalizing my car until she hates someone worse than she hates me?"

The bald guy didn't answer.

Jane's dad threw open the front door and ran down the long front steps. "What's going on here?" His voice boomed.

Stefan repeated the story.

The police sirens sounded in the distance, taking Jane back to the horrible morning she had found Bob. By the look on Stan's face it took him right back to two mornings ago.

Stan squared his shoulders and faced the officer just as though he had never been on the wrong side of the conversation before.

Making her complaint, showing the pictures, explaining the whole story seemed to take forever, but it felt cold and indifferent. *What is a car when the only thing flying through your mind is the people being remembered in the reception upstairs?*

Jane escaped to the house as soon as she saw the bald guy stepping into the back of the police car. As she went back upstairs, she made a mental note to find time to tape up the top of her little car. It was supposed to rain again.

The dull roar of conversation in the ballroom was comfortable after the to-do downstairs. She was glad to see that Marjory and Jake were eating at their table. They seemed to have no idea what had gone on downstairs. She looked around for Phoebe but couldn't find her. Isaac was at the buffet, but Phoebe wasn't with him or at his table. Perhaps she had gone to the bathroom.

Jane joined Isaac at the buffet table.

"Everything looks really nice, Jane. You've done a good job serving the Crawfords during their time of crisis."

"Thanks, Professor."

Isaac grinned "Sorry for sounding like a dork, but I mean it. I think having you here to help take care of all of this was a really good thing."

"I can't take too much credit. Every time I was ready to order something, Jake had already done it."

"That's good too. He needed something to do. Do you want to come sit down with me? Meet my parents?"

A shiver ran up Jane's arms. "In a minute. Have you seen Phoebe?"

"Not in a while."

"I'm going to hunt for her. I want to make sure she's okay, but I'll come and find you later." She didn't mention the car situation. It was bad enough that he wanted her to meet his parents. He didn't need to a reason to act protective as well. Not until May 25th, and then only if he was still interested in her.

Phoebe hadn't returned to the ballroom yet, so Jane went on a Phoebe-hunt.

She had come up by way of the front stairs, so she took the back stairs to the bedroom floor. Perhaps Phoebe had gone to her room for a rest. As she turned the corner into the hall she heard a door click shut.

Jane followed the sound. She hoped it was Phoebe. No one else had a reason to be on this floor of the house.

She popped open the first door, the one to Jake's room, but the light was still out. She left it ajar and moved to the next. The next guest room was dark as well. She popped open the door to the room Marjory was in, but it was dark and empty like the others. As she moved closer to Bob and Marjory's room, her blood pressure rose. She could hear the thud of her heartbeat in her ears.

She twisted the handle of the master bedroom door, but couldn't bring herself to open it.

A small squeal came from inside the room and roused Jane into action. She shoved the door open. It hit the wall with a bang.

Someone with thinning hair, wearing a shabby gray suit, had Phoebe pinned against the bathroom door. Phoebe's hands scratched at his neck.

"What are you doing?" Jane yelled as loud as she could, hoping to draw some attention to the room.

Fitch spun around and stared at Jane.

Phoebe wriggled her way out from behind him.

The last thing Jane had expected to find was the fully forty-year-old Fitch trying to have his way with the barely legal daughter of the deceased.

"I can't tell you, Jane. Five thousand dollars are on the line." Phoebe tugged at her dress trying to put it all back in place.

"Fitch—explain yourself before I call the cops." Jane wondered how far away the police were right now.

"You wouldn't." Phoebe made puppy eyes at Jane.

"The police aren't here?" Fitch's eyes darted to the window. "I thought I heard them."

"Phoebe, I saw him trying to-trying to…" Jane looked down at the floor. Phoebe's face was blotched red and the already low neckline of her dress had been pulled far enough down to exposure her slip.

"Trying to rape me, Jane? Is that word too icky for you to say?"

"I wasn't! I swear that's not what I was doing!" Fitch stepped farther away from Phoebe, and bumped into the Crawfords' mattress.

"Then explain yourself. What are you doing down here?" *And did the sound of police siren make you head here?*

"I just needed a little comfort, Jane. People need people at times like this." Phoebe batted her eyes at Fitch.

He turned violently red and looked away.

"That's enough, Phoebe. Fitch—I've got my finger on the phone. If you can't explain this I'm dialing 911." Jane held her phone out like a gun.

"She—I—She—I—" Fitch stammered.

"That's it." Jane moved the phone to her ear.

"No!" Phoebe screamed. Her face contorted as though she were trying to pull her scream back inside of herself. "Jane, don't do it." This time she spoke in a wheedling voice. "Some things need to be resolved, just, like, in the family, you know?"

Fitch inched his way towards the door.

Jane stuck her foot out and stopped him from scooting any further.

"You know what? I'm not entirely sure what I saw." Jane shut the door. She tried to scroll through her numbers casually, but her hand was shaking hard. She found Jake's number first and hit send.

"Let's see if we can think of three reasons for Fitch to be down here, shall we?" Jane leaned on the door to steady herself. "Maybe he needed a rest? Or did he follow the pretty girl in here? Or maybe there was something else in the room that he remembered when he heard the police sirens."

Fitch's face blanched.

"Sorry, Jane, you're wrong on point two. I followed him in. It just seemed very odd, you know, for the guy who orders new fry baskets to be coming in to my dead parents' bedroom."

"I agree. That is very odd."

Fitch let out an exaggerated yawn.

Jake answered his call, so Jane spoke in a louder voice, the phone still by her ear.

"No, sorry, that won't do it, Fitch. I saw the...energy you had earlier, with Phoebe in your arms. I don't think you are tired. Hi, Jake. Care to join a family pow-wow in the master bedroom?"

"No, Fitch, you aren't tired at all, are you?" Phoebe winked at him.

"Phoebe, I don't know what you are hiding, but I don't believe you came in here to snog Fitch, so you can drop that act."

Fitch shut his mouth. He narrowed his eyes, but wouldn't look at Jane. His face was pasty, shaven poorly, and puffy from too many Roly-Poly burgers. He had a thick middle, but skinny legs. He didn't look like a man driven by animal passions. His face was damp with sweat, and it smelled like fear.

"I think you wanted something in this room, but Phoebe followed you. You might have been overcome with passion, she does look really pretty this afternoon, but I think you were just trying to stop her or keep her quiet or something." The doorknob twisted behind Jane so she stepped aside.

"Hey, guys." Jake stepped into the room. "Thanks for inviting me to the shindig."

"Don't worry, Jake, I haven't said a word." Phoebe held a finger up to her lips.

"It's okay, Phoebe. Whatever you saw, you can tell us." Jake smiled at his sister, his eyes wide and innocent.

"Fitch, my brother offered me five-thousand dollars. Can you top that?"

"Offered for what?" Fitch flexed his hands open and shut.

"For silence, of course. For five-thousand dollars, what I saw gets no farther than this room. For ten, I won't even say it now."

"But I don't have that much money." Fitch's voice came out as a low moan.

"So she did see something." Jake rubbed his hands together. "You know, Jane, I really didn't think she had. I just wanted her to shut up about hating mom."

"I have an idea about what she saw, Jake. What about you?"

"Oh I have an idea too. A man who wouldn't order all new kitchen equipment for a poor orphan boy is capable of just about anything."

"Jake, Fitch came in here to get something when Phoebe surprised him."

"Is that so?"

"Very much so." Jane gripped her phone in her hand. She wished with all her heart she would stop shaking.

"And Phoebe saw something that Fitch wishes she wouldn't say."

"That much seems obvious."

Fitch was sweating copiously now, his hands still working nervously. He hadn't taken his eyes off of Phoebe for several minutes.

"Well, Jane, you know this room, heck, this whole house, better than any of the rest of us. What do you think he wants?"

"Only one thing comes to mind. I think he wants the bottle of potassium pills that is a little emptier than it should be."

Fitch dashed for the open door knocking Jane to the wall. He pushed Jake into the hall and ran for the stairs.

The sound of running feet echoed down the hall and Isaac flashed past them all. He stretched out his foot in a side kick and tripped Fitch as he reached the front staircase.

Fitch slammed into the banister.

The front door groaned open. "Jane?" Stanley Adler stood in the doorway. "Oh! There you are, perfect. This business with your car is taking forever and the police have more questions. I've been trying to call your cell."

Jane smiled at her dad. Her good old dad. "I'm coming." She ran down the steps, the beatitudes popping into her head, yet again. *Blessed are those who mourn.* It wasn't what followed Biblically, but the mourners were blessed today, for they were about to get some justice.

Isaac and Jake each took one of Fitch's arms and led him down to the police.

"We've got a few questions about this registration," the officer said to Jane. She scrunched her face up, the sound of her father's voice saying, "You bought a used car online?" echoed through her memory.

Jake stepped up to the officer. "Excuse me, I need your help." He tugged Fitch beside him. Isaac kept Fitch's other arm in his grip. "This man was tampering with evidence."

"Repeat that?" The officer said.

"Nothing of the kind." Phoebe lowered her eyelids and looked up at the cop. "It's just that my brother...he walked in on..."

"Please, Phoebe, not now." Jane placed a hand on Phoebe's arm. "Let's get the truth out, no matter how ugly it is."

Phoebe chewed on her lip and then turned her eyes to the ground.

"See, there's a reception upstairs, right now, for Bob and Marjory Crawford and I think they were murdered," Jane said. "From the beginning it just didn't seem right, their deaths. They were too young."

"According to the autopsy, they were a little bruised like there might have been a light altercation," Jake offered.

"And when I was looking at their medicine I saw that some of the potassium pills were missing. More were gone than should have been."

The officer stared at Jane with a bored expression on his face.

"Phoebe saw something but won't tell us what, and Fitch was sneaking into the bedroom," Jake said

"He heard the police sirens and headed to the bedroom where the pills were kept. Phoebe caught him and when I found them he was, I don't know. What would you say you were doing?"

Fitch looked at the ground. "I was just trying to stop her from making a scene."

"What were you doing in the bedroom during the reception?" The officer asked, one eyebrow lifted.

"I was—" Fitch looked up at the officer, and then clamped his mouth shut.

"Come on, Phoebe, just tell us what you saw," Jake said.

Phoebe took a deep breath. "I didn't used to hate my mom."

The cop didn't turn away from Fitch.

"But one morning, I had come over early to get some clothes and I saw her put a pill in a cup of coffee. Dad hadn't been feeling well, the heart thing, and I thought she was trying to make him worse. I was so mad."

"That's all you saw?" Fitch lifted his face.

"Then I saw her bring the cup to dad. He tasted it and said it was gross again, so I knew she had done it before. Neither of them saw me. I kind of snuck around all morning until I saw mom go back to her bedroom. She had put a bottle of pills on her dresser. She never keeps her pills there."

"No, she never does!" Jane added.

"Who are you?" The cop turned to Jane.

"I'm the housekeeper."

The officer nodded and turned back to Fitch.

Fitch was growing redder as Phoebe spoke.

"So I saw those pills there and figured they were the ones mom had put in the coffee."

"It was the potassium, wasn't it?" Jane asked.

"Yes. I looked them up later. They're deadly to someone with a heart condition."

"They weren't supposed to die!" Fitch blurted out. "No one was supposed to die."

"Repeat that?" The officer said.

"No one was supposed to die. We read everything we could. Weak, yes. Feeling unwell, yes. Not up to making big decisions? Yes! But no one was supposed to die."

Fitch looked around the crowd, eyes darting between Stan, Phoebe and the officers.

"I think you'd better come with us," the officer said.

"It was Pamela's idea—just to keep him under the weather for a while, to give him time to think his decision over. I didn't know it would kill him! I didn't know she would die."

"Can someone tell me how she died?" the second officer asked.

"According to the autopsy, she had a heart attack, probably caused by a lifetime of eating hamburgers and then having a light, physical altercation with her very large husband. I'm guessing he didn't want to be poisoned."

"Gotcha." The second officer turned away and spoke into a crackling walkie-talkie.

"Well done, knowing Fitch was going to go get that bottle of pills," Jake said to his sister.

"Oh, no." Phoebe looked at her dark red fingernails. "I thought he was going to try and steal mom's jewelry. He just kind of looks like a thief."

The first officer took Fitch from Isaac and Jake and put him into the squad car with the bald guy.

The second officer gave Jake his card. "We'll be wanting to talk to all of you very soon. No one leaves town, okay?"

They all said yes and nodded.

"And you—don't move that Volkswagen, understand? It's a stolen vehicle." He pointed up toward the back driveway.

"Yes, sir, of course." Jane looked back at her car. It had been a very good deal, and her dad had been completely against her buying it. Yet again, she should have listened to him, however this time God had used her mistake to provide just what the family needed.

CHAPTER 27

JANE SAT ON THE EDGE OF THE KING SIZED BED in her parents' suite at the hotel.

"Your roommate was both criminal and dangerous." Stan stood near the window, his arms crossed over his chest. His face was grim.

The room smelled of commercial laundry detergent and fresh brewed coffee. Nancy ran an iron over a pair of jeans while Jane listened to her father's lecture.

"Your car was in very poor shape, stolen, you were still paying the loan on it, and it smelled atrocious."

"Yes, Dad." Jane traced the gilded vine pattern that covered the duvet. *Deciding* to listen to her parents had been hard. Actually doing it, and considering what her dad had to say as he ran down every decision she had made in the last two years, was even worse.

"But, you have seven satisfied clients."

Jane tilted her head. "Yes?"

"I've made a few calls. Everyone is very happy with your work. You are a good little business woman."

"Thank you." She glanced at her mom.

Nancy smiled at her jeans as she ironed them.

"You handled yourself well through this crisis."

"Isaac really helped me stick with it."

Stanley grunted. "You are a young lady who finishes what she starts."

"Of course, Dad. That's what I always say."

"Yes, you do. Given that, I think you know that you need to stay here and finish school, but you are moving out of the Crawford house immediately, do you understand?"

She looked back down at the duvet. Sure, she understood it in theory, but that didn't mean she knew where she could go.

"I spoke with Pastor Barnes and he is putting you up in the dorm for the rest of the term. I paid the balance of your tuition, your book bill, and your room and board. I don't want to hear another word about it."

Jane wasn't tempted to argue. Staying on campus and knowing where her meals were coming from sounded divine.

"Before we leave we are buying you a car."

Jane picked at her fingernail. She had avoided that one for years. And why? So she could feel superior to the other girls at the prep school, like it had been somehow godlier to earn her own stuff? "Thank you." Her heart wasn't behind her words yet, but she said them.

"Now, this is the important part, so pay attention. After term is up, you are coming to Phoenix."

Jane's jaw dropped. "What?"

"We pay your way through the end of this term, and then you come home."

"But, Dad—"

"'But, Dad' nothing." Stanley crossed his arms over his chest. "I'd like to see a little gratitude from you right now."

Gratitude wasn't flowing, but Jane's blood was. She thrust herself to her feet, her face hot. "Dad, I am a grown woman. I do not have to move out of state just because you told me to."

"You might be a grown woman, but you have no car, you are homeless, and you just about got yourself kicked out of Bible school."

"Really, honey, who does that?" Nancy flipped the jeans off the ironing board. "It just wasn't like you."

"But what about my seven satisfied clients?" Jane sat back down on the bed with a thud.

"You're a good business woman. A good business woman who will be without a home by May 25th."

Jane stared at her father. May 25th. Her date with Isaac.

"Business people strike deals, Jane. Are you in, or out?"

Jane chewed her lip. "Let me be clear on this deal: I go to Phoenix in May or?"

"Or you come now." Nancy slipped her arms into a fuzzy pink sweater. "I'm so sorry, but things are a big mess here aren't they?"

Jane looked out the window behind her dad. Rain slashed at the glass, falling from the pewter gray sky. "I can make it on my own here."

"It's because of that Daniels fellow isn't it?" Stan stared at Jane over the top of his glasses, his jaw flexing.

Yes? No? Jane wondered. Didn't she want to stay here because she was established? There were her clients to consider, and her church family, the people who would eventually be sending her on the mission field.

Then there was the mission field. Wouldn't going to Phoenix slow her process down even more? She'd have to meet all new people, prove that she was serious in her intentions.

And then there was Isaac. How serious were her intentions if she could let him distract her from her goal?

Her trouble following the school rules, the way she had kept her troubles to herself instead of connecting with her parents and seeking help, and the overwhelming sense that she was puffed up with pride rather than faith, had shown her that her dream of heading to the foreign mission field was a bit farther in the future than she had originally hoped.

"Leave her alone, Stan. Isaac is a very nice young man." Nancy folded up the ironing board.

"I don't want to leave because Portland is home." Jane scratched at the gold vine on the bedspread again, but the shimmery color was in the thread, not painted on.

"You'll have to leave when you go on the mission field." Stan's voice had gone soft.

"I know."

Nancy rubbed Stan's back. "Don't worry about that yet, love." She turned to Jane. "This isn't easy on your Dad, even if you are 'all grown up'"

"Mom." Jane tried not to roll her eyes.

"Forget about it, for now, okay?" Nancy kissed Stan's cheek. "We've made you our offer. You consider it, and tell us what you decide.

Jane looked away from her parents. What was her choice, really? If she took them up on their offer to pay for school she was obligated to move back with them, at least for the summer. If she didn't take the bargain she would fail to finish the school she had put her heart and soul into.

She knew she couldn't quit school.

"Dad, did you talk to Marjory before we left the reception?"

"Yes. She is closing up the house and Jake and Phoebe are headed back to their dorm rooms and apartments. Don't worry about missing the Crawford paycheck, we'll make sure your ends meet."

Jane flushed. "I was just wondering what happened with Fitch?"

"He's in custody until the arraignment. They are talking manslaughter, I think. He planned the poisoning with Pamela for the sake of keeping the hamburger restaurants in business. The deaths weren't planned. I believe him about that. He didn't have the spine or the imagination for murder."

"But why wouldn't he want the family to run healthier restaurants?" Jane asked.

"Business is rough, and there was no promise it would work out. I think Pamela was behind the whole scheme, frankly. She liked the high life and turning the restaurants into something with a lower profit margin and no guaranteed customers was too risky."

"It will be sad when the restaurants are all gone," Nancy said.

"I wouldn't kill for a hamburger, but it will be sad when they are gone," Jane said with a grim smile. "Do you want to risk another run in with the protestors and get a burger for lunch?"

"Not on your life." Stan laughed.

"So, kids," Nancy said, "time to go car shopping?"

"Sorry, Mom. First I have to go clean the Larsen house, but I can meet you wherever you want by eleven." It felt good to have that one last bit of autonomy: Good, Clean, Houses. Her own business, where she was the boss. She didn't like the bargain her parents offered her, but she would have to make it work.

As she pictured the rest of her school term, cleaning houses, studying, and *not* kissing Isaac Daniels, the words of the beatitudes came to her mind again. Blessed are they who hunger and thirst for righteousness, for they will be satisfied. Not a promise from God to have all of her needs met by her parents who had means, but a promise from God that *He* would satisfy her hunger for holiness, if that was what she hungered for. Not independence, not adventure, just holiness.

May 25[th.]

She'd keep her date with Isaac, and then fly to Phoenix. If he was waiting for her when she came back to Portland, as she promised herself she would do, then she'd let him take her on a second date too.

NOW AVAILABLE!

CHAPTER 1

JANE ADLER SCRAPED THE GUNK out of the u-shaped pipe and flicked it onto the newspaper on the floor. She spread it thin with her gloved fingertip, but the missing wedding ring wasn't hidden in the blob of gunk. Either it hadn't fallen down the drain or it had washed away. She wasn't a plumber, so she couldn't vouch for the ring's ability to wash away, but it seemed unlikely. Especially with the huge diamond attached.

A tight knot had formed at the base of her neck, so she rolled her head from side to side. The sink parts had to go back together before her client came home, no matter how her neck felt.

Jane rocked back on her heels. According to the Youtube video on her phone, the plastic pipes should go back together without any kind of putty or tape. Jane started with the pipe from the drain to the pea trap. Despite the slippery sliminess of her gloved hands, it fit. So far, so good. If the pea trap would connect to the drain from the other side of the double sink, she was good.

It almost did.

She pushed it gently toward the back wall, and snapped it into the receiving end of the other pipe. She let go of it, and slid the screw connector into place, but the threads were crossed and it wouldn't twist on. She slid it up again. The pipe that led from the pea trap to the drain popped out.

Jane's phone beeped.

It was Isaac.

She tried to take the call, but the phone wouldn't read her latex and slime covered finger. She pulled her glove half way off, then changed her mind. Time was short, her boss was picky, and her boyfriend could wait.

She forced the PVC pipe back into place, but that made the pea trap pop out of the first connection she had made. She tried to slip it back up into the cap, but it wouldn't go.

She took a deep breath. She relaxed her shoulders. She thanked God that she wasn't the one who had dropped her client's wedding ring down the sink.

With slow, measured movements, she unconnected the twisty connection ring that supposedly held the pea trap in place, and slid it back onto the pipe in the right order, noting how much easier things came apart than they went back together.

She tested all of the connections. They were solid.

Then she pulled her gloves off and called Isaac back. "Sorry about the delay. I was plumbing."

"You know how to live."

"My client dropped her ring down the sink and wanted me to get it out." Jane crumpled up the newspapers she had used to protect the marble floor.

"And you tried, because you are awesome like that." Isaac had a chuckle in his voice, but the phone call was breaking up.

"Let me guess, you taught a class of eager, enthusiastic young seminarians under the shade of a grass roof, and then went to the beach to swim in the clear waters."

"Close. After class we went out back and kicked the ball around."

"Are you in heaven?"

"Are you kidding? You're not with me. It's paradise, at best, but it's not heaven."

Jane flushed. "I wish I was there." She mopped up the drips of grimy water that had missed the newspaper. "Only forty more days until you come home."

"Yup."

"Man, I do wish it was the other way around." Isaac's voice sounded far away, which was fitting since he was more than four thousand miles from home.

"You wish you were forty more days away from going away?" Jane rubbed her forehead. She wanted to engage in romantic banter, but she had limited time to get the plumbing mess put away.

"I wish you were coming here in forty days."

"I see! Sorry." Jane pushed the box of organic home cleaners back under the sink. "I'm thinking the Seminario Christiano de Costa Rica doesn't approve of girlfriend visits, though."

"They'd keep a close eye on us, that's for sure. But..."

Jane smiled. "But I could come, say, just for a week, right before you head home?"

"You could."

"Do you know how many houses I would have to clean to afford a trip to Costa Rica?" Jane swept the kitchen, though at first glance, it looked clean.

"Your parents?"

"Are about as excited for me to run off to Costa Rica with my boyfriend as your employers would be."

"Point taken. But I miss you." The phone crackled again.

"I miss you, too." The worst part of their summer apart was the patchy international phone calls.

"And I love you."

"I know."

"Jane, I'm serious." Isaac's phone crackled.

"I know. I'm just up to my armpits in Ajax and about to face a client who isn't going to be happy with me." Jane hedged. Love. Sure, she "loved" him, or she couldn't have spent the last year dating him. But after a point, love means the rest of your life, and that's where she hesitated.

The phone fritzed again. "I do, too, Isaac. You know I do."

"I've got to run. Call me later?" His voice was distant. Jane wanted to blame the phone, but she was pretty sure it was her own fault.

"Definitely." Jane racked her broom in the pantry. It was a balancing act, and no one knew it better than Isaac. Island life was getting to his brain, and she couldn't blame him. She hoped his summer away would light a fire for missions in his heart that matched her own, but only time would tell.

In the meantime, Caramel Swanson wasn't going to like it, but there was no ring in the kitchen sink pea trap.

Jane checked the house room by room to make sure all of the lights were out before she let herself leave for the day.

A bright red convertible pulled into the driveway just as Jane was locking the door. She had hoped to get out before Caramel returned, but she was a moment too late.

"Jane! I'm so glad you are still here." Caramel swept out of her little car, her heels clacking on the brick driveway. "Did you find the ring?"

Jane grimaced and shook her head.

"Did you take the sink apart to look?"

"Yes." Jane never knew what to say to Caramel. Isaac's mom had recommended Plain Jane's Good Clean Houses to the Swanson family, to replace their regular housekeeper while she was on vacation for the summer, but the thirty-something Caramel was as different from sixty-year-old Mrs. Daniels as a yappy little Chihuahua was from an Airedale.

"Did you check the mudroom sink?"

"You said you dropped it down the kitchen sink." Jane checked herself before she said, "Ma'am." Caramel's husband may well have been sixty years old and a former mayor, but Caramel was clinging to her youth at all costs.

"This is a very expensive ring, Jane. I assumed you would stop at nothing to find it."

Jane snuck a peek at the time on her phone. She wished with all her heart that she had to rush back to class, but nope. Her first year of business school was over and done. She had no reason to rush away.

Jane weighed the missing ring on a quickly manufactured scale of emotional importance. Her personal goal was to treat each family like the mission field, serving them with the heart of Christ... but finding a trophy wife's missing diamond didn't resonate with her.

"You were hoping that I would keep checking even if I didn't find it where you thought that you lost it." Jane went with "reflect so they will feel listened to" to buy herself some more thinking time.

"Indeed I did. And since you claim you didn't find it, I hope you have good insurance."

"Excuse me?" Jane took a step backwards.

"You claim you didn't find the ring. It went down the drain of my sink last time I saw it, so if it's not there now, there is only one reason."

"I'm sorry, what?" Jane couldn't reflect that sentence. "Are you accusing me of stealing your ring?"

"You tell me. Did you 'find' the ring in the sink or not? I would think if you honestly didn't find the ring you would have kept looking. That ring is worth half a million dollars."

"But, ma'am." It slipped out. Jane didn't intend to make Caramel angrier than she already was. "You told me to check the kitchen sink because you thought you dropped your ring down it. I took it apart, cleaned it out, and didn't see anything. You didn't ask me to look anywhere else." Jane's hand went to her pocket, where her instruction notes were folded carefully in a wallet, just for that purpose. Isaac Daniels' father was a small claims court judge, and getting to know the family over the last year had made Jane wiser and more paranoid. Apparently, just in time.

"You can get back in that house and find my ring, Jane, or you can leave, and hear from my lawyers." Caramel's cheeks were flushed pink, her red lips were parted and puffy, as though they had recently been shot full of fillers. Her eyes had done the buggy, crazy-eye thing they did when she talked about her husband's ex-wife or her neighbors.

Jane prayed again, begging God for the right words. "If you would like to have me come back tomorrow to help look, I can schedule you in." She exhaled slowly. "But I think you could get all of the sinks checked faster with a plumber."

Caramel stood between Jane and Jane's car. Jane measured the distance with her eyes. At least twenty steps, if she tried to barrel past her, but double that, or more, if she attempted to swing wide, walking around Caramel.

"My husband won't put up with this." Caramel put her hands on her hips. "When I tell him what happened here, you'll never work in this town again."

Considering Portland had half a million people, or more if you counted all the surrounding towns, Jane didn't take the threat seriously.

"Don't underestimate me, *Jane*. My husband may think you are the cutest thing ever, but that won't stop him from putting you in your place."

The husband.

Jane doubted that Douglas Swanson thought she was the cutest thing ever, as she had never met him, and didn't have a picture of herself on her website or flyers.

"So, would you like me to come back tomorrow or will you be calling a plumber?"

Caramel narrowed her eyes. "My husband won't be back for another two weeks, you know."

Jane nodded. "What time would you like me to arrive?" She attempted to smile. If she truly was coming back to dig through every sink in the Swanson house tomorrow, she'd be bringing Holly, her new employee, with her. When half million dollar rings were at stake, a witness seemed super important.

"Be here at 7:00 a.m. sharp." Caramel swept past Jane, pushing her into a concrete angel. "I'll be home the whole time, so don't think you can get away with putting the ring back. I'll be watching you."

Jane ran to her car. She drove away from the Swanson house as fast as she could. "Quirky," "spirited," and "particular" were the words Mrs. Daniels had used to describe the new Mrs. Swanson. They must have been synonymous for utterly bonkers, otherwise Mrs. Daniels was at risk for false representation.

The Swanson paycheck was a welcome addition to the bottom line, but Jane was willing to forego name brand coffee and other luxuries if it meant she could quit this job tomorrow morning, as soon as all of the sinks in the six-thousand square foot mini-mansion had been put back together.

Jane parked at the apartment she shared with her cousin. She had to take off her house-cleaner's hat now, even if the current situation seemed to call for some serious planning.

In a few short hours, she had coffee and dessert with her church's Mission Coordinator. Jane decided to spend as much time as she could this afternoon praying, listening to God, and reading the Bible.

Jane didn't know what Paula Ehlers had in mind, but a coffee and dessert get together with a couple of other mission-minded people and the woman in charge of the church missions program was something she needed to prepare for.

CHAPTER 2

AT SEVEN O'CLOCK SHARP, after two hours of prayer and petition, a nap, and a hastily eaten sandwich, Jane found herself in the cozy living room of Paula Ehlers, head of the missions department at Columbia River Christian Church.

While her time in the Bible had been solid, the scene with Caramel that morning had shaken her. She sat on an overstuffed leather chair across from Pastor Ehlers, feeling out of place and lonely.

The other two would-be missionaries sat on the matching sofa. Jane shifted in her seat. Long fingers of the bright summer evening sun filtered through the half-shut curtains, blinding Jane. Plus, she was hot. A fan kept the air moving around the room, but she was glistening and damp.

Paula was a thin, tan woman with wise eyes that crinkled when she smiled, and soft, straight hair that fell to her chin. Paula had a slow, steady way about her that spoke of the many years she had spent overseas, and reflected a life of patient obedience to God. She was exactly who Jane hoped to be someday.

Jane held a stack of papers on her lap that had crumpled a bit in her hot hands. She tried to smooth them out. A combination personality-test/resume, Paula had given a set to all three women a couple of weeks ago when they first met each other.

Paula gathered each set of papers. "I'm glad to see you all had a chance to finish the packets. We've found that a little time spent learning about our missions' candidates goes a long way toward helping them succeed on the field." Paula squared off the stack of papers and then slid them into a messenger bag that sat on the floor. "After I've had a chance to read all of them, I want to get together with each of you alone and chat." She folded her hands on her knees and leaned forward slightly, giving them the impression of rapt attention.

"I really enjoyed the opportunity to think and pray over the questions." Kaitlyn, a petite blonde woman sat across the room from Jane. Kaitlyn had a fifty-watt smile, glossy blonde hair, and a prosthetic hand, something Jane hadn't noticed last time they had met. "My fiancé is already overseas." She dropped her gaze to the diamond engagement ring on her fake hand. "I've been taking my future ministry for granted. It was good to step back and consider what God has prepared me for, instead of what I expect I'll be doing."

"Were you surprised by any of the answers you got?" Paula relaxed back into her chair. She picked up her teacup and sipped it.

"Nah." Kaitlyn laughed softly. "It was really good to see how well my hopes and my talents align."

"Remind me what Spencer does. I know he's in the Philippines, but what's he doing?" Valerie, sitting on the corner of the couch so she could face Kaitlyn while she spoke, was a plump, cheerful woman in her mid forties. Her eyes almost disappeared in crinkles when she smiled, and her curly hair bounced as she nodded her head.

"He runs a youth shelter in the Philippines. We're going to get married when he comes back on furlough next year, then I'm going back with him." Kaitlyn's prosthetic hand rested on her knee. Jane did her best not to stare at it.

"Congratulations on the upcoming wedding." Paula, herself a newlywed, glanced down at the simple gold band on her own left hand. "So what did the packet say you should do when you get to the Philippines?" Paula chuckled, and Kaitlyn and Valerie joined her.

Jane didn't feel like chuckling. She wanted to, but the missing ring kept worrying at the back of her mind. If Caramel decided to say Jane had stolen the ring, she could lose everything she had worked for this far. Trying to fight such a claim was one thing... but an arrest record would look terrible on an application for overseas mission work. Jane swallowed. A criminal record would likely keep her out of the closed-off countries called the "10/40 window" as well.

"I'll work with the women already there, leading Bible studies and Sunday school stuff," Kaitlyn said. "He will keep his focus on the young men, and I'll try and reach their mothers and younger siblings."

"What would you do if there wasn't a Spencer in the mix?" Valerie lifted an eyebrow. "I mean, it's awesome that you have a built-in ministry waiting, but what if you didn't?"

Kaitlyn lifted her hands, palms up. "Who can ever answer what might have been? I know that before I met Spencer I knew I had to go overseas. He was on furlough." Kaitlyn blushed. "It was pretty whirlwind, but our hearts and minds on ministry were pretty identical, so it wasn't hard to see how our lives could easily be joined."

Jane looked down at her hands. She rubbed her thumbnail. It was cracked from spending so much time in hot water. She knew she could wear gloves to protect them, but she always felt gloves kept her from feeling if surfaces were truly clean. Kaitlyn and Spencer. Two perfect missionaries joining forces. She sighed.

"That's fair," Valerie said. "I was just wondering. It seems harder for us single gals, if you don't mind my saying. I've wanted to go overseas for a long time, but found it hard to get the wheels in motion."

"I think that can happen to anyone." Paula gave her attention to Valerie. "And I don't think it's a bad thing. Sometimes God plants a seed in us because he knows it needs to germinate for a long time before it comes to fruition."

"Like you and Mark!" Kaitlyn's already happy face broke into a smile so wide Jane thought she might need sunglasses to look in her direction.

Paula glanced up to a huge photo hanging over her fireplace. "Yup," she said with a slight blush coming over her. "Just like me and Mark." After an embarrassed pause she started again. "Turning in your packets was a good sign that your intentions for missions are serious. Let's face it, dozens of students think they want to go overseas, but not all of them are willing to fill out fifty pages on the off chance their church will help support them."

"I bet not," Valerie said.

"We at Columbia River Christian Church get very excited about sending out missionaries. Kaitlyn, you probably already know this, since we support Spencer, but we feel it is our duty, as a sending church, to provide the bulk of your support."

A thrill raced up Jane's spine. The bulk of her support? That was unheard of, almost. She had taken a class called Perspectives during her days at Bible School and had heard that a few churches around the country had adopted the philosophy, but she hadn't known Columbia River was one of them.

"We don't make that public knowledge. For one thing, we get dozens of requests for support every month as it is. We prefer to get to know the missionary hopefuls in our congregation, invest in training them up and then support them in such a way that they don't have to spend their whole furlough drumming up more money."

"Furlough is much better spent resting and getting married," Kaitlyn said with a giggle.

"I don't know how much rest a wedding is," Paula said. "But yes, we believe that your furlough should be spent being ministered to, not fundraising. That said, obviously we can't fund everyone who applies."

Jane's mouth went dry.

"So far, you three are the ones we are most interested in, but to be honest, with the economy the way it is, we only have enough support available for one new missionary."

Jane closed her eyes. The Lord giveth, the Lord taketh away.

"So our time together over the next year is really important. It will help us determine who we will be funding. We wish we could fund all three of you, really we do. But we can't."

"We totally understand." Kaitlyn nodded her head, a bit overenthusiastically, in Jane's opinion. Of course Kaitlyn understood. They'd almost have to pick her, since they already funded her future husband for the same mission.

"The one thing most field missionaries wish their new recruits had is solid experience in leading small groups. It's such a simple thing to do, but sometimes sending churches forget to let their future missionaries lead in the church."

"Oh, I know what you mean." Kaitlyn flipped her blond hair over her shoulder with her prosthetic hand. "They almost sent Spencer home after his first month. They thought he was useless."

Paula smiled.

Jane squirmed. It was wrong to dislike someone with a missing hand, but the way Kaitlyn said "Spencer" and was so completely sure of what she was going to do with her life irritated Jane. She popped a quick prayer up, for forgiveness and grace, and tried to remember that her work-stress was the problem, not Kaitlyn. It kind of helped.

"The other thing new recruits need is strong teamwork skills, so I'd like to ask the three of you to start up a new small group together."

Jane looked at her new teammates out of the corner of her eye. If she had to guess, Valerie would plan everything, Kaitlyn would get all of the attention for it, and Jane would do all of the work.

Jane passed her hand over her forehead. Her heart was not in the right place, not even remotely. If her future were to be based on today's attitude, she wouldn't send herself to the foreign mission field, either.

"Why don't we all grab some coffee and dessert, and you ladies can get to know each other and talk a little about the kind of small group you'd like to lead.

Desserts were spread across the breakfast bar in the kitchen behind Paula. The aroma of freshly brewed coffee wrapped Jane in a comforting embrace.

"Come on in and help yourself."

Valerie got up first, with a little grunt. "I won't be shy. I have to admit those desserts have been tormenting me since I got here."

Paula laughed. "No need to be shy here. We're family."

From the relaxed smile on Paula's face, Jane knew she meant it. She saw the three potential missionaries as family.

Jane stepped into the hall to compose herself. When she felt half-way normal again, she joined the others in the kitchen. She poured herself a cup of coffee, hoping it was decaf.

"So, Jane, I hear Isaac Daniels brought you to Columbia River, is that right?" Paula asked.

"Yes…" Jane took a sip of her coffee.

"How does he feel about missions?" Paula passed a strawberry topped cupcake to Jane.

Jane's hand shook as she picked up the cupcake. That was the million dollar question.

Jane kept her eyes glued to her bright red berry set into the creamy pink frosting.

"Whoops! Excuse me." Paula patted her pocket. "My phone." She pulled out her cell phone and padded into the hall.

Jane's second narrow escape of the day. She pealed the sliced strawberry from the frosted cupcake and bit it. She wasn't sure which was scarier: finding out how Isaac truly felt about missions, or facing Caramel and the missing diamond in the morning.

Jane took her cupcake to the dining room table where Valerie and Kaitlyn were chatting.

Kaitlyn turned her one hundred watt smile to Jane. "So what kind of small groups do you like?"

"Bible studies are good." Jane licked a dab of frosting from her thumb.

"We're all single ladies—for now anyway," Valerie said. "Maybe we could offer a Bible study for single career women."

"Sure…" Kaitlyn said, her voice trailing off in an unconvinced tone. "That's a possibility. But what about single moms, instead? That's a really needy group."

"We could do that." Valerie sucked in her cheeks. "We'd have to get babysitters lined up, but it is a needy group."

Jane set her cup down. Nothing wrong with single women—or single moms—as far as an outreach was concerned, but they were going about this backwards. "Do we have a list of small groups that Columbia River already offers?"

"Oh, I am pretty sure I know all of them already," Kaitlyn said.

"Okay." Jane nodded, but found the claim difficult to believe. "Why don't we make a list of what we know is going on and see if we could identify an unmet need."

Kaitlyn pulled her tablet from her purse. She stroked it and poked it. "All right, here's the list from the website."

Before Kaitlyn could start reading it, Paula came back into the room. Her face was paper white. She gripped the back of Valerie's chair, her arms shaking.

"Ladies, I..." She choked on the word. "I need to ask you to leave. There's been an accident." Fat tears welled up from Paula's eyes, and rolled down her cheeks.

Kaitlyn jumped up, and put an arm around Paula's back. She pulled out a chair. "You need to sit."

Paula collapsed into the seat.

"What happened? How we can help?" Kaitlyn knelt down beside Paula so they were at about eye level.

"It's Marcus." Paula covered her face with both hands. "They found him... He was on his way home." She shook her head.

Jane reached across the table for Paula's hand. "What happened?"

"They said it was a hit and run." She took a deep, ragged breath.

"Paula, what do you need us to do for you?" Kaitlyn asked, her young voice business-like.

"He's at the hospital. Providence."

For a moment, Jane's heart lightened. Marcus would be okay.

"They need me to come identify his body." Paula crumpled forward, laying her head on the table, her shoulders shaking as she wept.

Kaitlyn stayed next to her, the prosthetic hand resting on Paula's shoulder, while she stroked the pastor's hair with her good hand. "When you are ready to go, we can take you there."

Jane and Valerie nodded in mute agreement.

A small voice at the back of Jane's head whispered, *at least it wasn't murder.*

About the Author

When not writing, Traci accompanies her mandolin-playing husband on the spoons and knits socks.

She is the author of the Tillgiven Romantic Mysteries, the Plain Jane Mystery Series, the Mitzy Neuhaus Mysteries, and *Hearts to God,* a Christian historical romance novella. She was the Mystery/Suspense Category winner for the 2012 Christian Writers of the West Phoenix Rattler Contest and has a Drammy from the Portland Civic Theatre Guild. Traci served as the vice president of the Portland chapter of the American Christian Fiction Writers Association.

Traci earned a degree in history from Portland State University and still lives in the rainiest part of the Pacific Northwest with her husband, their two daughters, and their dogs, Dr. Watson and Archie.

Traci's photo by Jessie Kirk Photography.

Find all Traci's books and sign up for her newsletter at TraciHilton.com.

Connect with Traci at Facebook.com/TraciTHilton or tracityne@hotmail.com.

Made in the USA
Lexington, KY
12 April 2017